Praise for Elizabeth Adler's previous novel

Please Don't Tell

"Brawn, bravado, and romance . . . Adler is in top form in her latest thriller. She delivers fascinating characters [and] twists that shock and surprise."

—*Mystery Scene*

"A page-turner . . . [These] are among the most appealing figures in a thriller." —*Publishers Weekly*

"Told with Elizabeth Adler's knack for terrific female characters and breathtaking twists, *Please Don't Tell* will keep you guessing, right up to the end."

—*Night Owl Reviews*

"Elizabeth Adler, veteran author of twenty-eight novels, is in top form in her latest romantic thriller."

—*Mystery Scene*

"A wonderful romantic thriller." —*RT Book Reviews*

Also by Elizabeth Adler

Please Don't Tell
A Place in the Country
From Barcelona, with Love
It All Began in Monte Carlo
There's Something About St. Tropez
One of Those Malibu Nights
Meet Me in Venice
Sailing to Capri
The House in Amalfi
Invitation to Provence
The Hotel Riviera
Summer in Tuscany
The Last Time I Saw Paris
In a Heartbeat
Sooner or Later
All or Nothing
Now or Never
Fleeting Images
Indiscretions
The Heiress
The Secret of Villa Mimosa
Legacy of Secrets
Fortune Is a Woman
The Property of a Lady
The Rich Shall Inherit
Peach
Léonie

LAST TO KNOW

Elizabeth Adler

St. Martin's Paperbacks

This is a work of fiction. All of the characters, organizations, and events portrayed in this novel are either products of the author's imagination or are used fictitiously.

LAST TO KNOW

For information address St. Martin's Press, 175 Fifth Avenue, New York, NY 10010.

ISBN: 978-1-250-06729-6

Printed in the United States of America

St. Martin's Press hardcover edition / July 2014
St. Martin's Paperbacks edition / June 2015

St. Martin's Paperbacks are published by St. Martin's Press, 175 Fifth Avenue, New York, NY 10010.

10 9 8 7 6 5 4 3 2 1

For my parents,
who were always there for me.

PROLOGUE

This will not be the first time I have killed, though I am not one of those roaming, spur-of-the-moment serial killers. I am discreet, careful, choosy in fact, about whom I want to kill, and why.

I am not an evil person; on the contrary I believe I am, if not good, then certainly kind. I am kind to animals unless they aggravate me, pleasant with babies because they are not worth the bother of aggravation, and I know how to use charm well enough to fool most people.

"Murder?" you might be asking. Am I talking casually, seriously, about murder? That is not the way I would put it. There is a reason I choose who should depart this life and it is always a logical one. Now I have picked out the next.

Rose Osborne is not dead yet, but she is going to die. And soon. Later, I will tell you exactly why.

How can I not be evil, talking so easily about killing someone? Believe me, I am as normal as you who are judging me.

You will never know me, never meet me. Not for me

the long, fantasy sexual bites of the vampire. If you want blood then the femoral artery at the junction of the thigh and the crotch cuts easily while at the same time giving access to the most intriguing and secret parts of the anatomy.

The knife is my favorite method. I have used it more than once, though sometimes other, more fitting methods work better, as you will see later.

So, be aware I am among you. I am the one who always helps out at the animal shelter, at the scenes of disaster, with the old people . . . that's how "normal" I am. And why you, like Rose, will always be the last to know.

1

Evening Lake, Massachusetts, 3 A.M.

Harry Jordan's wooden vacation house was certainly the smallest, as well as one of the oldest, on Evening Lake, a resort where nothing bad, like murder, ever happened, but which in recent years had become a little too smart for Harry's style: too cocktail-partyish; too many lonely blond wives with hungry eyes; too many miniature dogs peeking out of Range Rover windows. Mind you Harry's own car, a classic '69 souped-up E-type, British racing green with tan leather seats, was certainly a head-turner, but then Harry owned that car because he loved it with a passion, not for show. And the dog usually to be seen gazing from its windows was a large silver-gray malamute-mix that looked remarkably like a wolf, but with astonishingly pale blue eyes.

The dog's name was Squeeze and he went everywhere with Harry. Which, since Harry was a homicide detective on the Boston squad, meant that Squeeze had seen a cross section of hard life on the streets as well as the plusher environment of Harry's own Beacon Hill apartment. Not only did Squeeze know that the best place to eat in town was Ruby's Diner near the precinct, he also knew the locations of the best bars. Squeeze had it pretty good and so, Harry had thought, did he, until last week when the woman he was going to marry left him and went to Paris instead. Which was the reason he was here at Evening Lake. Alone. But for the dog.

Squeeze was Harry's alarm clock. At five thirty every morning, even on Harry's infrequent days off, he waited, eyes fixed on the flickering green digital display of the clock, zapping it with a fast paw at the first ring. Usually all that happened was that Harry would roll over onto his back. After another couple of minutes the dog would leap onto the bed and lay his massive head on Harry's chest, staring fixedly at him. Another couple of minutes and Harry would groan under the dog's weight, open his eyes and stare straight into the dog's. Squeeze would not move and Harry had no option but to get up. That was their morning routine. The difference now was that it was not yet morning.

It was 3 A.M., the darkest hour of the night. And they were on vacation at the lake. So what, Harry wondered, was up with Squeeze anyway. He always left the door leading to the porch open so the dog could push in and out as needed. Something must be wrong.

He sat up and looked at the dog, standing by the door, taut as a hot-wired spring, staring intently back at him. Knowing he had no choice he got out of bed and went in search of his pants.

At forty Harry looked pretty good, six-two, muscular despite a lack of serious exercise and his erratic diet of junk food eaten on the run. There were a few furrows on his brow now and his dark hair was beginning to recede a bit at the temples and somehow never looked as though it had been combed, and maybe it hadn't if he was in a hurry, which he mostly was; his level gray eyes under bushy brows seemed to notice everything about you in one sweeping glance and he never seemed to have time for a decent shave, so sometimes he had a rough beard. Stubble became him. At least that's what women thought. They found him attractive. His colleagues did not agree. They called him "the Prof" because of his Harvard Law degree, earned the hard and, for Harry, bitterly boring way. He'd given it up years ago and become a rookie in the police department instead. The reason he'd used was that he didn't want to waste his time getting criminals off on legal technicalities for large fees; he would rather be out on the streets catching them.

Harry had worked his way up from patrol cars to senior detective. And he was good at what he did.

What very few of his colleagues knew about Harry—because to him it was not important, and besides it was nobody's business—was that at the age of thirty he'd inherited a trust fund set up by his grandfather that made him rich. At least, rich enough to buy the brownstone on Boston's Beacon Hill, which he'd converted into apartments. He rented out the three top floors but kept the apartment on the garden floor for himself. He redid this to his own specifications, walled in the garden, and later bought himself a pup. The malamute.

Harry's fiancée had not enjoyed sharing her man with a very large, very present dog. She objected when Squeeze jumped first into the Jag and sat shotgun next to Harry, while she was expected to struggle into the small space in the back that almost could be called a seat. She also had not liked Harry's hours, especially the nocturnal ones. "You never take me out to dinner anymore," she'd complained, though she did like it when Harry cooked.

For a man who existed on food eaten on the run Harry happened to be a very good cook, though only old-fashioned things like pasta Alfredo, scampi Livornese, spaghetti Bolognese—all recipes taken directly from his rare and treasured copy of the Vincent Price cookbook with its menus and recipes from some of the great restaurants of the world, circa 1970. Exactly Harry's era, taste-wise. Forget today's avant-garde chefs and what Harry called tortured food: he liked it simple and, if he was lucky, good. If not then a burger was just fine.

He was fussy about his wine though. Harry enjoyed a good Claret. He never called good red wine "Cabernet," nor did he trust "Chardonnay"—he preferred a Graves or white Bordeaux.

Anyhow, Harry thought now, swinging his legs out of bed and gazing out the window at Evening Lake, glimmering blackly on this moonless night; anyhow, the fiancée whom he'd loved dearly, Mallory Malone, the girl of his dreams, had had enough. Paris, she had told him, would be more fun than another night alone in Boston waiting for the phone to ring or sharing more takeout fried chicken and a bottle of his good red. "I can share a bottle of good Bordeaux with anyone I like in Paris," she'd added.

Harry had seen the tears in Mal's eyes as she walked out the door for the last time, not slamming it, though he guessed she had every right to. He had not gone after her. It would not have worked; he knew it, and she knew it. Not the way things were, with him dedicated to his work. While she had given up her own successful special investigations TV show, which looked further into unsolved crimes of the past, for him.

He'd called his best buddy and colleague, Carlo Rossetti, broken the news, and for the first time in his police career said that he needed to take time off. He needed a break. He wanted time out from stabbings and shootings and killings on the streets. He needed to rethink his life. He needed to be alone and the old gray wooden fishing shack on the lake that had been his grandfather's was just the place.

It consisted of two sparsely furnished rooms, a corner kitchen with a hot plate and a microwave, a white-tiled shower that needed regrouting—a job Harry promised himself to do while he was there—a porch with an old three-legged orange Weber barbecue with a lift-up lid and several years' worth of burned-on grease. There was a narrow wooden jetty and a small rowboat with a little outboard motor. Powerboats were not allowed on the lake, only sails and boats like Harry's. A copse of birch trees, trunks gleaming silvery in the night, protected him from the sandy road that led around the lake, giving him privacy, though he did have an excellent view of nearby houses, much larger and grander than his own, and also of those on the other side of the lake, the largest of which was owned by a flashy blonde with a daughter who looked about eighteen, though when Harry glimpsed them in the mini-market, he thought that with her pale straight hair and elusive blue gaze, she might be closer to thirteen. It occurred to him looking across the lake now, that it was odd, with such a big house, so little entertaining was done. Unlike with the rest of the summer people there were no cocktail parties, no barbecue nights, no boozy laughter. And apparently no friends for the young daughter. Quite different from the Osborne family who lived a couple of houses away. He'd encountered Rose Osborne on his early morning walks. She too, seemed always to be alone. They'd exchanged morning pleasantries. She'd said please come by, they kept open house, but Harry never had. He found Rose attractive: a sumptuous-looking woman, round and full and . . . welcoming . . . was the best word he could use to describe her, with her wildly curling long hair, often pulled in a messy ponytail, her intense brown eyes, her long legs and—of course he had noticed—her slender ankles. She always seemed last-minute thrown-together in a sweatshirt, capris, and sneakers, and sometimes she was on her bike: "Getting my morning exercise in," she'd call cheerfully in passing, throwing him a smile that, lonely man that he was now, Harry really appreciated. Still, maybe because he was attracted to her he had never taken Rose up on her offer, never gone by for that cup of coffee or that evening drink. He respected marriage and married women were not his style. Besides, he was still a man in love. With Mallory Malone. Or at least he thought he was. Thought maybe she was too, in love with him. Maybe a little bit.

Every now and then, though, he would see other members of the Osborne family dashing in and out, a remote-looking college-age son, who gave off "keep away from me" vibes that spelled a problem to Harry; a couple of fluffy teenage girls; and a boy, elevenish, small, skinny, ginger-haired and, unlike the rest of that busy household, always alone. Harry noticed things like that and it made him wonder why the kid was always alone. He also noticed that the boy would hide up in the fig tree where a branch led, he guessed, to his bedroom window. So the kid sat up there and spied on his family and the rest of the world. He would probably make a good detective.

And then there was the husband, Wally Osborne. The famous writer. Wally wrote scary novels that could make the hair stand up on the back of your neck and which were made into films that made you want to shout out loud, "Look behind you, the killer's there!"

You might expect a writer of evil books to look evil, or at least a bit mad. Wally Osborne looked neither. He was tall, lean, and handsome with permanently tousled blond hair, deep blue eyes, and a light summer tan which, Harry knew, must send the local women into raptures. He thought Rose Osborne probably had a hard time keeping tabs on a husband like that. But that was none of his business.

Anyway, he was at Evening Lake, it was three in the morning, and he was climbing into the sweatpants he wore to the gym and a soft dark blue sweater, a present from his ex, thrusting his feet into sneakers, grumbling as he laced them up, glancing at the dog, still expectantly waiting.

"So, okay, let's see what's up, Squeeze," he said resignedly. He wasn't sure what it might be but the dog surely knew something, and since he was still a cop, even though he was thinking about quitting, Harry needed to investigate.

2

The Osborne house nearby Harry's sat squarely on the edge of Evening Lake. "Sat" rather than "perched" because this was a solid house, built to last, ninety years before by a generation that respected solid workmanship and the art of a true craftsman.

It still sat, rather than perched, all these much-lived-in generations later, a white clapboard structure, raised on stilts at the waterfront with a veranda, or "porch" as it was always to be called, running the length of it lakeside, and a jetty where variations of small boats were moored. Omar Osborne was one of the first settlers and certainly one who voted for the irrevocable rule that no motorboats be allowed. Evening Lake would remain unpolluted, he hoped, for his descendants.

New houses now edged the lake, some of them Gatsbyish in their size, but local laws kept them to "simple" splendor, and many of the first old shacks were still there, the brown wood faded to a silvery gray, a reminder of times past though still lived in and enjoyed.

The house was traditional. A row of French doors opened onto the porch, fronting a spacious light-flooded room with oversized "lived-in" sofas covered in nut-brown heavy linen, and comfy chairs with rarely plumped-up cushions, covered in cream brocade, obviously brought from some other house to join the mix-and-match melée, because this house had never felt the hands of a "decorator."

"It all simply came together, the way it should," was what Rose Osborne told her visitors, apologizing for the trek up the wide creaking wooden staircase—she never knew when asked whether it was oak or chestnut, and was always surprised by the question because she was too worried about guests having to march up three floors to their rooms.

The main guest room was on the second floor and had gables jutting like eyebrows over the short windows. Rose's favorite color was turquoise, and she'd had the gables painted that cheerful color, though now because they weren't too keen on having the upset caused by repainting every three years they had faded to what Rose called her "passionate blue."

"Why 'passionate'?" guests would ask and be rewarded with a smile and Rose's answer that many people had asked her that, but it was her secret. Hers and her husband, Wally's. She had never even told her three children what it meant. Which, in fact, was that it was exactly the color of the pure silk nightgown her husband had surprised her with on their honeymoon, bought in some outrageously expensive boutique and which they certainly could not afford, but that he'd said he'd just known would look wonderful on her and that he wanted to make love to her wearing it.

So he had. They had. And the nightgown was still there, wrapped in special tissue to preserve the silk, in the second left-hand drawer of her vanity, under lock and key. A memory preserved. Occasionally, dreaming of the past, Rose would unlock the drawer, take out the package, carefully unwrap the tissue, and look at the most beautiful garment she had ever owned. Its pale champagne lace trim was as delicate as ever, its blue as turquoise as the Mediterranean on a summer evening when that coast turned luminous in the fading light.

In back of the house a forest of birch mounted the hill, silver at dawn and evening, blank and peeling in the full light of day. Atop the hill, brambles tangled at a walker's feet, thorns scratched childish hands seeking blackberries, and old wells, dry now but once the area's only source of fresh water, crumbled, away from the main paths with warnings posted to "take care."

The small town of Evening Lake, only a village really, lay two miles down the sandy road that led behind the house, which had a sharp gravelly turnoff that you had to watch out for or you would miss it. There was a lean-to on the left where cars could park, and a would-be vegetable garden struggled on the right where tender Boston lettuces pushed through the sandy earth and radishes grew to giant size and where, if left unnetted, birds or animals ate all the tiny sweet tomatoes that here were more true to their fruity origin than mere salad fixings.

Two chimneys sat atop the Osborne house and in winter smoke plumed straight up. The builder had done a good job on those flues, as he had on everything else.

There was a "mudroom" to the left of the front door. It was called the "front" door because it faced onto the road, though no one ever used it, they always walked directly into the kitchen by the side door, now painted Rose's turquoise blue. Fishing tackle and wellington boots, tennis rackets, dog leads and raincoats, a vacuum cleaner, buckets and a whiskery old broom were stored in there.

Rose and Wally's "boudoir" was above the living room, a spacious sprawl with a big old brass bed. Dylan's song "Lay Lady Lay" (across my big brass bed) used to be Wally's favorite song: they had played it endlessly on their old hi-fi in those early days, so of course Wally had finally had to buy his big brass bed. A long white chaise stood under the window where Rose would read; there was a pretty vanity against the wall where the light fell perfectly onto the mirror; and a smallish bathroom in pale marble with a tub deep enough for soaking, and big enough for two.

Beyond that, down the hall, was the twins' room, a girly pastel horror of dropped clothing, still-plugged-in curling irons, spilled powder and abandoned tubes of lipstick. The cat they had rescued from the side of the road as a minute kitten that had to be fed by an eyedropper slept on their beds. Now hefty, he was called Baby Noir because of his luxuriant black fur, and he scared the hell out of everybody who came near him, except, of course, Madison, whose beloved he was. There was also Peggy the Pug: beige, flat-black-nosed, soppy and snoring, and Frazer's best friend.

Roman rarely allowed anyone into his room, which he kept in almost total darkness. He had the whole top floor to himself, accessed by a stairway leading from the kitchen, as well as from an outside flight of, by now, rather rickety wooden stairs, something Rose had always had her doubts about, especially with a teenager. When he was younger she had locked that door and pocketed the key. Now Roman was eighteen and objected to "being locked in." His father had come out on his side and the key had been handed over, though not without misgivings on Rose's part.

"What if he escapes at night, runs off in the dark, partying, drinking . . . doing lord knows what?" she'd asked Wally. But her husband had laughed her fears off with the same old same teenager get-out card.

"Look at him," he told Rose. "He's a quiet, well-behaved, responsible young man. He works hard, gets good grades, he's on course for a scholarship to a good college, let him have his fun."

It was Wally's opinion that his son was far too quiet and could use a bit more "fun," and should get out alone more. He stayed home too much, hung around the house, always on his phone or his tablet, always somewhere else in his head.

"That's teens for you," Wally emphasized to Rose. But Rose wasn't buying in to that cliché and she worried. She wished he was more like the twins, outgoing, lovable, touchable, hugs and kisses all round. As well as "teens" she guessed "boys would be boys." In fact all the clichés seemed to suit her son. Right now, that is.

A big house, then, though never grand. A true family house, filled with friends and people of all kinds. This was the Osborne house. Charming, calm, friendly. Until that night. When everything would change.

3

Somewhere in France

Mallory Malone, now Harry's ex-fiancée, had thrown it all in. She'd given up her successful career as "The TV Detective"; famous for pursuing forgotten murder cases, reenacting them on her show, jogging old memories, old resentments, old feuds, and often coming up with the truth—and sometimes the killer. Beautiful, blond, cooler than any cucumber on camera, she had been a toughie to be reckoned with. Not anymore.

Now, she sat alone at a café table somewhere in France, sipping a too-expensive café crème, staring into the small cup as though the remnants of froth could foretell her future. Which of course, since she herself had no idea what her future held, was a ridiculous notion. When you simply threw away your entire life in one fell swoop—your job, your man, your heart—what was left? Paris, she had supposed.

This time, though, Paris had let her down. On that first day, alone in a tiny room in a small inexpensive Left Bank hotel, she'd leaned out her window on the rue de l' Université, listening to small children in the school across the street singing what sounded like nursery rhymes, though since they were in French, and her grasp of French was minimal, Mal could not be sure. It only added to her despair. She was not sure of anything anymore. No job. No fiancé. Certainly no children.

After a couple of days, unable to bear being a woman alone in beautiful Paris any longer, she'd gathered up her stuff, pushed it into her single suitcase, paid her bill, collected her rental car—a dusty white Fiat Uno almost too small to fit both her and the suitcase inside, and which, naturally, since she had parked on the wrong side of the street, already had a ticket tucked under the windscreen wiper. The way things were going it was par for the course.

She tore up the ticket and scattered the remnants in the Left Bank gutter. They gave her tickets, she gave them litter. About to open the car door, she stopped in her tracks and looked aghast at what she had just done. She, Mal Malone, upholder of all that was good, destroyer of all that was bad, really bad, like thieves and pedophiles and killers, had become a litter lout. Her head drooped. Her whole body drooped. She crouched and picked up every scrap then searched for a trash can. Nothing. Where did Parisians put their trash anyway? In their handbags, she supposed, which is exactly what she did now.

She got in the driver's seat and checked how she looked in the rearview mirror, running a hand through her shoulder-length dark blond hair before tying it back with a scrunchie. She wore no makeup. You couldn't hide crying eyes with shadow and mascara. It didn't work. That was okay, nobody was looking at her anyhow, and she had been scrutinized so long on her TV show she felt anonymous without the war paint.

She looked at the dashboard, checking where all the

familiar things should be but in this French car were not. She pressed a button. The windscreen wipers swished noisily in front of her. Another button. Hot air swirled around her. Accidentally she touched the horn, jumping at its sudden loud bleep, waving apologetically at the man sitting in the car in front of her, who gave her a glare that she guessed said "dumb foreigner," which, right at this moment, she was.

Her heart sank. Right at this moment she also missed Harry Jordan more than he or any man had a right to be missed. He had left her alone one too many times, not called until it was too late; not shown for dinner. His work came first, though she had been the one to voluntarily give up hers so they could be together without clashing schedules. Hers and his. Now, though, there was only his and his was all-consuming. Mal had thought they had a future; it had suddenly become clear they had not. Not, at least, the kind of future she wanted: the cozy couple spending their time together, vacations, a house, normal stuff like every woman wanted. At least she guessed they did, and every woman she knew but her had gotten it.

Mal wondered if it was her fault, after all she had a complicated past, a rough childhood with no money and a pot-smoking single mother constantly running from the law and unpaid rent, snatching Mary Mallory, as she was called then, out of schools where she had only just begun to try to fit in. "Fit in" was not meant to be in her and her mother's future. Her mother was "complicated": sweet and kind and loving one day, withdrawn and silent the next.

Mal was away at college. Her mom was living in a trailer in Oregon, on a big wide beach where the waves rolled, in mounting glassy green fury, spurred on by thousands of miles of wind all the way from Japan. She had come "home" for Thanksgiving, only to see her mom standing on the shore, arms raised as though daring those lethal, energy-filled waves to come and take her. Mal had cried out to warn her. She ran down the slope of the cliff to get to her, stood horrified as her mother was lifted into that wave. She saw her curled aloft on it as it peaked, and then it slammed back onto the shore. Her mother's body was never found, and a new Mary Mallory Malone had been forced to emerge.

The experience strengthened her resolve to become somebody. She'd started at the bottom as a "minor" assistant at the local TV station, gradually moved on and slightly up, gaining an understanding of how it all worked sitting in the director's booth, pressing all the right buttons, marveling at the poise and confidence of the people in front of the cameras.

She spent every penny she earned, after rent and ramen noodles, on improving herself, learning how to use makeup by watching the women applying it to others and asking the right questions. She'd trained herself to stand up to her tall height without slouching, forced herself to leave her past and inferiorities behind.

In classic fashion there had been an emergency at the studio; a presenter had not shown for an interview, and Mal was called in as the only one who looked camera ready. She'd done so well she was offered a tiny fifteen-minute segment of her own, talking about local matters. Things had gone on from there.

Ten years later, she ended up in New York with her own important show, a luxurious penthouse apartment, and a life, apart from work and the social events that she was invited to, of complete loneliness which she refused to acknowledge. Until, under strange circumstances, she had met Harry Jordan. Nothing had been the same since.

Harry had truly "saved" Mal. Of course she was already a success, but inside she was still that same scared Mary Mallory Malone waiting for the ax to fall and everything to go back to "normal," meaning the way it was when she started out, alone at eighteen.

Harry Jordan was so straight, so sane, such a regular guy under his macho cop persona it was impossible for her not to fall for him. Harry made love to her like she was the only woman in the world, he made her feel beautiful in a way no camera angle ever could; Harry made Mal feel loved. When he showed up, that is. And there was their problem.

So, there it was. She had left him. Flown on impulse to Paris, found herself more alone than she had ever been on any of those long nights waiting for Homicide Detective Harry Jordan to show up and tell her how much he loved her, but he was sorry, something had come up and he had to leave immediately. A woman can take only so much of that sort of thing.

And then Paris let her down. She found that hard to believe. The City of Light had never let anyone down before. Was it only she who felt alone, rejected by its busy citizens, its sightseers in groups, its lovers kissing over tiny sidewalk café tables, its patronizing waiters at the smart restaurant where she had ventured. "A woman alone" their eyes had said when they asked if she was expecting "monsieur." There was no monsieur, her glare had told them back.

Negotiating the surging traffic around the Arc de Triomphe almost undid her; she must have circulated half a dozen times before managing to exit onto something she hoped pointed south. Three hours later, she stopped at one of the immaculately clean roadway cafés, where, hands still shaking from the nerve-shattering drive, she downed two espressos and ate a bread roll without butter, because that was all they sold at that hour. The provincial French, Mal was soon to find out, ate between twelve and two and not one moment after. They reopened at six for "dinner" and closed early, like around eight. God help you if you found yourself starving, as she did, in the in-between times. A vending machine produced a snack of potato chips and a fizzy Fanta orange soda which she saved for later, "just in case." She could, after all, end up somewhere for the night where nobody served dinner, let alone a drop of red wine to nourish a girl through the long lonely hours, in bed, alone. And very probably crying.

Now, a couple of hours after she had left Paris, numb from being stuffed into a car seat too small and narrow for her long-legged five-ten frame, she had ended up here. In France. In the middle of nowhere.

Despite her vow not to think of him, she wondered what Harry was doing. Catching killers, she supposed. Oh where was Harry Jordan? Why had he not come after her? "Oh fuck," she said out loud, then remembered she was a lady. She should not even be thinking that word, except under special circumstances. Or about Harry Jordan.

But she was. So she called him.

4

Evening Lake

The 3 A.M. silence at the lake was broken by a muffled ringtone. Walking by the lake Harry shuffled in his pocket, found the phone, and stared stunned at the name of the caller. There was a joyous upward lilt to his voice as he said, "Mal, thank God, you're back." Then he saw the incoming call was from France. His phone was global but even so it was pretty good reception, somewhere in France to Evening Lake.

"You're not back," he said, flatly.

"I'm in France."

"I can see that."

"I ran away."

"Why did you do that, Mal?"

The dog tugged at the lead, staring intently into the trees. In the distance a boat slid silently across the lake. Preoccupied as he was, Harry still had time to notice it was an odd hour for someone to be out and about. He thought it might be the boat belonging to the local oddball, Len Doutzer, though from where he was standing, on the sandy path just where it curved, he couldn't be sure. It made sense though, because Len had lived here forever, and if anyone was out catching something at night, it would be him. Anyway, what did he care? He was on the phone with the love of his life.

"I'm in France because I needed some good coffee," Mal said. "And a bottle of good red."

Harry sighed into the phone. She sounded a million miles away, though in truth she was only hours by plane. He said, "You could catch a flight home first thing tomorrow."

"It's already first thing tomorrow here. Remember there's a time difference. So what are you doing up in the middle of the night anyway? Do you have a woman with you?"

Harry's sigh was exasperated now. "Mal, for God's sake."

"Oh no, of course you don't, how foolish of me even to think that, all you have time for is finding criminals, no time for love and kisses and forever and ever . . ."

"Mal, I promise you, it is forever."

"Then come to France. I'm lonely here without you, Harry. We can be together. I miss you, I miss your body next to mine in bed, naked the way we like to sleep, my leg over yours, your arm under my neck . . . I want to smell you, kiss you, taste you . . . dammit I want to lick every bit of you, you detective you . . ."

Harry no longer hesitated. "I'll do it," he said. "I came to Evening Lake to try to sort out my life and now you've just sorted it. I'm coming to France to get you. Where are you in France, anyway?"

"I really don't know," Mal said, laughing, surprised at her ignorance.

"Text me," Harry said. "And trust me, I'll be on a flight to Paris tomorrow."

"I trust you," she said. "Let me know the flight information, I'll meet you at the airport. Don't bring much luggage, my car is pretty small. Oh . . . and please, for God's sake, Harry, don't bring the dog."

"Not this time, babe, I promise," he said.

She rang off and Harry and the dog stood for a minute sniffing the fresh clean air, savoring the silence, the aloneness. He slipped the chain round the dog's neck because he wanted to keep tabs on him and then they were off, leaves crackling underfoot on the sandy path that led around the lake.

Harry's annoyance at being woken had disappeared. He was going to see Mal. He found he was enjoying this deepest, blackest part of the night, liking the rarity of being completely alone. At least he thought he was alone until he heard the squeak of oars on rowlocks; the faint splash of water.

He stood listening, the dog alert in front of him. Perhaps this sound was what had disturbed the dog. He wondered who else besides Len could be out on the lake at this time of night. Teenagers, he decided, looking for trouble and hopefully not finding it. Drugs didn't seem to be a problem here at the lake, but you never knew. What Harry did know, though, was that if you wanted trouble enough you would find it.

A small boat slid into view, being rowed from the opposite shore. The rower pulled up to the Osbornes' wooden jetty. A man got out, quickly stowed the oars, then slid the craft into the boathouse. Moments later, keeping to the shadows, he walked silently toward the house. Harry recognized Wally Osborne. And then, emerging from the woods, came his son, Roman, also keeping out of sight of his father, who he followed back to the house. Harry gave a soft surprised whistle. He wondered what Wally had been up to. And young Roman, though he guessed the teenager had been partying.

Suddenly, a pink glow spread across the night sky. Surprised, Harry glanced at the house across the lake and saw the young blond girl standing at the open door. Her face was distorted in a scream. Her hair was a ring of fire. And then she was running, plunging into the lake, just as the house behind her burst into an inferno. And Harry was thrown to the ground with the force of the ensuing explosion.

5

EVENING LAKE, 3 A.M., Rose Osborne

Rose Osborne woke at the same time as Harry Jordan. Startled out of a bad dream, she reached nervously across the bed for her husband but Wally was not there. The covers were thrown back and Wally's side of the bed was cold, which meant he'd been gone for some time. It wasn't unusual these days. Her husband had not been sleeping well; Rose thought he'd probably gone down to the kitchen to get a cup of the chamomile tea she recommended, though she suspected it was more likely to be a shot or two of vodka.

They had come to the family vacation house on the lake, as they had every summer since their first child was born eighteen years ago, when Rose was a mere girl of twenty-one. Married too young, as she realized ruefully later, but so hotly in love nothing else mattered but being with Wally who wanted her "forever." So what else could she do but marry him.

Wally called Rose his "lavish" woman. She was round and soft, always hoping to be a size twelve but mostly sticking at fourteen. She loved that Wally enjoyed the way she looked, the way she felt under his hands. She was still the same size now, still round and soft with a mass of curly, coppery-brown hair worn shaggy to her shoulders because it was easier that way, and big brown eyes that Wally had once told her were definitely not "spaniel-like." More of a Labrador, he said. Rose had not been sure if that was a compliment but decided it was better if she took it that way. Her long legs and racehorse-slender ankles were her best features, that and her smiley mouth and pleasing expression.

Wally didn't tell her he loved her "Labrador" eyes until after she agreed to marry him and he'd actually put the ring on her finger "just to make sure," he said with that smile that twisted up her heart and melted her bones and made her tremble with desire for him. He wanted her! Rose Gothorpe, born to an American father and English mother who Rose thought must have been a direct descendent of Queen Victoria, whose mores and moral code her mother followed perfectly, imposing them on her own daughter, making Rose feel wicked for her desire.

Being an only child wasn't all bad though, Rose remembered now. She was thinking of her own brood and their sibling squabbles and the times she'd had to separate them like sparring wrestlers fighting over which twin had taken whose ballet slippers and which one had deleted whose homework and who had eaten the last of the ice cream and put the empty carton back in the freezer. Guilty on all counts, she thought with a fond smile. Kids were kids and that's just the way life was.

She was living in Greenwich Village when she met Wally, sharing the smallest apartment possible with two other girls, yet even so, paying the rent was a continual worry.

If there was one thing Rose could be thankful for

though, it was the year's cooking lessons she'd taken, and the joy she got from them. And the weight she gained because of them.

Her curves certainly hadn't kept the guys away; Rose could have taken her pick; she could, as her mother told her after she'd accepted Wally and brought him home to meet the family, have done better for herself than a penniless would-be writer who picked up the occasional script job on a TV series that almost paid his way, with about enough left over for them to share a pizza and a beer and a cozy night, for which no money was needed, spooned together in his single bed after they had made earth-shattering love, unable to let go of each other because if they did it was so narrow one or the other of them would fall out.

With money earned from the sale of his first story Wally bought her a ring, the flattest, thinnest diamond ever seen but at least it looked big. Rose recalled their celebration, at a proper restaurant. Was it the Sign of the Dove? Something like that, somewhere in Manhattan on a rainy night clasping hands across the table, her with her left hand pointedly up flashing her new status, wearing the tight black cashmere sweater her mother had given her last birthday and a white pencil skirt that clung sexily to her rounded rear, with beige suede heels soaked from the walk in the rain because financially a taxi was out of the question, her hair a-frizz from the damp, curling all over the place, her brown eyes golden with love for him. Wally, her all-American boy. They were all of twenty-one years old, both of them. Old enough to vote, old enough to drink liquor, and old enough to marry. Certainly old enough—or young enough—to have so much sex Rose would hurt from the love-bruises on her inner thighs as she walked to NYU the following morning, worried about her degree in English Lit and

Anthropology though what she would do with either of them was debatable.

Those were the good times, Rose thought now, when their only problems were how to be together and how to make enough to pay the rent and to eat, with a little left over for a bottle of Italian red. Inevitably, she had gotten pregnant. Marriage followed. Not the small "family-only" ceremony Wally had pictured, but an outrageous blowout, a Christmas garlanded church packed with family, some of whom Rose hadn't seen in years; her friends in fancy getups and staggeringly high heels; huge football player buddies of Wally's; their college professors; even Wally's great-grandma made it from Seattle, Washington. Looking at her, serene and smooth-skinned, cheekbones still holding everything up, Rose glimpsed her future children in that face.

Oh, she had been such an outrageous bride though, in long, clingy scarlet silk-velvet, strapless, with her golden breasts spilling out under a little white ermine shrug and the string of good pearls her parents gave her as a wedding present. Wally said he thought a new car would have been a better choice, but, hey, that's who her parents were. And she was their only child.

She could remember the look of love and pride on Wally's face even now, as he waited for her at the end of that long white-carpeted aisle. Rose had chosen white carpet rather than red because of the contrast with her dress, and Wally was drop-dead handsome in the pinstripes and tails her mother had insisted on. Even rented, Wally made them look good, a red carnation in his buttonhole, one of the old-fashioned kind that were so hard to find especially at Christmas time, flown in to a pricey Manhattan florist. Malmaison, now Rose remembered the name. She had thought it odd to call such a beautifully scented flower "bad house," which was the literal translation from the French. Anyhow, it was beautiful, it smelled divine, and Wally was hers. Later, she even managed to grow some Malmaisons, out at the lake house; a permanent souvenir.

The champagne reception, the dinner, the party, the dancing till all hours, then slipping away to a hotel room and the next morning to a honeymoon in Barbados courtesy of Wally's parents. Ten days of pure blue: sea, sky, and sunshine. Then back to reality and the two rooms in Greenwich Village with Wally writing at the kitchen table under the single window while she picked up her diploma and got fatter with the baby growing at the rate of knots, as her yacht-club father said.

Either the gods were kind or Wally was really good because his first book of horror stories was accepted by a reputable publisher, a modest advance handed over and they moved, just in time, to a small cottage near Rose's parents, with two bedrooms and a proper kitchen and a bathroom with a real bath, important when you were about to have a baby.

Their first child was born, and named Roman because they decided Rome was the first place they would take him when Wally had a big success and made enough to afford it. Show him Italy young, Wally said. He was a very proud father, adored his son, found beauty in his every squall. Wally could not have been a better dad.

Then suddenly he made all that money and they did take Roman to Rome. He was all of two years old and they sat late into the night with him dozing on Wally's knee while they dined on scampi and porcini pasta and foi gras ravioli and sipped soft dark-red wine, gazing awed at the ancient buildings around the tiny piazza glowing under the scattered lamplight of trattorias, enlivened by the Italian voices speaking a language Rose longed to know, and the violins and accordions of strolling players who smiled at their baby and nodded thanks for the small donation slipped into the extended tricorne hat.

Memories, Rose thought, alone now in bed at the lake house, were what held lives together. Without memories to share you had only the present, perhaps not even a future.

Rose loved her husband, she loved her children: eighteen-year-old Roman and the twin girls Madison and Frazer who were sixteen and full of themselves, into hair-flicking and texting and keeping secrets from her. Rose worried they were heading for teenage trouble. And then there was eleven-year-old Diz, named for a great-uncle Disraeli and known as "the afterthought" because the boy was an unexpected surprise, just when Rose thought she had completed her family.

Diz was different from the others, a small, skinny, gingery-haired kid; he looked nothing like his mother or father. Wally said he must be a throwback to his Irish ancestors, though Rose had no idea who those might be. "Don't worry, it'll only be a long line of peasants," Wally had told her, laughing.

With her lavish overblown looks Rose radiated "earth mother" and, anchored as she always seemed to be in her cluttered kitchen with its long table where mostly you had to shove stuff aside in order to find a place to put your coffee cup, she looked the role. She was a good if messy cook; there was always soup on the go, always a bottle of wine on hand for whoever dropped by, always kids running in and out though not so much her own these days, since hers had grown up. Why, she wondered, was it that kids got more secretive as they got older. They shrank from confidences though she did her best not to pry. Even Diz kept to himself, but then Diz was different, a loner the way children coming late and last into a family often were.

Lying back against the pillows in her white satin nightshirt—she'd chosen white because it was virginal, satin because it was sexy, and a nightshirt because somehow these days she never slept naked—Rose thought about her marriage. Where, she wondered, had it gone wrong? And where was Wally anyway?

Wally was a successful writer of, of all things, horror stories, two of which had been made into movies. Rose did not like his stories; she found them sinister and wondered how they could have come out of the mind of a man so handsome he could be a poster boy for clean living and good health. Which, she guessed, just went to show how you could not judge a book by its cover, especially the ones Wally wrote. He was supposed to be writing now, getting on with his next "epic," but all he seemed to have done for the last few weeks, here at the lake, was take the sailboat out when the wind was up, and if not then he would row himself out of sight of the house, fishing rod in hand, and be gone all day, returning late with nothing to show for it and nothing to say for himself.

Of course, the thought of another woman crossed Rose's mind. This was a resort community with plenty of vacationers like themselves whose families had been coming here for decades. In fact now that she thought about it the place was probably full of bored wives drinking too many martinis and looking for a spot of trouble. A man like Wally was a prime target; successful, good-looking, and undoubtedly sexy. At least he used to be and she was sure things had not changed in this department. Was it simply that boredom had set in?

She thought of him now. Was he downstairs, alone

in the kitchen, drinking? She could stand it no longer, she would have to find him and ask what was going on, why they were like this.

But suddenly the door was flung open and there Wally was, still fully clothed in jeans and sweater, staring at her as though she were a ghost. Rose stared back, astonished.

Then without warning the whole room turned red, the glass in the windows crackled like tissue paper crushed in the hand, and the following explosion knocked Wally off his feet and Rose out of her bed.

6

Evening Lake, 3 A.M., Madison & Frazer Osborne

Madison and Frazer Osborne were not identical twins, something for which every time they looked in the mirror, they thanked God. "At least I got the blond hair," Madison would say, smugly. And, as Frazer would tell her, she was a bit too smug for her own good, which Madison said sounded like a threat, and inevitably that led to a row.

"Getting on" was what you were supposed to do as a family, their mother informed them, exasperated with their continual bickering.

Rose had her own set of commandments, one of which was "thou shalt not hit each other." Another was "thou shalt not curse at each other" (the word "fuck" was definitely out). The third was "thou must remember thou is—" Here Rose had become a little confused with the "thou's" and the girls giggled. "You are sisters," Rose had finished firmly. "Sisters don't fight, they stick up for each other, regardless of who got the blond hair."

"So why am I the one with the horrible ginger?" Frazer had demanded.

They were standing on the deck at the lake house

some weeks ago when this happened. It was evening and the sun was a molten red ball sinking rapidly into the rippled lake, turning Frazer's orange hair into a true fiery red and her normally blue eyes into spitting red fireballs. Rose told her to ask her father. Wally's ancestors were Irish redheads. Frazer decided it was all her dad's fault anyway, but Rose calmed her down, told her her hair was beautiful and that one day she would be really glad she had it. It was what made Frazer different, Rose said firmly.

It was also what made it easy for Rose to distinguish who was who in their darkened bedroom at night, when she stole in to check on her sleeping girls: one pale head on the left pillow, one true redhead—nothing carroty about it—on the right.

Plus always on Madison's bed, on her chest, practically tucked under her chin, was her black rescue cat, Baby Noir. Sleek, and so fat Rose wondered how on earth Madison could stand the weight, though sometimes later when Rose peeked in again, she'd spot Baby Noir at the foot of the bed, yellow eyes glowing menacingly at her in the dark. A one-person cat, Baby Noir's devotion to Madison was total. Nobody else could so much as get near him and if they tried were rewarded with a swift swipe of a black paw.

Oddly, the cat got along fine with Frazer's dog, Peggy the Pug, who took up her own small slice of Frazer's bed: compact, beige-furred and with squashed nose, and always snoring loudly. Rose didn't know how the girls could stand it but they didn't even seem aware of it.

Not only was Madison blond, she was also taller than Frazer, a fact of life Frazer also blamed on Rose. "All I did was give birth to you," Rose countered her accusations calmly. At that time the girls were seven. She'd added, "Anyhow, you'll grow." In fact Frazer ended up a mere five-five while Madison was a modelly five-eight.

All their lives, the twins shared a room, complaining about who was hogging the bathroom (their own private attached bathroom so Rose didn't know what they were grumbling about anyway), so when they were at the lake where each could have had their own room and instead opted to share, Rose was astonished. The bond between twins was there for life. Nothing would ever separate them.

They vowed this to each other, lying on their beds, talking into the middle of the night about anything and everything: school, the prospect of college, what choice to make and if they were both accepted would they go together, or should they finally be separated. And of course, they talked about boys. "Men," they called them.

With Peggy the Pug snoring at Frazer's feet and Baby Noir with one yellow eye open keeping an eye on his territory, nightly the two girls hashed out the teenage problems of their lives. Madison would wrap her hair sideways round her head, securing it with a plastic clip that dug into her scalp but which enabled her long blond hair to fall smooth as satin every morning. Frazer's hair tumbled, like her mother's, in a chaos of curls around her shoulders. No matter how she tried to tame it, it was what it was. "The red riot," she called it, and it was true. One day she planned to sneak out and have it cut off, without telling Rose of course because she knew her mom would cry.

Sixteen, the girls decided, was a tough age, neither here nor there, considered by parents still to be a child, by boys to be fair game, and by themselves to be terrified of new feelings and emotions.

"And responsibilities," Madison whispered to Frazer, still awake though it was almost three o'clock. They were both wearing old T-shirts, soft from many washings, and boys' boxers which made them feel kind of one up on "them." "Them" being "men." Scary as hell and just as exciting, and thankfully, there was a pretty fair assortment of them out here at the lake, some of whom they had grown up with, played with as children, learned to swim with at the long icy pool under the tutelage of April Morecombe. A champion from the grand old age of the sixties and still going strong, with shoulders like a pro wrestler and a heavyweight at that, no child could fear drowning with April standing in back of her, urging her to put her face under the water and just blow a bubble, then kick, girl, for God's sake kick, don't you know how? A groan would follow this instruction, but everybody learned to swim and not only that, learned to swim really well. They lived on a lake, on a vast stretch of water, and safe swimmers were what April needed to turn out, and every member of the Osborne family had benefited from her tuition. Even Rose, who had been timid though graceful in the water, became stronger and easier and unafraid of being submerged.

Still awake for some reason at three in the morning, too much talk of boys, no doubt, Madison unearthed a Kit Kat chocolate bar from her hiding place under the mattress. Rose did not allow candy in their rooms, worried about their teeth, but of course they had found a way around that rule, and anyway were dutiful about the toothbrushing after. Madison cracked it into two and handed half to her sister.

"Look how nice I'm being to you," she said, lying back against the pillows and taking a giant bite of the chocolate, which crunched satisfactorily in her mouth.

"Only because I'd tell on you if you didn't," her twin retorted.

Giggling, the girls sank back against their pillows,

then all of a sudden the tall windows overlooking the lake, which had been left open to catch the breeze, shimmered rosy-pink. They jerked upright, staring at this phenomenon as it darkened to coral then to a fiery red. And then came the explosion that rattled the entire house, shattering their windows, sending the cat hissing under the bed and the dog out the door and down the stairs, with the twins, screaming, after it, and their brother Roman not far behind.

7

Evening Lake, 3 A.M., Diz Osborne

Eleven-year-old Diz Osborne was sitting on the branch of the fig tree that stretched almost all the way to his bedroom window. The tree, he'd decided, must be thirty, maybe fifty years old, broad in the trunk like the prow of an old sailing ship except with sprawling solid branches and enough footholds and grips to accommodate a snoopy little kid like him. It was the end of summer and he couldn't sleep. TV was forbidden, his iPad confiscated, and there was nothing to do but crawl out on his branch and contemplate the silent night.

Much earlier that evening though, around sevenish, just as dusk was falling, there had been a ruffle of "excitement" when he'd observed through his ever-present binoculars the blond girl from the lake house opposite emerge stealthily from her own window. He'd wondered why she had not used the door, then decided obviously she did not want to be seen. She was holding two large plastic bags, carrying them carefully in front of her.

Diz had watched her run, crouching low, to the narrow strip of shore, climb into the small boat beached there, place the bags in the stern, then row her way across to the island a couple of hundred yards away where he'd observed her get out, take her plastic bags, and disappear into the bushes.

She'd emerged a short time later without the bags and gotten back into the boat. Pushing off, she rowed expertly, with hardly a rustle of water, he'd noticed admiringly, back to the coarse sandy shore where she beached the craft. Diz had watched her walk back to her house, keeping to the cover of the trees, and climb back in through the kitchen window.

At the same time, something else, a movement, had made him glance back at the island. Surprisingly, he'd seen a man there. He couldn't quite make out who the man was, but now he was carrying the white plastic bags. Diz watched him wade to a waiting dinghy and row slowly out of sight.

At the time, Diz had wondered what the two were up to, what was in the bags, whether they'd had a secret rendezvous. He'd shrugged it off. Girls were a mystery. It probably had something to do with sex. It always did. At least with his sisters it did.

Actually, even though it was now 3 A.M. it wasn't totally silent. Not many people knew it but there was always something doing at night. No hooty owls and dumb country stuff like that, but a lot of slithering and grunting went on when the rest of the world was safely asleep in their beds. Voles rustled through the grass escaping the talons of the silent, watchful owls; rats scratched in the wooden boathouse, shredding it to bits, his father complained, but then his father was always complaining about something these days. More interestingly, a set of badgers gleamed in the dark like they were headlamps, making Diz wonder how they could not expect to be noticed by other, more predatory creatures.

Just went to show you, he thought, picking another

fig off the tree and shoving it, whole, into his mouth so that the juices slid out the corners and ran down his chin. He wiped it off with the back of his hand, bored. And then he saw a light go on in the downstairs window at the house across the lake.

He checked the time again. Three A.M. Immediately alert, he grabbed the binoculars strung around his neck. Curious, Diz had been observing the family for the past few weeks, though he had never met them. He knew that his own mother, Rose, who almost always liked everyone regardless, did not approve of the way the girl's mother dressed, flashily, in too-short shorts and too-tight tank tops and always with her oversized white sunglasses. Too sexy for her own good, he'd heard his sisters comment the other night when he'd been out here on his tree branch which was conveniently close to their bedroom window. Not that he spied on them, just snickered when they talked boys and stuff. Were all sisters as stupid as his, he wondered, and decided probably all girls were. Though not the one who came with the woman across the lake, and whom he had observed earlier that evening, rowing to the island and back. Now she was quite something.

Tall, skinny as a snake, long pale hair that hung straight to her shoulders and swung when she walked, which was always right behind the cheap blonde he guessed must be her mother. "Walk, Goddammit," he'd heard the mother snarl when the girl dawdled to look at the horses grazing in the field or the red-tailed hawk flying overhead, or something equally important and anyhow probably the reason she was on vacation there, to enjoy nature, etc., like the rest of them. The woman had a hard mouth and narrowed eyes, and something about her gave Diz the impression she drank. Unlike his dad, who Diz knew was drinking. Diz guessed Wally was considered good-looking and very probably attractive to women, which might be the reason now, in the middle of the night, he saw his father rowing back across the lake from the direction of the woman's house. Shit! It couldn't be! His dad wouldn't do that, and not with her! God, he could never tell his mom, never tell anyone, not even his older brother, Roman . . . Wait, though, could that be Roman? Hiding in the trees, watching his father? Why didn't Roman call out, a simple "Hi, Dad, what's going on?" What *was* going on, anyway?

Diz watched his father dock the small, lightweight craft, pack the oars, drag the boat into the boathouse, then walk silently toward the house, followed seconds later by Roman. Diz pressed back against the tree trunk, rustling the leaves. For a second his father paused and looked directly at the tree. Roman was in the shadows behind him. Diz thought surely they must see him . . . but no, his father walked on and went into the house, while Roman simply disappeared into the night.

Two minutes later, the whole world lit up in a surprising rose-tinged glow.

Astonished, Diz immediately focused his binoculars on the house across the lake. The door was flung open. The blond girl stood there for a second, then ran screaming, toward the lake. It was odd, Diz thought, because she seemed to be surrounded by a halo that lit up her face, illuminating her open screaming mouth. And then he realized the girl's hair was on fire . . . Oh Jesus, oh Jesus . . . he was down that tree in seconds, knees skinned, palms raw . . .

The girl flung herself into the water, submerging like a terrified porpoise. And then the explosion rocked around, knocking Diz to the ground and the breath from his lungs with its force, and the house behind the girl seemed to disintegrate in slow motion, pieces flying in the air, in a ball of fire that radiated heat to the lake itself.

8

Moments after the explosion, Harry picked himself up. He saw the girl plunge into the lake and begin to swim toward the island. He grabbed his little outboard boat kept for lake emergencies, and headed fast toward her, but even with the shock and her house in flames with debris falling all around her, she made it before him. She dragged herself onto the sandy strip of shore, where she lay on her stomach, arms stretched out sideways.

All the houses on her side of the lake were now in darkness, the power knocked out by the explosion, but every light was on on the opposite shore. The boat he had noticed earlier and thought might be Len Doutzer's had disappeared, as had Wally's.

He scrunched ashore, running toward the girl who sat, knees hunched under her chin, face in her hands, sobbing.

Harry stood over her, dripping lake water. He said urgently, "Are you hurt?" She did not answer.

Diz suddenly waded out of the lake. "Jesus H. Christ,"

he yelled to the girl. "Your hair was on fire, you must be burned."

Harry pushed back the girl's hair and inspected her. She closed her eyes, seeming to await his verdict, as though, Harry thought, she felt nothing. He saw there were no burns on her face, but that she was in shock. In the background, fire engines clanged along the lake road.

"We've got to get her out of here," he said to the boy. "I'll carry her to the boat, you come back with us."

Even in her soaked jeans, Harry thought the girl was light as a child. The word "waif" came to mind as he laid her down in the stern while Diz, who knew a thing or two about outboards from many summers at the lake, jerked the motor to life. They skimmed toward the Osbornes' jetty where his family stood, illuminated like a row of cardboard figures, as were the occupants of every other lake house, all staring stunned at the inferno.

A police helicopter clattered suddenly, its searchlights beaming down on the boat. The girl moaned again, hiding her eyes with her hands. Harry wished he had a blanket to cover her but there had been no time to think. All he had on were his soaked striped boxers; his sweatpants and sweater were still on the lake path where he'd left them, along with the dog, while he swam first to his own jetty to get the boat, because a boat was the only way he was going to get to this girl in time. Oddly, despite the burning hair, as far as he could see her face was unharmed; even her hair seemed okay, thanks no doubt to her quick thinking, diving into the lake like that. He would never forget the halo of fire around her head, though.

Suddenly, she opened her eyes and looked at him; big clear blue eyes drowning in terror. "My mother," she whispered.

Harry turned to look back at the inferno. He knew there was no hope.

The search-and-rescue squad brought the helicopter in low. Harry told Diz to switch off the outboard motor. The small boat floated silently as the rescuer swung himself down and with Harry's help got the girl into the mesh stretcher to be hauled up and inside. She was already being wrapped in a foil blanket as the pilot gave the thumbs-up and took to the skies again. She would be in a hospital in Boston within half an hour. Not knowing the extent of her injuries, Harry hoped it would be soon enough.

He was thinking about that second boat he'd seen on the lake and about who was in it. It had to be a local, someone who knew how to maneuver the lake in darkness, knew what he was doing. He'd thought it might be the local oddball, Len Doutzer, it had looked like him anyway, but he could be wrong. Later, he would check Len out though, ask if it was him, and if so exactly what he was doing there when that house caught on fire.

9

Boston, Massachusetts

It was close to four that same morning when Homicide Detective Carlo Rossetti pulled his five-year-old stick-shift black BMW, tires screeching, into the lot outside the converted waterfront warehouse, now known as the Moonlightin' Club. He ground through the gears into park, slid out of the front seat, slammed the door shut, and gave the car an affectionate pat.

He stood for a minute in the lemon-yellow streetlight, hearing the silence. Rossetti was thirty-six years old and good-looking and he knew it. He fastened his Italian leather jacket, buttoned his immaculate white shirt to the neck, adjusted his Hermès tie—the one with the tiny gold dragons, a gift from a woman who liked him—slicked back his already slick black hair, then, satisfied, sauntered casually into the club.

A wall of sound blasted from gigantic speakers, enveloping the dancers still pounding off their energy even though it was late. Most of them had nowhere else to go. The Moonlightin' Club had been Harry's idea, financed anonymously by him in an attempt to get troubled kids off the street, give them a place to hang, a place where they knew they belonged no questions asked, though there were strict rules: no discrimination, no drugs, no weapons, and no gangs. So far, Harry's investment had been successful: the rules were respected, kids played basketball, worked out, made amateur music videos, invented games for iPads, looked around for a life other than trouble. Harry had seen too many go the wrong way, seen too many lives ruined.

Rossetti knew his buddy was a caring, concerned man who somehow could never get his own life into gear. Now the fiancée had had enough and ditched him. His friend was in emotional trouble and Rossetti knew he might be considering quitting the force.

He grabbed a cup of coffee then went to check the gym. Even this late the machines were jammed. The "high" gained from working out was better than roaming the dark streets looking for the high of danger.

He leaned against the wall, sipping coffee from the cardboard cup (Styrofoam was not allowed, everything must be recyclable, Harry had been adamant about that), watching the action, keen-eyed, always looking for tensions that might erupt into something. But all was quiet, everyone keeping to themselves, racing on treadmills, sweating over weights, feeling good.

Rossetti was whistling his favorite tune, the Italian opera aria "Nessun Dorma," through his perfect teeth, slicking back his already slick black hair, when his phone rang. He glanced at his Rolex Oyster Perpetual. The watch was a gift from Harry at the conclusion of a case when Rossetti had gone more than overboard and put himself in great personal danger to nail a notorious killer. He treasured that watch and always arranged his cuff so that it showed a little. Now it said almost five minutes after four. Shit.

Unfolding himself from the wall, Rossetti removed

the phone from his inner pocket where he always kept it, even though it disturbed the hang of the jacket, but he was damned if he was gonna wear it stuck on his belt where anyhow he already had his detective badge clipped. He checked the name of the caller. Wally Osborne—the Wally Osborne? Jesus! And in the middle of the night.

He clicked on. "Yes, sir, Mr. Osborne," he said. "How can I help you?"

"It's me, Rossetti," Harry replied. "I'm on a borrowed mobile, I'm okay, but someone else is not. She's being helicoptered, as we speak, to Mass General, probably with burns and certainly with severe shock. Her house just exploded. It's opposite mine on the lake. I saw her run into the water with her hair on fire . . . I got her out of there. She's around eighteen years old and her name is . . ."

Rossetti waited. He could almost hear Harry thinking.

Then Harry said, "Jesus, Rossetti, I don't know what her name is. I only knew her by sight, her and her mother."

"So where's the mother?" Thinking of what Harry had said about the fire Rossetti almost didn't want to hear the answer but "God knows," was all he got.

"Detective," Rossetti said, sighing, "I thought you'd gone to the lake for some peace and quiet and now look what's happened. I swear you take it with you . . ."

"Take what?"

"Trouble, asshole, that's what." Rossetti groaned. "It's the middle of the night . . ."

"I know what time it is." Harry could hear music blasting behind Rossetti's voice. "So why are you at the club instead of in your bed anyway?"

"Just amusin' myself."

There was silence, then Harry said, "Detective Rossetti, you and I are a couple of lonely guys, using our jobs to keep out of real relationships with real women, hangin' in clubs at four in the morning drinking stale coffee out of cardboard cups and checking that the rest of the world is okay while we are not."

Rossetti drained his cardboard cup and tossed it into the waste bin. "And finding out why young women get themselves burned up in a house fire and their mothers go missin'. Ever think the girl might have wanted to get rid of her mother, Harry?"

Harry's laugh was without amusement. "Not a shot," he said. "This one's just a poor kid who survived an inferno that should by rights have killed her too."

"That mean you think the mother is dead?"

"I'd bet on it," Harry said. "Now, will you please go to Mass General and check on that motherless young woman for me? I'm gonna get some clothes on, I'll be with you in a couple of hours." Harry paused, suddenly remembering. "Oh God," he said, "I'm supposed to get a flight to Paris tomorrow. Today. Mal said she'd meet me."

Rossetti straightened up, slicked back his hair, and unbuttoned his black leather jacket. "Story of your life," he said. "Better call her. And don't leave Squeeze behind in your hurry to check the girl."

"I'd never do that," Harry assured him.

Walking through the parking lot to his black BMW, Rossetti thought that was probably part of Harry Jordan's problem. That and his relationship with women. One woman. Namely, Mallory Malone. "Love of his life."

10

Here I am again, and you can see, I am getting closer, not on target yet but then, I like a little foreplay. You really thought my target was that mother? Think it was the hunky detective who's always saving folk that should not be saved? What about the little kid who's always looking where he should not be looking and might, in the end, be the one who proves to be the greatest danger to me. Spyers, voyeurs, call them what you will, always have a sharpened sense of normalcy; they know through seeing it so often what is usual and what is out of sync, out of place. Different.

I've seen him up in that fig tree, "spying on the spy" you might say. Though of course he would not have seen me. Nobody does when I don't wish to be seen. Funny, I've always had that ability to disappear in front of your very eyes, almost to become invisible by becoming someone other than who I truly am. Which, in my heart, and yes I do have one, is a perfectly attuned killer who loves getting away with it, loves fooling everyone. Why not go to your local library and look me up in the many manuals on psychological and sexual deviants. Or just Google it.

Diabolical, you might say. Depraved. A demon. Don't put all those labels on me. I am perfectly normal. I look normal. I look like anyone in your neighborhood. I look like you. I could be you. Or a friend of yours.

Well, now, we'll just have to wait and see, won't we, what happens next, and to whom.

11

Back at the lake, the helicopter had left. Diz saw his siblings waiting on the shore as he stepped out of Harry's boat and trudged through knee-high water to the shore. Cold water, Diz realized now, with a shiver, he hadn't noticed that earlier, in the "heat of the moment," you might say. His brother Roman was already there. He flung a friendly arm over Diz's shoulder, something he had never done before. Diz guessed mostly big brothers were like that, keeping their distance and not letting you into the lordly high place where they "lived." But now, he seemed to think he had done something remarkable, jumping into the lake and swimming to the rescue of the girl whose name Diz still did not know. He had suddenly become a hero, even though he had not been the one to rescue her. Harry Jordan had done that. Jordan had pretty much rescued Diz as well because by that time Diz had been running out of breath and might simply have had to strike out for the island instead of the girl.

Roman was tall and muscular and good-looking, like his dad. He was everything Diz was not. His twin sisters were standing there, wrapped in blankets against the cold. The girls' long hair was blowing sideways in the wind that had gotten up, and they were looking admiringly, not at him but at the soaking wet and half-naked Harry Jordan.

His mother rushed forward and wrapped him in a blanket. Tears gleamed in her eyes as she said, "Oh God, Diz Osborne, don't ever scare me like that again or I'll have to strangle you myself."

Harry Jordan had dragged the rowboat out of the water and now he came to stand next to them. Rose gave him a blanket and Wally lent him his cell phone so he could call Detective Rossetti.

"Cover your nakedness, sir," Rose said to Harry with that wonderful caring smile which, though she was unaware of it, hit Detective Jordan right in the place his heart was. He hadn't been the recipient of that kind of smile, of that personalized deep look of caring, for too long a time. In fact, not for a very long time, even before the end was flagged by his fiancée.

"Sorry about that." He wrapped the rough plaid blanket over his wet boxers. "I took off my pants before I jumped in. Left them on the bank near my house."

"I'll get them for you if you like," Roman volunteered. "You must be freezing."

Harry thanked Roman but said it was okay, he'd be getting back, his dog was still there.

Then without warning, the air was rocked by another explosion. They turned as one and looked at what was a large expensive house being flattened to glowing red rubble with flames shooting out, and fire trucks swarming and a swooping aircraft dropping water.

Neighbors drifted over in hastily flung-on shorts and bathrobes, and Rose, taking charge, said, "I have soup for everybody in my kitchen. And brandy. I think we all need it."

Privately, Harry thought the explosion did not look like a normal fire, it was too grand, too all-encompassing; there was almost something planned about such an inferno.

He thought again about the mother, wondering if she'd been in there, and what little must remain of her. Or had the girl in fact been alone in that house?

He decided he'd better get over to Mass General and ask her some questions.

Diz was with Wally, still staring at the faint light that was all that could be seen of the fast-disappearing rescue helicopter. Wally told him they'd better join the others in the kitchen, where Rose always had soup ready for emergencies.

"Well, this time she really has an emergency," Harry said.

"There's also brandy," Wally added. "I could use one myself. What d'you say, Detective?"

Harry hadn't known that Wally Osborne even knew his name, let alone that he was a detective. He thanked him, but said he must be on his way.

Wally said, "To Boston, I guess. To the hospital, see about the girl."

"My partner's already there; gotta know she's okay, and hopefully hear what she has to say."

"About her mother, you mean?"

Harry wondered if Wally knew the mother, but the man fell silent, staring across the lake to where firefighters were still attempting to douse the flames.

Harry thanked him for the loan of the phone and went to retrieve his clothing from the lakeside path. Back at the house he gave Squeeze the leftover steak grilled earlier on the Weber. He hadn't felt like eating much so the dog got lucky. Then he took a hot shower, pulled on his jeans, a gray tee, and a black leather bomber jacket. He and the dog were in his car and en route to Boston while Wally Osborne was walking down the side of his house to the jetty and the boathouse, where he cleaned off the still-wet rowboat.

He checked the oars, still slimed with greenish weed, cleaned them too, and slid them back into place. Then keeping to the trees he walked back to the house. He did not notice his son Roman, who was waiting in back of the boathouse, go in and, when his father had disappeared, relaunch the boat and row across the lake.

Rose turned as he came in. "Wally!" she cried. "I was beginning to worry. Diz said you were still out there, I thought you might have taken the boat and gone across to try to help."

Wally shrugged as he poured himself a drink. "Nobody's over there but the firefighters and cops," he said, avoiding her eyes. "A mere civilian couldn't get near it, not even a detective."

"You mean Harry Jordan?"

"I spoke with him. He's on his way to the hospital to see that girl. He thinks she's unharmed but in shock. I guess he wants to know what happened."

Rose clutched a hand to her heart over the heavy wool sweater she had thrown on over her nightshirt. "To her mother, you mean?"

Wally's eyes challenged his wife's. "I don't know who she is. I never met her."

Diz's brows raised in surprise. He knew his dad was lying. His gaze swiveled to his mother, but she was nodding sympathetically. One thing you could guarantee about Rose was her sympathy. Sometimes, like now for instance, Diz thought she might sharpen up a bit, catch on to his dad, see what was going on. Suddenly scared, he thought he couldn't, after all, tell his mother that her husband was lying; that he'd just seen him rowing from the other woman's house before it exploded in flames. Could he?

12

Rossetti was waiting in Boston, lounging against the wall near the emergency entrance, arms folded over his neatly buttoned chest, dark glasses on. Seeing him, Harry thought he looked more like one of those guys holding the velvet rope, the ones who decided whether you could be allowed into a popular nightclub, than a homicide detective.

Rossetti was thirty-six and hot, yet he still lived at home with his mom, who ironed his shirts, fixed his favorite pasta, and never allowed him to bring home a girl. Harry knew Rossetti kept his own apartment but he simply couldn't bear to hurt his widowed mother by letting her know about it. He was a good old-fashioned Italian son.

Harry hit the brake, told the dog to get in the back, then put down the window. "Hey, mama's boy," he yelled, grinning as Rossetti glanced quickly from side to side to see if anybody had caught the insult.

"Fuck you." Rossetti circled the Jag and clambered in. "Daddy's boy."

Harry grinned. "Never. Not even a shot. In fact I'm

surprised 'Daddy' ever talked to me since I always did what I wanted and not what he wanted me to do."

Rossetti shrugged. "I hope you called Mal and informed her you were not gonna make it to Paris tomorrow," he said, as Harry slid into a No Parking spot and slammed the blue police light on top of the car.

"I'll text her," Harry said. Right then, his mind was on other things than flights to Paris.

"Anyway," Rossetti said, changing the subject to the matter at hand, "Talking real now, the girl's name is Beatrice Havnel. The woman in the house is—was—I guess we can assume she is dead—her mother. Name of Lacey Havnel."

"How do you know all this?"

"She spoke."

Harry looked at him, astonished. The last time he'd seen the girl she was being airlifted after almost being caught in a fire and then drowning.

"She hasn't said a lot yet, the docs are not letting us near her until they make sure she's okay and that we won't stress her out, though how we can stress her out any more than she already is beats me."

"Doctors always think cops stress their patients out. And maybe we do," Harry said, thoughtfully. "Besides, they are right, she's just seen her home go up in flames, probably with her mother in it."

"Jesus." Rossetti took an emery board from his inner breast pocket and filed a nail, stone-faced. He'd heard it all before, seen it all before, though maybe not quite like this. "Poor kid," he said, suddenly sympathetic.

Harry cracked open a window for Squeeze, and climbed out of the car. "Get your ass out of there, Rossetti, we have to talk to her. We have to know if the mother was in there, who in fact she is, what she is, and how that fire started anyhow."

"But the doctors . . ." Rossetti hurried after Harry as he strode through the emergency room door.

"Fuck the doctors. We may be looking at murder here, Rossetti, and I'd like to know who my suspect is."

"Shit, you don't mean you think the girl . . ."

"I never just 'think,'" Harry said, already heading toward the nurses' station. "I find out."

Bea Havnel was in a small private room at the end of a very long corridor, far enough away, Harry guessed, to make it difficult for the media to access her. Not that TV cameras or even a cell phone would stand much of a chance; the nurses were on full alert and a uniformed cop stood guard outside her door, which was firmly closed. And anyhow Harry and Rossetti were accompanied by the doctor who had attended her in Trauma.

The doctor took her chart from the slot on the door and glanced at it, brows raised, in astonishment. "She's amazing," he said, turning to Harry, "coming through a fire like that practically unscathed."

"How exactly 'unscathed'?" Harry asked.

The doc shrugged as he opened the door. "See for yourselves," he suggested, lifting a hand in greeting to his patient, who was sitting up in bed sipping orange juice through a straw.

The doctor introduced them and Bea Havnel threw the detectives a soft glance from under her lashes.

Unburned lashes, Harry noted. And unburned hair. Apart from a bandage on her right wrist, there was no evidence of what the girl had just gone through. Except perhaps the scared look in the back of her eyes, behind the sweet-little-girl smile that Harry had to admit was endearing.

"I'm so sorry for what you just went through," he

said. "I have to ask some questions but if you feel unable to talk we can come back later."

"No. Please." Bea waved a slender white hand at the chair next to her bed. "I need to talk to someone, I need to ask you . . ." She hesitated. "I need to know about my mother."

Harry's eyes met Rossetti's briefly. He hated being put in the position of messenger of doom.

"It's all right," Bea said quietly. "I can guess what your answer is. I was with her when it happened."

"When exactly what happened?" Harry asked. He and Rossetti were still standing by the bed, uncomfortable in their roles.

"It was all so sudden." Bea put down her glass of juice. She crossed her arms defensively over her chest, clutching her shoulders with her hands. She was wearing a blue-flowered hospital garment that was way too big for her and in which, Harry thought, she looked even more childlike.

"I saw the explosion," Harry told her. "I was on the opposite side of the lake."

"Oh God, then it must have been you who saved me!" Bea reached out to him and instinctively Harry took her hands in his. "Oh my God," she said again, gazing at him in wonderment. "If it were not for you I might not be here."

"Yes, you would," Rossetti said briskly; this was after all a police inquiry. He checked his notes again. "You ran from the house with your hair alight, dunked yourself in the lake, saved your own life, in fact."

"I remember now, there was also a small boy," Bea said. "He wanted to save me. So sweet, so very sweet. But it was you who loaded me into the helicopter." She was looking at Harry.

Her wide-blue-eyed smile not only touched Harry's

heart but reached into the pit of his stomach. He had never met a girl quite like this; even in her shocked state with the loss of her mother looming he knew she would be the kind of good polite woman who later would send a thank-you note written in her own hand, not simply a printed card. Whatever the mother might have been, she seemed to have raised her daughter properly.

"Please," Bea said softly, "you have to help me."

"Anything we can do, miss—er, ma'am." Rossetti stumbled over his words, succumbing to her charm, making Harry smile too.

"Detective Rosssetti is correct, Ms. Havnel," he said. "Just tell us what we can do for you."

Throwing back the covers, Bea slid out of bed. Clutching the short flowered hospital gown around her, she stood silently, all long white legs, long blond hair wisping over her shoulders. There was something eerily childlike about her yet Harry had the gut feeling she knew exactly who she was as a woman, and how to use the power of her gentle beauty.

Now she turned that full power on him. "You came to tell me about my mother," she said. "I know she's dead. I was with her when it happened. I just wanted to know if you'd found her body."

She was shivering and Harry reached for the terry bathrobe hanging behind the door and put it around her shoulders. She seemed to sink into it, then sink into the chair Rossetti held out for her.

"Tell us how it happened," Harry said gently, standing directly in front of her. Rossetti stood to one side. They were in the classic interrogation positions of "good cop, bad cop," though neither of them believed they were interviewing a criminal. Bea Havnel was a victim.

Bea clasped her hands in her white terrycloth lap. "My mother's name is Lacey Havnel. She is fifty-four years old. I am twenty-one. My father . . ." She hesitated, looking embarrassed. "Well, the truth is there never really was a father, at least not one I ever met. There were always men with my mother but never a father." She smiled hesitantly up at Harry. "I had to learn to fend for myself. Especially with a mother like mine."

"Like what, exactly?" Harry asked.

Bea seemed to think for a moment, then she shrugged. "If you'd ever seen my mother I believe you would know what I mean. She was wild. 'Flirtatious' would be a kind word. Oh God," she wailed in sudden despair. "The truth is my mother was a mess! She drank too much. She abused alcohol. She'd been in rehab many times, and was doing drugs whenever she could get her hands on them." She lifted her eyes and stared from one man to the other. "What do you think caused the explosion anyway?"

Harry shrugged while Rossetti stared silently at his neatly filed fingernails.

Bea answered for them. "It was methamphetamine. She knew how to make crystal meth. It's so simple even I could have done it. Not that I would of course." She glanced up at them again. "She had a friend. His name is Divon. I never knew his last name. I never really knew him at all but she went out with him, partied with him . . . he got her the fixings, taught her how to make it."

"And where were you when all this was going on?"

Harry's question seemed to take Bea by surprise. "Why, I was just . . . home . . . I guess. Holding the fort, you might say."

"You were not in college? Working at a job?"

"I dropped out of college after a year. Mom needed me. She was in rehab again, killing herself with all this other stuff."

"What other 'stuff' exactly?" Rossetti focused in on her again and Bea gave him that wide blue-eyed look again.

"You name it, she used it. The first I remember as a kid is cocaine. There was always bags of it around, little piles on coffee tables with rolled-up ten-dollar bills just waiting to scoop it up."

"You never tried it?" Harry's tone was neutral but he knew she sensed his skepticism.

"You forget, I grew up with this. I saw what it did to people. One thing I will never touch in my life, Detective Jordan, is drugs."

Remembering what she had said about her mother's promiscuity, Harry wondered if she had the same negative reaction to men as she did to drugs.

"It's funny," Bea was saying now, smiling as though indeed it was something amusing she was about to tell them. "I always thought she would blow herself up with the meth; the ingredients are notoriously volatile. But you know what really started it?"

They stared silently at her, waiting for her to tell them.

"My mother smoked, Detective Jordan. She also liked her hair in a bouffant style, backcombed, piled up on top, and sprayed firmly into place. She'd gotten all dressed up in this sparkly top and white pants, she'd put on her lipstick, her lashes, arranged the hair. I can see her now, sitting back in her chair looking at herself in the mirror, misting her hair from the spray can. And then she lit a cigarette."

"And . . . ?"

Bea Havnel looked up at the two of them and said, "And then the hair spray ignited and she just sort of went up in flames. Then everything else caught fire and I was running out of there. And then the meth exploded . . ."

"Jesus," Rossetti said.

"Your hair was on fire," Harry said. "You threw yourself into the lake . . ."

"Actually it was a wig, my mother made me wear it when she could no longer stand looking at her young blond daughter."

Bea's tone was bitter, the first time Harry had heard that.

"I was trying to get the wig off, I burned my wrist." She showed the bandage. "It must have come off in the water when I fell in."

Harry thought the story about the wig was odd, and besides she had not "fallen in," but he let that pass. He was simply glad she had survived without major burns. He reminded himself to ask if the wig had been found, washed up maybe near the house. As a detective he was used to checking every piece of relevant information, nothing against Bea Havnel, who he now had to help.

"Thank you for telling us. You were very brave," he said gently.

"What will happen to me now? Am I going to be arrested?"

"On what charge?"

"Well, you know, sort of . . . accessory to drugs, her death. Isn't that what usually happens?"

"Only under suspicious circumstances," Rossetti hastened to reassure her.

Bea smoothed the terry robe and gave him that smile. "What will I do now, then?"

"I'll call social services," Harry told her. "They'll fix you up tomorrow, take care of you, get you some clothes, find you a place to stay."

"Oh, please," Bea said quickly. "There's money. Just book me into the Ritz-Carlton. I'll ask one of the nurses to rush out to Target, pick up a few things for me. Target's so good," she added, solemn now. "They have everything. I always shop there."

Harry was surprised that she had money of her own. "And what about relatives, Miss Havnel? Who should we call, ask to come and look after you?"

"I have no relatives." Bea looked astonished he had even asked. "I don't even have friends. We never stayed in one place long enough, and also because of my mother, you see. I mean, nobody ever wanted to know me . . . except maybe that nice woman across the lake, the one with the lovely family. Rose Osborne. She always had a smile and a wave. I used to watch that family. Roman, the twins, Diz, I envied them . . . I thought they were like real people."

Lost in thoughts of a family she had never had, Bea looked infinitely sad. Tears stood in her eyes. "I wish I could live with them," she said suddenly. "The Osbornes. They are my ideal."

Looking at the pathetic child-woman standing in front of him, wrapped in the voluminous folds of the too-big terry robe and with that lost look in the back of her wide blue eyes, Harry wondered if he could do something about that. The Osbornes' busy, bustling family house would be a better place than a hotel room for a recently bereaved young woman, alone in the world.

He and Rossetti said goodbye and walked away, then his phone buzzed. "Yeah?" He clamped it between chin and shoulder, turning to wave to the girl. Rossetti marched alongside him, phone also in hand, checking with the precinct. Then, "Jesus," Harry said. "Okay, we'll be right there."

Rossetti looked inquiringly at him.

"They found Lacey Havnel's body near the house an hour ago, it's on its way to the coroner now."

"Bingo." Rossetti grinned, high-fiving. "Now we can wrap this whole thing up and let that young woman get on with her life."

"Maybe," Harry said, heading for his car, but then Rossetti always thought Harry stuck to the noncommittal until he was super-sure of his facts. That's what made him a good detective.

"Except this time," Harry said, "there's a knife sticking out of her right eye. We're looking at murder, Rossetti."

The cold white room at the morgue was lined with refrigerated steel cabinets where bodies were stored pending autopsy and release for burial. If there was an ongoing investigation, as there was now, the body could be stored indefinitely.

Rossetti turned up his coat collar. "I hate this part," he muttered, standing next to Harry in front of the wall of cabinets, each with a label giving the name of the deceased. If it was known, that is. Often it was not.

Lacey Havnel however had not yet graduated to a cabinet. She lay on one of the metal tables, zipped into a dark-blue plastic body bag under which Rossetti could make out her toes and the bump that was her head. He thought she looked very small under that plastic.

Murdered bodies were never a pretty sight but this time Harry had to stop himself from drawing in a shocked breath as the assistant unzipped and he found himself looking at the charred flesh and the staring still-open left eye of the woman who was Bea Havnel's mother. A knife, approximately six inches long, protruded from the right eye socket. The flesh of the forehead was burned black, her hair was gone, and the rest of the face was unrecognizable as that of a woman.

"She might be anybody," Rossetti said, turning away. "How do we know she's who we think she is?"

"We won't until we confirm dental records," the assistant said.

"She was found just outside the burning house," Harry told him. "Bea told us her hair was in flames and that she had run."

"She didn't tell us about the knife in her eye." Rossetti's gaze met Harry's. "Tell me now, Detective, why did she not tell us that little detail? And anyhow, why would anyone knife a woman already burning to death?"

Harry looked again into the open staring left eye of Bea Havnel's mother. "Who the fuck knows," he said.

The police photographers had already taken pictures at the scene, now they came to photograph the body in detail. One more gruesome fact that Harry would not tell her daughter.

"I'm certain drugs are involved," he said to Rossetti. "One way or another. And our first task, Detective, is to find who Divon is and exactly where he is."

Rossetti stalked thankfully outside with Harry.

"That was an old kitchen knife in her eye," Harry said, "A Wusthof." As a cook himself, Harry knew about knives and had a collection of which he was proud. "It takes a lot of force to stab somebody, you need to put a lot of weight behind it."

"Even in the eye?"

"Our killer may not have been aiming for the eye, maybe Lacey Havnel moved, tried to get away and that's just where he happened to get her."

"Lucky him." Rossetti hunched into his coat collar, still cold. "The question is why."

"Find Divon," Harry said, "and we'll find out."

13

Paris

Mal knew it was trouble when instead of the text with the flight information she got a phone call.

She was back in Paris, sitting at a tiny faux-marble table in the Café Les Deux Magots on boulevard Saint-Germain, peacefully occupying herself looking at the small stone church in the square opposite, which she knew to be one of the oldest, if not the oldest in Paris, which information gave her a nice sense of history and of being part of a greater scheme of things. If only it were not for the phone ringing. Of course it was Harry.

"What?" she asked, knowing it was trouble.

"You know what," Harry said. "Mal, it was unavoidable, I'd just finished talking to you when right before my eyes the house on the opposite bank burst into flames, and this girl with her hair on fire threw herself into the lake."

"And the brave detective rescued her."

"To serve and protect, that's the police motto."

Mal listened while he told the whole story. Then, "Tell me something, Harry Jordan." She signaled the waiter to bring another glass of the champagne with which she had been celebrating Harry's imminent arrival. Now she might as well drown her sorrows in it.

She said, "Tell me, Harry, do you find trouble? Or does it always just find you? And anyway, since you've already rescued the female swimmer with her hair on fire and I assume the house has burned down, what's stopping you from getting on that flight to Paris?"

Harry held the phone away from his ear; he knew he should just get on a flight to Paris, that's what he should do. But, "Her mother burned to a crisp," he said flatly.

"Oh, oh." Mal was crushed, she felt small in the face of such disaster. "I hope the girl will be all right."

"She's a survivor," Harry said.

It wasn't what he said but the tone of voice when he said it that raised Mal's female antennae. "I'll bet she's blond and nineteen," she said, taking a swig of the fresh champagne, suddenly very much aware of being a woman alone in Paris, again. For a while, knowing Harry was coming to join her, she had lost that feeling. Now it was back in full force.

"Twenty-one," Harry told her.

The cute guy she'd noticed earlier at the next table caught Mal's eye and smiled. He looked so attractively French: lean, dark, mid-thirties, in jeans and an impeccable tweedy jacket, it even had leather elbow patches; and with a scarf tied that certain way all Frenchmen tied their scarves. Fuck it, she didn't have to sit here and wait for Harry Jordan to get his ass on a flight, to join her in her petite Left Bank hotel room, to make love to her . . . she could trade him in for this French guy right now.

"You've broken my heart, Harry Jordan," she said, quietly so the Frenchman would not hear, if indeed he spoke English, which she guessed he did because somehow all foreigners did. Tears stood in her eyes and she blinked them away, turning her head, careful not to grab a tissue and blot them. She wanted no one to see her cry over a man.

She had to shuffle in her bag for that tissue because those tears simply had to come out, and the Frenchman was gazing sympathetically, leaning toward her, offering a fresh supply, calling to the waiter for more champagne.

"Please," the Frenchman said, looking into Mal's teary blue eyes with his concerned brown ones. "Allow me to help."

Mal thought maybe she should.

At the same time, though, she was thinking if she wanted to hold on to Harry, she had better find out who exactly the new competition was. Harry had not mentioned the girl's name but Mal was not a TV detective for nothing. She immediately texted her office. Her assistant, Lulu, would know what to do. Within hours, Mal would bet, she would know more about her new "rival" than Harry. Even sooner perhaps because she wasn't caught up in "helping" the poor burned girl, though it was actually the poor mother who had, as Harry so succinctly put it, "burned to a crisp."

Mal's sharp woman's mind couldn't help but wonder, among all the other questions currently crowding her head, how much the burned-to-the-ground house was insured for. It didn't take a genius to know the poor-twenty-one-year-old-homeless blonde would inherit it.

It was, Mal thought, smiling back at the attractive French guy and accepting that glass of champagne, a classic situation. Or perhaps not. Perhaps it was just that she was acting like a jealous bitch, which truthfully, right now was exactly what she was. And what woman wouldn't be, who'd just been dumped, alone, in Paris, for a young and now homeless fire victim who had lost her mother in the blaze and who now Mal's lover felt compelled to take care of.

She sipped her champagne and, leaning closer, smiled at the French guy. *"Bon jour,"* she said. Adding silently *c'est la vie*.

14

Back at Evening Lake, Len Doutzer was the first person Harry questioned.

Len was the eyes and ears of the lake. Unlike young Diz, who saw only what was going on from his tree, Len missed nothing. He lived up on a hill in a fifties A-frame painted mud-green, "to blend into the background like me," he angrily told the curious who came panting up the slope to take a look at the view and also at the man known locally as "the janitor" because he kept his small compound under meticulously "green" conditions. No insecticides, no sprays of any kind. It was said real worms actually existed under his earth, which was the reason his vegetables grew so prolifically, especially zucchini, which once it got a grip was hard even for an experienced gardener to control. Still, its yellow blossoms looked lovely in spring, and Len's single apple tree gave a goodly crop of crab apples, which he never seemed to mind the kids pinching, though he kept his plums for himself, swathed in netting to keep the birds off.

Should you ask any of the locals, that is, the people

who lived there year-round, of which there were not that many since Evening Lake was mainly a resort area, but should you bump into them on the High Street, or in the Red Sails Bar or Tweedies Coffee Shop, or any of the small stores or takeout places, and ask about Len, all you'd get was that he'd been there forever, kept himself to himself, and that he drove an '80s Chevy woodie, which he maintained himself. Len was the kind of guy, they said, who could turn his hand to anything. He lived alone with not even a dog for company on the long silent winter nights. No family had ever surfaced for a visit, certainly no wife or grandkids.

A loner, he seemed to have enough to subsist on. He owned a TV, drank the occasional beer at the Red Sails, ate pancakes at Tweedies, always wore the same faded brown cords—in winter with a gnarly gray sweater, summers with a faded T-shirt—he grew his salt-and-pepper beard bushier in winter, clipped it shorter in the warmer months. He was short and lean to the point of emaciation and his face was nut-brown and lined from exposure to all weathers, his faded eyes constantly slitted against the sun. And as far as anyone knew he'd never needed a doctor or a dentist. In fact, they said Len Doutzer needed no one but himself. He asked nothing of anyone.

Sometimes lately, he would not be seen for weeks. Somebody might notice his car was gone, or that he wasn't picking up his usual meager groceries, eggs and bread and suchlike as well as the case of Jameson that fueled his solitary life. Occasionally someone would worry and check the A-frame, peering through the dust-encrusted windows, knocking at his door, but when there was no response and they saw the car was gone, it was assumed Len was off on his travels. Wherever those might take him.

In fact Len Doutzer was so much part of the background, those around him barely registered his presence. His life was his own. He shared it with no one.

Len knew everything about the lake and would tell anyone curious enough to ask about its history, about its steady evolution, from its beginnings as a little-known fishing spot, where guys like Harry's grandfather went to be buddies and camp out and get drunk on warm beer, to its transition into a place where those same men, married now, brought their families, wives and kids, swimming and hollering and building new frame houses with shingle roofs and porches and wooden jetties; to more recently, when the lake had been "discovered" as a resort and grander homes built, painted white or pastel with proper green-tiled roofs and expensive professional boats moored outside though never, never had powerboats been allowed to desecrate the ecology of the lake, which to this day, as Len would verify, was as pristine as the day he'd first arrived.

"And when was that?" curious listeners to the lake history might ask. And Len would say, as he always did, it was some time ago now.

In fact Len was sixty, and looked older. Thirty of those years had been spent at the lake and he considered it his own. He lived in his green A-frame, drank his Jameson, and every now and again went off on his "travels." He helped out for a fee when a neighbor needed a hand—he was good at things like electrical wiring, small plumbing disasters, the occasional flood. He carved soft pine tables to go out on terraces, made bookshelves, anything people wanted at modest prices. And if he had any other little business going on the side, nobody gave a damn. Len was a fixture, the place simply would not be the same without him.

Harry and Rossetti were on their way to question

Len. "Why are we doin' this?" Rossetti grumbled, chugging his precious BMW up the dirt slope leading to the Doutzer compound. "It's killin' my car."

"Nothing kills BMWs." Harry closed his window so the dust would not blow onto Squeeze. The dog hunkered down in the backseat, not enjoying the ride. "Len Doutzer is the eyes and ears of Evening Lake. Anything untoward, he would be the one who'd know about it. Besides, I believe it might have been him in the second boat that night."

"So? Then why wasn't he down there immediately with the others when the house blew up? Where was he when the girl was drowning? Why has he not come forward since to offer any information he might have, instead of us trekking to his goddamn shack to question him?"

Harry shrugged. He had asked himself that question and come up with no logical answer. "Maybe he's a man who knows more than he wants to tell," he said. "Just maybe he knew things about the Havnel woman, he could see her house easily from his perch up here on the hill, see the comings and goings."

"Seems there were not too many of those," Rossetti said, as Harry swung the car to a stop in a flourish of dust, in front of the seedy A-frame with its grime-encrusted windows and the front door fastened with a ridiculously large padlock.

"Why a padlock?" Rossetti asked, because it was obvious all a would-be intruder had to do was smash the window and he'd be in inside a second. And anyhow, from the look of the place, there would be nothing worth breaking-and-entering for.

There was no doorbell so Harry knocked. They waited. Rossetti traced the toe of his shoe in the dust, writing his name. Squeeze refused to get out of the car and sat with his snout sticking out the window, watching. Nothing was happening.

"He's probably in his work shed in back," Harry said, walking round the corner. Rossetti ambled distastefully after him. Give him urban squalor any time.

The shed was probably less than six hundred square feet, hand-built, without a permit, Harry knew, years ago by Len. Nobody had thought it worthwhile objecting. Len kept his gardening stuff and work tools in there. Oddly for such a rough man who cared nothing for his appearance, Len was known to wear yellow rubber household gloves when he worked. Jokes had been made in the bar at his expense, about him needing a manicure, which he took with silence and a small twisted smile.

Harry and Rossetti stood outside his workshop and hammered on the door, calling his name.

Suddenly that door was inched open and Len was looking back at them, his eyes narrowed in a squint as always, a truculent expression on his face as always, and a power saw in his right hand. Rossetti did not like this one bit.

"Hey, Len," Harry said easily, giving him a half salute since he obviously could not shake the man's hand, already occupied with the Black & Decker power saw. "Long time no see," he added, searching for a response.

Len's dour expression did not change. "I keep to myself," he said. "More folks should be doing that, there'd be less trouble."

Harry had known Len—that is, he'd seen him around, passed the time of day, seen him fishing, and like that, for years, but they had never gotten beyond that point. Now, though, he had questions.

"I see you're busy," he said, indicating the saw and the wood shavings swirling in the breeze, out of the cracked-open door. "I'm sure you know some things have been happening here, at our lake." He carefully put the "our" in front of the word "lake"; he wanted Len to feel they were comrades in arms against anything that disturbed their peaceful retreat.

"Bad things." Len put down the saw and carefully closed the door behind him. He wore a T-shirt that had once been gray, and smelled strongly of sweat. Rossetti took a step backward though Harry did not flinch.

"Why not let's sit down a while, Len," he said. "Here on your good bench, you and I need to talk."

"That bench is not mine," Len said, standing right where he was while Harry took a seat then immediately felt wrong for doing so. "It's that Havnel woman's. I guess she won't be needing it now."

Harry hoped his jaw had not dropped at the mention of the name Havnel. He ran a hand through his dark hair, adjusted his dark glasses, gave Rossetti an inquiring glance out of the corner of his eye.

"Didn't know you even knew her," he said casually.

Len's face twisted into what might have been a skeptical grin, though under the beard it was hard to tell. "If you've come here to ask about her, you've come to the wrong place. All I did was take her order for a bench and a table for her terrace. She didn't look like the kind of woman that sat on redwood benches admiring the view but," Len shrugged, "she offered good money and I took it."

"Have you seen her since?" Harry asked.

"No, sir, and I won't, not now she's dead. All burned up in the fire they said."

"A fire you could see easily from here, Len, but you didn't bother to come down the hill to ask if you could help, until it was too late. Remember? When you and I met?"

Harry watched Len's face close, his eyes narrow into slits, his mouth become a tight line.

"Wasn't none of my business."

"Did you see the girl, the young daughter, run into the lake?"

"Didn't see her." Len looked straight at Harry as he said it.

"Then you didn't see her hair was on fire, see her throw herself into the lake to save herself?"

Len shrugged and turned away.

Harry said, "Len, I'm asking you as a cop now, did you see anyone else on that lake that night? It was three A.M. Len and I know there were two boats because I was there and I heard them. I saw them. I know who was in one, but I'm still puzzled about the other. Now you and I know you miss nothing. If anybody would know who that person in that second boat was, it would be you. I'm talking murder, Len. Better tell me if it was you."

Len wiped his hands on his shirt, stood looking up to the sky for a long moment, as though seeking inspiration. "I saw the one boat," he said finally. "It was Wally Osborne." He glanced back down at Harry. "Don't know nothing about a second boat."

"And the girl with her hair on fire?"

Len shrugged. "Too far for me up here on my hill to save any swimmer, besides you did a better job, the helicopter and all that."

Harry got to his feet. So did Rossetti. The dog gave an impatient yup from the car.

"Thanks, Len." Harry did not give a little salute goodbye. "I'll need to talk to you again, later."

The two men walked to the car, both aware of Len's eyes on them.

Rossetti got in, found a tissue, and wiped the dust carefully from his shoes. He handed Harry one and told him to do likewise. "Not fuckin' up my car for a truculent bastard like that," he said. "What did he tell us anyway?"

"Not as much as he knows," Harry replied. "I'll bet even money it was him in that second boat."

15

Len watched the two detectives drive off down his hill. When the cloud of dust raised by the car settled, he went back into his shed and shut the door. There were no windows. The inside was lit by a single hundred-watt lightbulb dangling from the ceiling. A hand-carved worktable occupied the far end, with tools for gardening hung neatly along the left wall, power tools attached by clamps to the right. A collection of knives fronted the workbench, behind which were stretched the drying skins of two small animals, a badger and a coyote, both shot and dismembered by Len.

It was a kind of hobby with him. Amateur taxidermy. The smell was terrible at first but it disappeared after a while into a kind of mangy fustiness he barely even noticed. A third skin hung on twin cables from the slatted wooden ceiling, a larger rougher pelt, which, since it still had its head, was immediately identifiable as a German shepherd whose thick coat and erect ears closely resembled Harry's malamute, Squeeze.

A few weeks ago a local family had lost their dog, combing the woods, calling its name, but Len had spotted it first and thought it would be the making of his collection. The lost dog had come eagerly to him when he whistled; it had no reason to fear humans. Except this one. Len had slit its throat, carefully because he did not want to ruin the pelt, carried the dead dog back to his shed, and shut him up in there for a few days until the hue and cry died down, dousing him in an insecticide, the use of which was normally against his principles but he had to prevent flies and maggots.

He had enjoyed skinning the animal, enjoyed burning the entrails, the tissue, the detritus of a body, in his homemade barbecue oven, its stones glowing hot, smoke streaming straight up into a flawless sky. If anybody noticed, they assumed Len was burning off his plant waste, getting his crops in order for the next season. Anyhow, nobody ever bothered to go up there to see what was what; Len had become enough of a background creature to warrant no attention, an oddball of no importance, a bit crazy maybe but harmless.

Len was lying when he said he did not know Lacey Havnel. Of course he knew her. He'd met her years ago when he was around thirty and she was in her twenties and called by some other name, in Miami, Florida, where he was working at a marina, servicing boats and drinking a lot, and she was a bar girl living in a studio apartment that qualified in squalor as well as in glitter, because "Lacey" adored sequins and rhinestones, though she would have preferred diamonds. There was no kid then. Later Lacey had attempted to palm off the paternity of her daughter on Len, but he was sure the kid was not his. No way. He was too careful a man for that. That was many years ago now, long enough to be forgotten. It was because of their old connection, though, that Lacey Havnel had found him again.

She traced him, via old bar acquaintances, and

newspaper ads. She called him, told him she was in trouble and it was his duty, for old times' sake, to help her. "Don't have no money," was what he told her.

"Don't need none," was her reply. "All I need is to hide."

The name she'd gone by when Len first met her was Carrie Murphy. She'd gone through various marriages and aliases since then and had finally taken the name of a dead woman, Lacey Havnel, she told Len, because she had been able to get her hands on her social security number and driver's license. The daughter, she also told him, was the remnant of a marriage gone wrong. Len did not believe this.

Their encounter, when all this had been discussed, had taken place in Miami a few months ago. Lured by Lacey's promise of money from a big "business deal" she was about to be involved in, Len drove there in his woodie, carefully of course, because it was an antique car that caused a few admiring comments en route. When he saw her again for the first time in more than thirty years—he was in his sixties now, she, he guessed, in her fifties—he told her she had not aged one bit. And thanks to plastic surgery she appeared not to have.

"You don't know it, Len, but I've already been to Evening Lake, inspected the area with an eye to my business."

Lacey told him this, sitting in a bar over glasses of his favorite Jameson, something she'd remembered he liked, which kinda pleased him.

He was wearing his cleaner summer pants and had bought a new T-shirt for the occasion. He'd also taken a shower at the Dade County motel Lacey had recommended. Len had not been out of his own environment, mixing with real folks, in years. He felt wary as a stray cat, felt like everybody was looking at him, hated the cars, the noisy streets, the endless flatness of the Florida he had driven through.

"Why am I here?" he asked finally. She sat opposite him at a corner table in the dark bar. It was late afternoon and the place was practically empty. The bartender wiped down his counter with a slick cloth, and rearranged his bottles, disinterested. A fan smeared the thick air around them. Len felt sweat trickle down his neck. He wiped it with his hand, then wiped his hand on his pants. Lacey's chin lifted, her mouth pulled in distaste.

"I have a package for you to deliver," she said. "It must be at this address by five tomorrow morning. You are to leave it in the mailbox at the front gate of the house." She showed him a piece of paper with an address in Boca Raton. "You do this for me, Len, and I will pay you five hundred dollars."

He looked at her, still silent.

"Cash," she added. "And if you get this right, there'll be more where that came from."

"It's illegal," Len said flatly. The fact that what he did himself, in the privacy of his own shed, was actually criminal, was different.

"Of course it's illegal. Why the fuck else would I pay you to deliver something practically round the corner. You take the risk, you get paid, and I am in the clear."

"Drugs," Len said.

Lacey patted the blond ponytail pulled through her white visor, fluffed her bangs, looked away.

"You don't need to know what it is. None of your business. You are simply a messenger, a delivery man. And nobody knows you. That's why you're perfect for the job." She sat back and gave him the kind of smile he remembered from when they were both young. "You owe me, Len," she said. "You had my best years and you know it."

Len didn't know about that but still, she was the closest to a human relationship he had ever had. "I'll do it," he said. "Gettin' older, could use a little money for my retirement years."

Lacey said, "I also thought I could use a new house in a location like Evening Lake, out of sight for a while, from people who might be after me, people who might want my neck in their noose."

Len said nothing.

"I've managed to come into some money lately," Lacey was saying. "I already bought a house on your lake. A 'hideout,' you might call it." She paused, thinking about what she had just said. "Well, something different anyway, I'll still be in business, just a smaller kind of business, enough to keep a girl busy."

She pushed a heavy plastic bag across the table at Len, then she counted out five hundred, in tens, and pushed them over to him too. Len pocketed the money, picked up the plastic bag, put the paper with the address in Boca in his pocket, drained his glass, nodded abruptly at her, and walked to the door.

"Hey," she called after him.

He turned and looked.

"See you in Evening Lake," she said with a grin. "Me and my daughter."

In the three months since Lacey moved to Evening Lake, Len had been "helping her out" with small transactions, such as hiding the packets of drugs, cocaine or heroin or whatever, he supposed, in plastic bags on the island where Lacey told him the people who were after her would never find them. A couple of times she'd have him deliver stuff out of state.

And now Lacey was dead and blown up in that house and Len was afraid he would be caught and charged with her murder.

16

Rose Osborne, barefoot, in old cutoff jeans and an even older soft white cotton gypsy blouse, was in her kitchen when she got the call from Harry Jordan asking if they could meet: he needed to talk to her about the young woman rescued from the fire at the lake house. He told Rose the girl was alone in the world and that both he and she needed Rose's advice.

"Your advice as a mother of course," Harry said, an hour later, sitting opposite Rose at her kitchen table piled with several days' worth of newspapers as well as a jumble of flowery fabric samples. Rose was thinking of redoing the living room, but then she was always thinking of redoing the living room while never quite getting around to it. Also on the table were several half-empty mugs of cold coffee, a quart of milk in a paper carton, a pair of grubby sneakers (Diz's), and a few old pages of typed manuscript (Wally's).

"Make yourself comfortable, Detective," Rose said cheerfully. "I'll give your dog a bowl of water." Squeeze was in his good-boy "waiting" pose on the terrace. "And as a mom I'll tell you what little I know. For a start, there's not a lot to know about mothering. It's a craft, not a talent. We simply learn on the job as we go along, so to speak."

"So to speak." Harry nodded. Rose was a chatterer. He said, "Actually what I've come here to talk to you about is a girl without a mother."

"Of course. The lake house girl."

Rose went to put another capsule into the Nespresso espresso machine. "It's stronger," she explained. "I like it better than regular filtered for tough moments, like for instance what you are about to tell me. I get the feeling it's not good," she added, pouring the espresso and shoving a small cup across the table and sitting opposite him again.

Actually, though she did not appear to be, Rose was uncomfortable with Harry Jordan. She sort of knew him, sort of didn't, sort of liked him—well, anyway liked the interesting way he looked, hard-edged and keen-eyed and with abs to die for. She was not beyond admiring a man's abs, that was for sure, though she no longer had much chance to admire her husband's since he was gone so much.

Rose wished now she had at least brushed her hair instead of leaving it slopping messily around her shoulders. Besides, the twins had told her the color needed re-revitalizing, whatever that meant, more "golden" than "brown" they'd said, but never "copper." Jeez. At thirty-eight she had to learn to reinvent herself and now she wanted to, all because suddenly she was looking at a man who was, she admitted, very fanciable. But he was here on business. About the girl rescued from the inferno.

"So, what's happening with her anyhow?" She clutched her coffee cup in both hands and sat back, large brown eyes alert. "Poor child," she added, "though I suppose she's not really a child. How old is she anyway?"

"Twenty-one," Harry said. "Good coffee, by the way." He drained his cup and put it on the table in front of him. Rose took a sip from hers then put hers down too, suddenly nervous. She asked herself why she was behaving like a silly girl while somehow, inside, knowing the answer. Which anyway she was not going to acknowledge, even to herself. "What's to become of her?" she asked instead.

"Her name is Beatrice Havnel. She's a college dropout. She left to look after the mother."

Rose sat back, astounded. "She left college to look after that harridan? I'll tell you something, Detective, I've never met a woman like her, she dressed like a slut, trailing that daughter along behind her like some kind of slave, to carry her bags I suppose. Oh, I know I shouldn't make quick judgments, after all I didn't know her, but then nobody around here did. A woman like that, well, you know, she would not be popular with the wives."

"The daughter is very different," Harry said. "Whatever her mother was, she seems well brought up, good manners, a gentle quality about her. The fact is, Mrs. Osborne . . ."

"Oh, please." Rose pushed a self-conscious hand through her hair. "Rose."

Harry's eyes met hers across the table. He said, "Rose, I have a favor to ask of you. Bea has no family at all. She has nowhere to live. In fact one of the most tragic things I've ever heard was when I asked the girl where she would go and she said simply to book her into the Ritz-Carlton." He spread his hands wide, amazed. "There seems to be no one she can turn to, nowhere to go after her home burned to the ground, no woman she knows to offer advice or help. In fact it was then she told me how much she admired you, how she envied your family, merely glimpsed from across the lake. 'Like real people,' Bea said." Harry's eyes were linked with Rose's now. "It was," he added softly, "one of the saddest statements I ever heard."

Rose sat back in her chair. She stared down at her empty coffee cup. A silence fell. Harry did not break it.

After a few minutes, Rose met his eyes again. "Why do I have the feeling I know what you are going to ask? But before you do, I want to ask you why? Why me?"

"Not just you, Rose. It's your family. Bea needs a family, if only for a short while. Someplace she can feel safe, maybe for the first time in her life. All she's ever done is look after her mother, instead of the other way around."

"Did she ask you to ask me?"

Harry shook his head. "Bea did not ask me to ask you. Not directly anyhow. It was simply the way she talked of you, a woman she scarcely knows, but it's the image of you as the mother she would liked to have had, of your family, doing what families do. It's something she never had, and perhaps never will. She's a damaged young woman, Rose, I won't pretend otherwise. She needs help and I've come to you to ask for it, instead of simply turning her over to therapists and doctors."

"And the Ritz-Carlton," Rose added, making him smile. "It sounds as though money is no problem. Ritz-Carltons do not come cheap."

"I'm sure we could make some financial arrangement . . ."

"Oh God, really, Harry Jordan!" Rose flounced, irritated, over to the stove where she gave the perennial pot of soup into which all leftovers were tossed another stir. "I'm not asking for money. Of course we'll take the girl in, but she'll have to get it straight about how things work in this family."

Rose was flustered, her cheeks were pink, her eyes flashed, and her gypsyish blouse had slipped from one rounded, lightly golden-tanned shoulder.

"So?" Harry had noticed the blouse. "How do things work around here?"

"Er, well . . ." Rose was thinking of Roman and of what effect having an attractive, sexy young woman about the house might have. Because there *was* an aura of sex about Bea, and "vulnerable waifs" could be very appealing. "Everybody's supposed to do their bit to keep the place running. Wally likes the quiet—for his writing you know."

Harry nodded. He was remembering Wally Osborne rowing back home across the lake immediately before the explosion. He said, "I'm sure Bea would be happy to help any way she could. What I'm wondering now is about your husband. He already has four kids around the house."

"So? Another one?" Rose shrugged and the gypsy blouse slipped a little lower. "Actually, I like the idea. Give the twins a role model, that kind of thing. So I'm saying yes, but only for one week. Just to get her over the hump, so to speak."

"So to speak," Harry agreed again, relieved. "Right now, I've left her in the care of social services, I could not allow her to be alone in a hotel, after what happened."

Rose nodded, understanding. "She's upset, heartbroken perhaps."

Harry did not think Bea was heartbroken. He filled Rose in on Lacey Havnel's background as told to him by her daughter, and also the fact that Bea was probably now a rich young woman since she stood to inherit everything her supposedly wealthy mother possessed, as well as the insurance, though he had yet to check out that information. "Including," he added, "the burned-out wreck of a house we can see from here."

He walked over to the window and Rose went and stood next to him. They looked over the lake. Firemen were still sifting through the wreckage making sure nothing smoldered.

Harry said, "They found her mother, you know. She's at the morgue now."

Rose turned and stared at him, stunned. Somehow he had just made it real for her.

"The poor child," she said quietly, feeling bad because she had not wanted to take her in. "What happens now? There'll be a funeral I suppose."

"Not for a while. We have to complete our inquiries first, into the cause of the fire." Harry shrugged, leaving the exact reason for stalling vague.

"Oh." Rose looked shocked. "That makes it even worse. Of course we'll do all we can to help her. I'll get Wally to go pick her up if you like." Rose wasn't sure it would be a task her husband would enjoy, but she could not go herself, she was needed here for her family.

"No need. Not yet. And anyhow we can have social services take care of that."

"Maybe she'll need a limo," Rose said with a hint of a grin, thinking of the Ritz-Carlton.

Harry was looking across at the island, remembering Bea half drowned in the water. "So who owns that island?" he asked.

"I really don't know," Rose said, surprised. "I've never been asked that before, never thought about it either I suppose. It's just a place the kids always swam to as soon as they were old enough. There's a fair current under that still water, as you no doubt found out, Detective."

Harry was very aware of Rose standing close to him, aware of the faint smell of clean linen, of just-washed hair, of a "good life" that hung around her. He had never met a woman like Rose Osborne. She had not come on to him, she had not in any way set out to attract him, yet he found himself attracted. He reminded himself that she was the busy wife of a famous writer; that she was the mother of four children, one of whom drifted into the kitchen as they spoke. But Rose Osborne was a sexy woman. Harry wondered if she knew it.

Diz stood in the kitchen doorway, hands stuffed into shorts pockets, T-shirt on backwards, feet bare—those were his sneakers on the kitchen table. There were several deep scratches on his legs and arms—gained, Harry guessed, from hurling himself out of the fig tree and into the water to try to rescue Bea.

Diz said, "What's going on?"

"Hey, Diz." Harry stepped forward, offering his hand. "I was thinking of applying for a medal for you, after that rescue attempt."

"It was you that saved her." Diz shook his hand reluctantly.

His hand was sticky with fig juice and Harry wanted to wipe his own on the back of his pants but restrained himself.

"Anyhow," Rose said, fetching a piece of paper towel dipped in water for Harry. "Guess what. You're to have a new sister for a week."

Diz's gingery eyelashes blinked in horror. "What? Another girl!"

Rose explained about Bea, and what was to become of her. "So we must all do what we can to help," she added.

Diz eyed his mother carefully. Then he looked at Harry. He was thinking about the blond snake of a girl he'd watched from a distance. "Are you two sure you know what you're doing?" was all he asked.

Later, when she thought about it, and talked to Wally about it and her other children chorused their disapproval and reluctant acceptance, Rose was not sure that she did.

17

How sweet that Rose Osborne is. I mean, how could you find anyone nicer, more willing to give of her time and energy and her sympathy, than plumply pretty Rose? Is the woman merely stupid? Willing to be used? After all, Bea Havnel is not her responsibility. And nor for that matter is she Harry Jordan's. One is a housewife and mother; the other is a cop. And now they have taken on the job of straightening out a "disturbed" young woman when in fact neither of them need have bothered. Jordan could have simply passed her over to social services; Rose could have said no. But those are the ways life turns, on small seemingly simple decisions, almost always made impulsively. Would the Osborne family's destiny be different had Rose not talked them into "caring for" the twenty-one-year-old orphan?

Meanwhile, I am keeping watch, getting closer to my goal, keeping to myself, in the background of real life. I don't like that kid, though. He's a nosy little fucker and he's far smarter than anyone but me thinks he is. It seems clear now that I will have to take care of him first, which is troubling because it's bound to sharpen up public interest in the Osborne family.

I am asking myself that question as I remember the fire-ravaged house that was once home to the glitzy drug-addicted woman who had more money than she ought to have from a "business" which, though dangerous, provided her with that money, though first it was simply gained from three husbands who fell for her cheap line of flaunting and glitter, always laughing, always ready to drink anybody under the table, always the party girl, even at age fifty-two. Which is what Lacey Havnel was when she died. Right there, in that terrible house.

It was a cadaver dog that finally located her body, not exactly in the ruins, but just outside. As though, Detective Jordan was heard to say, she had been trying to escape the fire. Odd, that she was found outside, and with a broken knife blade in her eye.

How do I know that?

Of course, I know everything about that woman. I also know that daughter better than she knows herself. I know exactly what happened, and trust me, it's not what Bea Havnel told those cops. Those detectives are being bamboozled, and I, for one, am enjoying watching events unfold.

Who, I wonder, in the end, will be the smarter. Detective Harry Jordan? Or me?

18

Mal wasn't taking Harry's defection lightly. There was a responsibility to loving someone. Being "in love" is a decisive act. You choose to be in love. His duty was to her as well as his work, yet somehow, same as always, his job had come first. Wounded from what she deemed as her rejection, Mal went immediately to the rue du Cherche-Midi, her favorite shopping street in all of Paris. She did not lead the kind of high-society life that needed avenue Montaigne couture which anyhow she could not have afforded, but much preferred the chic funkiness of the Left Bank boutiques. Especially the shoes. No need for a huge outlay when stores like L.K.Bennett sold the very same shoes the lovely young British duchess wore. Or was she a countess? Soon to become a princess and after that, queen. Anyhow, that Kate bought her shoes from the same shop on London's King's Road, and if they were good enough for a princess, they were good enough for Mal. Not to say that Maud Frizon didn't have a nice little quirky sandal or two, and Sabbia Rosa made only the best and most expensive lingerie in Paris, and maybe the world. One pair of chiffon boy shorts there and she had exhausted her budget.

On to Galeries Lafayette, where she was distracted for a while by the outdoor stands showing glorious costume jewelry going for a song. A clunky ring with pearls and shiny stones, and a necklace that looked to be made of expensive Limoges crystal leaves but was of course fake, put her budget back on course. Not that she really had one. Heartbreak never has a price.

But it did make a woman hungry. Shouldering her way along the street, Mal stuck out her arm to signal a taxi. Miracle of miracles, in Paris, one slid to a stop immediately. Mal tossed in her shopping bags and climbed in after them.

The driver gave her a raised-eyebrow glance. "Madame?"

Oh. Right. She was supposed to go somewhere. "Véfour," she said, out of the blue.

Le Grand Véfour was only one of the oldest, most expensive, and most revered of Paris's restaurants. It was lunchtime, she had no reservation, and anyhow she really couldn't afford it. It was a place to be taken to by a rich and attentive lover, something she did not have. Too late, the traffic thinned and they were already there.

A valet opened her door and Mal stepped out. She paid off the taxi, overtipping wildly in her new panic because what she should have done was gotten right back in and told the driver to drop her off on boulevard Saint-Germain, where there were dozens of decent inexpensive eateries, but she had acted like the grand dame and now she must carry it through.

She was escorted into one of Paris's oldest and most revered restaurants, grand with gilt and cherubs on the ceiling, yet intimate with its burgundy booths, some of which bore small brass plaques with the names of famous customers from the past: Colette, Alexander Dumas, even Napoleon!

Mal's shopping bags were gently removed, her warm jacket whisked away, a small table along the wall found for her. "Madame is lucky, a cancellation," the headwaiter murmured as he handed her the menu, then asked if she would care for something to drink.

"Oh, Perrier, please."

Mal smoothed her hair then, worried that her lipstick had worn off in the long spree of shopping, quickly fished her Burt's Bees Peony lip balm from her purse and smudged it over her mouth. She took a sneaky peek at herself in the mirrored wall. She was still wearing the blue scarf! A quick glance round told her that was okay, half the men in this place were still wearing their scarves. Obviously it was the accessory du jour.

Perking up, she took in her surroundings, which she was free to do without being accused of staring since every booth and table was occupied with happy-looking diners, sipping wine, and chattering away in various tongues, some of which she did not recognize. One thing was sure, though, the women looked good, and the men were not bad either. Lucky women, Mal thought with a frown. With their men.

Summoning the waiter, she ordered a glass of the house champagne. The waiter arrived minutes later with a chilled glass and the bottle of Taittinger. Of course the champagne house owned the place. He filled her glass gently, allowing the tiny bubbles to fizzle and the aroma of the wine to come through. Mal thanked him, took a sip, and sat back and relaxed. Harry Jordan did not know what he was missing. She pictured him in Ruby's, eating yet another cheeseburger and downing another Bud. Maybe she would get him to progress to Stella Artois, add a little of the Euro spirit to his Boston cop life.

The waiter brought small dishes of what he called "*amuse-gueule,*" little nibbles to "tempt her appetite." Slivers of artichoke in a lemon and oil dressing and tiny chicken wings.

In between sips, she studied the menu and decided to splurge on oysters and then a fish called "*rouge,*" which turned out to be red mullet. She would choose dessert or cheese later.

This is great, she told herself, sitting up straight at her single-woman table, discreetly eying her fellow diners. She was the only person dining alone. Some businessmen, of course, that was to be expected; and at least one pair of lovers, directly across from her on the opposite side of the room, holding hands under the table, eating with their eyes linked. Tricky, Mal thought, enviously. She must learn how to do that.

A basket of breads that smelled deliciously of the oven arrived and with it a round flat dish of butter. She took a roll and broke off a piece, layered on the butter, and put it in her mouth. Oh. My God. Where did they get this delicious yellow creamy sweet ever so slightly salted butter that if she ever was lucky enough to live here and dine in this place more often, would ruin her usual diet. Never had she wanted butter more.

Sitting back, she took a contented sip of the champagne. Odd, how quickly it disappeared when you were having a good time. Was she having a good time? Okay, so she was. The only trouble was she was projecting how it would be if she were with Harry, and she had come to realize it was never going to happen. Harry would never come to Paris. They would never sit in a gorgeous restaurant like this, holding hands under the table while gazing adoringly into each other's eyes and eating divine food.

She summoned the waiter for a second glass of champagne. What the hell, she thought, remembering that old saying, in for a penny, in for a pound, or was it about burning your boats? Stuff like that, anyway. She might as well forget Harry and just enjoy her lunch.

A phone rang somewhere. She took another sip, noticed heads were turning in her direction. Oh my God, that was her phone. "Sorry, sorry, *je m'excuse*!" She waved an apologetic hand at them, fished the phone from her cavernous bag . . . why had she gotten a black phone, she could never find the friggin' thing. Finally she had it. She breathed a sigh of relief and pressed the one button.

"Mal, are you there?"

She closed her eyes, leaning back in her burgundy padded velvet banquette, the phone clasped to her chest. It was Harry.

"Of course I'm here," she said, smiling to herself, "and you'll never guess where I am either." She lowered her voice and tucked the phone under her hair, keeping Harry close to her. "Are you calling to say you are getting on that plane?"

"Not this time, Mal. I just wanted to say . . ."

The phone went dead. Mal rattled it furiously, clamped it to her ear again, but he was gone. She couldn't call him back from here, it would be positively rude and to the French, no doubt indiscreet, to call one's lover from a public place so everyone could hear you fighting about getting on a flight and getting your ass over here to be with her . . .

She would call him back later, if she could ever get him, of course. You never knew where Harry might be from one minute to the next.

Still, he had called her. And she was surrounded by

beautiful people so she might as well people watch, and enjoy a fabulous meal in one of Paris's most beautiful restaurants. And the hell with Harry. Well, almost. Anyway, the food was fabulous! Oh God, she was so alone without him.

19

It was latish, after ten that night anyway, when Harry finally sat himself down in his favorite red-vinyl booth at Ruby's Diner, the one with the perfect view of the door so he could check who came in, who went out. The dog hunkered on its haunches awaiting its own "Squeeze special" raw burger, which it practically inhaled in one ecstatic mouthful. The procedure was always completed before Harry even put in his own order, though, like Squeeze's, his was always the same: a Ruby cheeseburger, Swiss, charred, well done. Lately he'd been trying to do without the fries but the night seemed to call for comfort food. After looking at a particularly gruesome murdered body in the icy morgue and hours spent fruitlessly searching for a drug dealer by the name of Divon, who'd had a rap sheet since he was a kid with probation orders and time for drugs, and who seemed to have skipped town, he needed a burger and a beer. Besides, Mal was on his mind. He wondered what she was doing. Alone. In Paris.

Ruby's was jammed. The plate-glass windows with their looped-back red-checked curtains gave a view of the cold and still-busy street, making inside seem even cozier. The Formica tables were the same ones that had been there since Ruby's opened and the matronly waitresses might have been from the same decade. Doris, Harry's favorite, came over as he sat down. Without asking she placed a cold bottle of Miller in front of him, took the iPad from the pocket of her white apron, and looked expectantly at him.

"Not that I need it," she said, putting the iPad back into her pocket. "It'll be the same old same old, So, where's the Eyetalian tonight, then?"

Harry sighed. "Come on, Doris, you can't go on calling Rossetti that."

"Takes one to know one." Doris's dark eyes crinkled in a grin. "Only an Italian can call another Italian an Eyetalian. So? Is it the usual?"

Harry nodded. Pulling off his old black leather bomber jacket, he checked the room. He'd sometimes brought Mal here. She had never liked it, and nor, he thought now, had Doris liked her, though both had been scrupulously polite. Mal had complained about the smell of fried food and chicken gravy that somehow always hung around the place, and Doris had decided the fiancée felt she was slumming.

Harry took a long cold gulp of the beer, closed his eyes, and tried to think good thoughts. He heard Squeeze give a warning growl and looked up.

A young woman was sliding into his booth. She sat down opposite him, not smiling, just looking, brows raised in a question. Then, "Hi," she said.

Even sitting he could tell she was tall. Late twenties. Fire-red bangs over pale eyes, and a short swinging red bob. Roundish face but nice cheekbones; definitely not skinny but neither was she plump. She looked, Harry thought, like a woman who might enjoy the occasional french fry without too much guilt.

She held out her hand to him. Her short nails were polished shiny black and she wore a thin gold band on the third finger—right hand, though, not left. She had on a black leather bomber jacket, not unlike Harry's own, with a white T-shirt under and though he could not see her feet because they were already under his table, Harry would bet she was wearing towering heels and a short skirt. She was just that kind of woman. Young, confident, and very much of today. And Harry very much did not have time for her.

"You'll excuse me," he said, icily polite, "I'm about to eat my dinner."

"No trouble, I'll join you." She gave him a wide smile of such dazzling confidence Harry almost succumbed to his curiosity.

Squeeze emerged from under the table. Harry put a hand on the dog's collar.

"Jeez," the girl said, amazed, "I didn't even see him. Is he supposed to be in here?"

"Special dispensation," he said.

She took away the hand she had offered Harry and which was still unshaken, and instead offered it to the dog who sniffed it curiously then settled back down under the table.

"Such wonderful blue eyes," she said. "I've never seen a dog like that."

It was a direct line to Harry's heart: love me, love my dog. "Squeeze is part malamute," he said. "Arctic dogs, sort of like Huskies."

"Must be useful in the Boston snow," she said.

"So, to what do I owe the pleasure?" he asked, thawing a little.

"Ah . . . well . . . it's kind of complicated . . ."

"I thought it would be." He met her wide gaze across the table, just as Doris arrived bearing a foaming glass of Miller Lite for the girl.

Harry glanced suspiciously from Doris to the woman and then back again. She had not ordered the beer, yet Doris had known what to bring her. He said, "Why do I get the feeling this is a setup?"

"Because you're right," Doris agreed. "This is my niece, Jemima Forester. She's an investigative reporter. Right up your alley, I thought."

"A would-be investigative reporter, more of a blogger really," Jemima said.

At least the girl had the grace to look embarrassed.

Harry took a long drink. The beer turned his throat to ice. It was a wonderful feeling. He watched Jemima lift her glass to him then also take a long drink. Despite himself, Harry was interested.

"Later on, we could go to the Mexican down the street," Jemima suggested. "Do tequila shots."

"And then who would drive you home?"

"*Moi*?" She gave him a mischievous smile that, cliché though it was, Harry thought really lit up her face. Her skin was the color of alabaster, her lips as ruby as Ruby's curtains. She took a card from her cavernous black handbag and tossed it across the table at him.

"A good taxi service, should you ever need one, though I guess cops can always call on their own to pick them up, see them safely to their beds."

"Then you think wrong."

Doris arrived with his burger and a wire basket of still-sizzling fries.

"God, how great, I'm starving." Jemima's hand hovered for a second or two over the fries then she pulled it back, biting her lower lip, embarrassed. "Shit,

I've done it again. My dad always said I was too impetuous."

"Your dad got it wrong. I'd call you 'pushy.'" Harry shoveled fries onto a side plate and passed it over to her, along with the ketchup bottle. "And since you're eating my dinner shouldn't I at least know why you chose my table to sit at tonight?"

"You looked lonely." She paused. "Well, that's not exactly the reason, though it is true. Actually . . . well, the fact is . . . I know you are working on the mystery of the fire at Evening Lake, the one where the mother burned to a crisp . . . and the girl escaped. Her name is Bea, I saw her on the evening news."

"Jesus!" Harry stared at his burger, suddenly unhungry.

"Ohh, sorry," she said, "I didn't mean to put you off, I mean, aren't you supposed to be used to that kind of thing? The cops on TV always are."

Harry pushed his plate aside, put his elbows on the table and rested his chin in his hands. "Shut up," he said, "and then think about exactly what you want to tell me."

Mortified, Jemima Forester sank back against the quilted red vinyl. Eyes lowered, she seemed to be considering what he had just said.

"I earned that, I guess," she said.

"You have the nerve, Jemima Puddleduck, to intrude on my dinner, on my space." Harry was getting really angry now. "Without any explanation. And then you question me about a current case that I would never talk to you about, even if I could. I am not a TV cop," he added. "Don't ever forget that."

He finished his beer, pushed away his food, and clipped the lead onto the dog's collar. It got to its feet, looking expectantly at the door, anticipating the biscuit treat he would get on the way out.

"I was always called that at school," Jemima said. "Puddleduck. The Beatrix Potter nursery rhyme character. Sometimes I feel like her."

"Then try not to behave like her."

Jemima sat up straight. Her pale eyes were not merry now, her look was deadly serious.

"I know where Divon is," she said.

Harry thought of all the things Jemima might have said this was the most unexpected. He sat back down and called Doris over.

"Two Cokes, please, Doris," he said. "And plenty of ice."

"I didn't know I'd gotten you that hot," Jemima said.

Harry wondered if she was flirting with him. Shit, she was smiling at him with that mischievous look that made him wary of her. He also wondered how much she really knew and how much she was trying to find out.

"So," he said, as Doris came back with the drinks. "How do you know Divon anyway?"

"I went to high school with him. Same class. We all worried about him even then because he knew such shady characters. We liked him, he was a nice guy, always polite, always helpful, never gave the teachers attitude . . . I mean he was a regular kid like all of us. Apart from the trouble he'd get into."

She clasped her hands around the icy glass of cola, staring thoughtfully into its depths, as though, Harry thought, she was conjuring up a scene, or a story. He did not trust her.

Jemima said, "Divon's father murdered his mother. Stabbed her to death. She was in the bathtub at the time." She shrugged in an effort, Harry thought, to appear nonchalant. "Made the cleanup easier, her being in the bath, I guess. But Divon was never the same. The father disappeared and Divon had to go and live with some relatives, an aunt I think, yes in fact now I remember it was the mother's sister. His mother's name was, unbelievably, Fairy Formentor. That was fifteen years ago, probably before your time on the force," she added, giving Harry a long look, as though checking to see if he believed her.

"I believe you," Harry told her, making a mental note to check on the murder fifteen years ago of Fairy Formentor.

She said, "Anyhow, every now and then, over the years, Divon just kinda showed up. He knew where I was at college—Oberlin, a small school, I loved it there, the best time of my life."

Harry was not interested in her college years. "Divon," he said.

"Oh, right. So Divon would show up, sometimes with his pockets bristling with money, sometimes to beg for a few bucks just to get him through. He always repaid it though, he'd send money orders. He was a very responsible young man really." Jemima's eyes met Harry's. "Even though he was doing drugs. Heavy-duty stuff," she added. "And then recently he called, told me he'd let me have the hundred he owed and as much more as I wanted. What he said exactly," she said seriously, "was, 'Jemima, honey, I've hit the friggin' jackpot. I'm working with a woman who has all the contacts, and knows what she's doing, and I know what I can do, so it's mutual.' Of course I asked him who the woman was, I was worried, he sounded so high. At first he just laughed, then he said, 'She's money and class, baby, and she has a lake house you would just die for.' "

Jemima drained her Coke and heaved a sigh. "And I guess she did just that," she ended.

"Do you know where Divon is now?" Harry asked.

Jemima looked worried. "He'd told me he was going

to Evening Lake that night to see her," she confessed. "But what will you do with him? I know he's innocent, after what happened to his own mother he could never kill a woman. Never kill anybody for that matter."

She looked so concerned Harry knew her heart was in the right place. She had told him the story in order to protect Divon, not to see him jailed for murder.

"I'll stand up for him in court, if I have to," Jemima added, reaching suddenly across the table for Harry's hand. "He's a good guy, Harry Jordan. Just on the wrong path, that's all."

Harry had heard that story before, seen it a thousand times. Jemima's hand felt cold in his, probably from clasping the icy Coca-Cola glass. Somehow it made him feel protective toward her. "Thank you for telling me," he said gently. "And for trying to help him. Running is the worst thing he could do right now. Do you have any idea where he is?"

Jemima lowered her head and gazed, shamefaced, at the now-cold basket of fries. "At my place," she said.

20

Harry drove Jemima to her apartment in a row house in North End, on a newly gentrified street that once housed Boston's Irish immigrants in squalid tenements. Now, the buildings had been refurbished, the brick was bright, there were even trees. Of course, Jemima had to sit in the back since Squeeze was not about to give up shotgun. Still she told Harry she liked his car. She even said "wow" when he parked where he was not supposed to, right in front of her door, and clamped the police light on top.

She waited for Harry to open the door for her, then wiggled up and out after the dog, showing a great deal of thigh. "Sorry, not used to such smart sports cars," she said, leading the way up the front steps and buzzing them in.

"Third floor," she called, already heading upstairs. There was only one door on the third floor landing and she unlocked it.

"Okay, Divon," she called, "it's only me. And Detective Jordan," she added as Harry followed her inside.

There was no hallway and they walked directly into

the tiny apartment. Divon Formentor was sitting on a blue sofa, head down, hands clasped in front of him, as though waiting for the cuffs that would inevitably be placed there. He was very thin, youngish, in his late twenties, Hispanic-looking like his mother. His bald head had that recently-shaved shine. His eyes were dark and frightened.

Squeeze went and sat right in front of him, fixing him with that blue stare.

Divon shrank back, afraid. "I didn't do it, sir," he said to Harry. "I don't do murder."

Jemima hurried over and sat next to him, taking one of his hands in both of hers. "I already told Detective Jordan that," she reassured him. "He'll help you, Divon, all you have to do is tell him the truth."

Harry stood by the door, his face impassive. "I have to take you in, Divon, you understand that, don't you."

"Yes, sir, but, like, I didn't kill her."

The click of the cuffs as they snapped over Divon's wrists sounded to Jemima like the knell of doom.

"I should have helped you get away," she said, suddenly terrified of what she had done. "I should have helped you."

Harry said, "And I'll remind you that if you had, you would be accessory after the fact to a murder."

"Jesus." Jemima subsided onto the sofa. All her former bravado and brilliance at Ruby's seemed to have deserted her. Even her flame-red hair seemed suddenly paler.

Harry got on the phone and called for a squad car, then he got Rossetti on his phone, told him what had happened and that he was bringing Divon Formentor in. Rossetti said he was already on his way.

"You're coming with us for questioning," he told Jemima, who shriveled under his gaze.

"I'll only come to help him," she said defiantly, making Harry smile.

Rossetti was waiting at the station. It was a busy night, cops in uniform filling out paperwork, detectives conferring in corners over cold coffee, a smell of pizza over all. Divon was quickly processed. He already had a rap sheet; arrests for drugs, juvenile probation, no violence. Social services had had their hands on him early, but once he was sixteen he'd eluded them and gone his own way, dealing small time on street corners.

"Until I met that woman," Divon told them.

They were in a small interrogation room. Jemima had taken Squeeze for a walk. Harry was sitting opposite Divon at the bare table. Rossetti fetched coffee and set it in front of the young man, who was now without the cuffs.

"Drink it, son," Rossetti said. "You'll feel better."

"I'll never feel better," Divon blurted suddenly. "Not with this hanging over my head. I don't do murder," he said, panic sending his voice higher. "I tell you it wasn't me . . ."

"Why not start by telling us how you knew Lacey Havnel," Harry suggested. "She wasn't the kind of woman who'd hang in your hood."

"I didn't find her. She found me. You guys know me, you know all about me," he said, suddenly quieter. "You know I dealt, small time. One day she just drove up the street, she spotted me on the corner, she was looking for cocaine, Oxycontin, heroin, whatever. She told me to get in her car, we needed to talk, she said she would use me as her only dealer, she'd pay me well if I could keep quiet."

"So?" Harry said. "Did you become Mrs. Havnel's dealer?"

"Yes, sir, I did. And she paid me well. And I didn't ask for none of the sexual favors she was offering either," he added, angrily. "She was what good women call a cheap bitch, even if she did have money to burn. Always in short skirts and sneakers and her blond hair in a fluffy ponytail pulled through that visor she always wore, pretending like she was a young tennis player or sump'n."

There was a knock at the door and a cop entered with a file marked "Lacey Havnel," which he gave to Harry, who opened it and quickly read the two pages it contained. He raised his eyebrows and handed the pages over to Rossetti.

The info on Lacey Havnel was spotty: she had moved around a lot, born in a small town in Idaho to a single mom. Her name was then Carrie Murphy. She had dropped out of school at sixteen. No known family. Resurfaced age eighteen in Florida, where she got work as a waitress. They had that information because she had lost her social security card and applied for a new one.

The next time her name surfaced officially was for a marriage license, to a Florida man, in his sixties. The time after that was a year later, for a death certificate. The husband was out in his backyard, chopping logs for the house. The ax slipped and he cut right through an artery. The police report was consistent with an accident.

Lacey was left comfortably off and also left the area. She surfaced officially again with a second marriage several years later. This time the husband died of a heart attack. Again Lacey inherited, though this time not without a fight from his distraught family. Again, she left town. Neither of the husbands was named Havnel. If there had been a Mr. Havnel, which Bea claimed there had not, then he had been in one door and out the other, and the presumably pregnant Lacey was left holding the baby. There was no official birth certificate for Bea, which seemed to mean Lacey had failed to register her birth, and had been using faked documents. She and the kid moved to Boston where she started a new life as a merry widow and party girl.

It was Harry's guess that Lacey had been running out of funds. She had needed a new business. He guessed there had been no willing new wealthy suitors waiting in line for her to say yes. She had found drugs an easier way. And had died because of it. There was no doubt in his mind that Divon had supplied the necessary, if simple, ingredients to manufacture methamphetamine on a large scale.

Rossetti brought more coffee. He said to Divon, "So, tell us, son, were you at the lake house that night?"

Divon's eyes flashed panic. "I wasn't sir, no, no . . . not me . . ."

"Come on, Divon," Harry said. "Wasn't that you rowing over to the island?" He just threw out the question, thinking of Wally Osborne, and maybe Len. But it could have been Divon on the lake that night.

"I never rowed, I don't like water, I can't swim, it scares me, that lake . . ."

"Bullshit." Rossetti was losing patience. "You were there and you know it."

There was a long silence. Divon did not drink the coffee.

Finally, "It wasn't me," he said, in that same shrill, scared voice. "It was him. That writer."

Harry flashed a glance at Rossetti then back at Divon. He said calmly, "Which writer would that be?"

"The famous one. He was at the house after I left, I saw him coming when I was getting into my car."

"What car was that, Divon?"

"The old Corolla I'd bought so I could access her at the lake house, bring her the stuff. He—that writer—came rowing over, I saw him and so did she and she told me to get lost, so I did."

"Was he in the house when you left?" Thinking about Rose Osborne, Harry almost didn't want to hear Divon's answer.

"He was rowin' up, like I said."

"And you're sure it was Wally Osborne?"

"Yes, sir, I'm sure."

"Did you see him get to the jetty, get out of the boat, tie it up? Did you see Wally Osborne walk up to the house?"

Divon shook his head. "No, sir. I was outta there like I said. And then I wasn't only halfway down the road round the lake, when it all exploded and like I just kept on movin' because I thought they'll pin this on me sure as hell and now it's all happening and I'm tellin' you, Detective, it was not me . . . I don't kill women . . ."

Somehow, Harry didn't think he did. But what about Wally Osborne?

"But I did see the son at the house earlier," Divon added, as an afterthought. "The older good-lookin' one. Roman, I think she called him. I know he and Bea knew each other. That's for sure."

"How did they 'know' each other?"

"Well, like I said, I seen 'em together. Sometimes. Walking by the lake."

Harry fixed his eyes on Divon's; could he be lying? Seeking to lay the blame elsewhere. But why Roman Osborne?

"When did you see Roman with Bea?" he asked.

But Divon shrugged. "Could be I was mistaken," was all Harry could get out of him.

21

It was late and Diz was on his branch, listening to his mom and dad talking. Rose and Wally were on the terrace looking out at the lake. Tiny white lights marked the perimeter and the lake shimmered like black ink. Wally's face was angry as he said, "You will cancel the arrangement, tell the cops to get somebody else, we want nothing to do with those people."

Diz didn't really want to hear this, he hated that his parents were fighting, and especially over the skinny blonde who he didn't want here anyway. As if his vote counted. But his mom was determined to do good and his father was determined she should not.

"I've given my word," Rose said. "Come on, Wally, she's having a hard time, losing her mother and her home, she has no one else, poor child . . ."

"She is not a poor child. She and her mother were involved in drugs. Why do you think that house exploded, anyway?"

"Wally! How do you know this?" Rose pulled her hand-knit cardigan closer.

"I heard it around town," Wally muttered. "You know

I always keep an ear tuned for that sort of thing, for my books."

"So what you know about Mrs. Havnel was purely research?"

Rose's voice was colder than Diz had ever heard it. He did not like what was going on. He did not like that his dad was lying to his mother. He didn't know for sure why he was lying, only that he was, and that he could say nothing. He could never tell his mom.

Wally had stepped away from Rose. He seemed to be holding himself in tight check when he turned to look at her. "Rose, I didn't know that woman. I just knew about her. Okay?"

Rose was silent, looking at him. Diz was silent, also looking at him. Had they both got it wrong? Could Wally be telling the truth?

"Look, okay, I give in." Wally took a step back toward Rose. He ran a hand through his already rumpled blond hair, gave her a sort of half smile. "I'm sorry," he said. "I got a bit carried away. Our life here is so peaceful, nothing like this has ever touched us in all the years we've been coming to Evening Lake."

"Nothing's different, Wally," Rose said quietly. "Only you."

In the silence that fell between them, Diz could hear his dad breathing heavily, as though he was holding back from saying something more. The lake rippled under the freshening night breeze. A bulb went out with a tiny hiss on the string of lights slung around the terrace rail.

"Okay, I'm sorry," Wally said bitterly. "I'm wrong, and you are who you are, the person you are, the loving caregiver. How could I expect you to turn down a young woman in need, when I know if it were your own daughter you would expect someone to help her. I'll just get out of your way early tomorrow, go fishing, let you get her organized. Okay? And I promise I'll back you up. Okay?" he asked again. Diz heard his mother's answering sigh.

"Oh, Wally, I know we're doing the right thing," she said so softly Diz almost could not hear. "Trust me, she'll be fine."

Diz wondered why his mother thought that and his father obviously did not. He thought about his father rowing back from that house right before the explosion. Of course he could be mistaken, Wally might simply have gone for a row around the lake, working off steam; he did that sometimes when he got uptight when he was writing. Diz hoped so anyway. And he hoped the skinny snake wasn't gonna wreck their family.

Wally had already departed when Bea Havnel arrived the following morning. Rose was surprised to see her alone; she'd expected Harry Jordan to be with her. She was also astonished to find her prediction come true when a long black limo crunched up the driveway. The driver opened the door and Bea stepped out clutching a bunch of plastic Target bags. Her hair was pulled back into a braid held by an elastic and her smooth face was unmadeup. She was long-legged in tight washed-out jeans and skinny, as Diz had earlier observed, as a snake. She stood uncertainly as though wondering if she'd got the right place. Rose noticed that her new T-shirt still had a size sticker on the shoulder. S for small. She looked so pathetic Rose's heart went out to her. She knew she was doing the right thing.

"Bea," she called, "I bet you thought there was no one here to greet you. Welcome, dear child, welcome to our home. I thought Detective Jordan would have brought you."

"I wanted to come alone," Bea said.

Rose held her close. She could feel the girl's ribs under her hands. Harry Jordan had said how frail he thought she was. "Come on in and let me show you your room," she said. "I hope you don't mind I had to put you next to Diz. He's only eleven but he's a quiet child and you won't be disturbed by loud music. We insist he wear headphones because the rest of us can't stand the racket."

"Oh, I wouldn't mind." Impulsively, Bea took Rose's hand in hers as they walked together up the shallow steps into the house and into the large open living area with its view through the birch trees of the lake. And also, unfortunately, of the blackened remains of Bea's home. Rose thought it better not to mention this right now and walked her guest quickly to the kitchen.

"Just put your stuff down on the table, honey," she said. "Take a seat while I get us a cup of coffee. I'm sure you could use one after the horrible stuff they gave you in the hospital."

"Oh, it wasn't too bad. Not really."

Bea was looking around and Rose noticed the pleased smile on her face.

"It's lovely here," the girl said. "So much nicer than our house ever was. It's just so . . . well, homey, I guess is the right word."

"Then I'm glad you feel at home. We aim to please. Take a seat." Rose swept the copy of the local newspaper, *The Lakeview Monitor,* to one side and placed a steaming mug of coffee in front of Bea.

"A Peter Rabbit mug," Bea exclaimed. "I always loved those books as a kid."

"It was Diz's when he was small, somehow it's survived the years. There're also banana muffins fresh made this morning, though, I confess, not by me. Madison did it, she likes to cook. Maybe she'll end up a chef somewhere."

Bea took a sip of the coffee then took a small polite bite of the muffin Rose placed on a handy saucer in front of her.

To Rose, the girl looked as though she had not had a decent meal in a long time. She wondered about that mother. Even though the woman was dead and she should not be thinking badly about her, it was apparent the daughter had been neglected. Not only had she obviously not been eating properly but Rose would bet she was also emotionally starved.

Bea hunched over the table, her eyes fixed on the muffin on the saucer as though wondering what to do with it, and Rose wondered if after all she was doing the right thing. Harry Jordan might have talked her into the biggest mistake of her life, looking after this troubled young woman.

"Madison, the girl who baked the muffins, is one of my twin daughters," she explained. "The other is Frazer. They've just turned sixteen and are full of teenage angst."

"I don't remember any teenage angst." Bea frowned. "I don't think angst was allowed in my house."

The Havnels had only lived at the lake for a couple of months and now Rose wondered exactly where that house, where Bea had spent her angst-less teenage years, was.

"You a Boston girl, then?" she asked casually, biting into a muffin and the hell with the calories; this girl made her nervous as no other child ever had.

"Idaho," Bea replied, picking up her muffin too and inspecting it carefully.

"That's where the potatoes come from." Diz's voice

came from the doorway. He stood, hands shoved in his shorts pockets as always, feet bare as always, his sneakers on the table, as always. Though Rose did notice her son had put on a clean T-shirt. It was too big for him and she knew it belonged to Roman.

To Rose's surprise Bea smiled at Diz. "How do you know that?"

Diz shrugged. "We wrap 'em in foil and put 'em on the barbecue. When you unwrap them an hour or so later they smell great. Don't even really need the butter." He walked to the table and picked up a muffin. "Mom," he complained. "I hate banana."

"Blame Madison, she made them. And anyhow, say hello to Bea, she'll be staying with us for a while."

"I know. I heard all about you." Diz stood by the table looking at Bea. "I used to see you across the lake sometimes. I saw you rowing to the island the day of the fire," he added, eyeing her warily, carefully not mentioning the plastic bags and the man he had also seen there.

Bea looked innocently back at him. "Do you know there's a badger sett on that island? I've no idea how they got there, but there they are. At first they would hide when they saw me but I just stuck around day after day and they got used to me, I guess."

Rose wondered about a young woman spending her time on a small uninhabited island watching badgers. Looking after Bea would be a long haul. Then the front door slammed and her daughters came rushing in, all brown legs and short white shorts, chambray shirts with the sleeves rolled, long hair flying free. A breath of fresh air. Rose sighed, relieved. Even if she didn't mean to be, Bea Havnel was hard work.

"Has she arrived yet?" they called in chorus, the way they sometimes did, because they were twins and thought alike. Now, though, they stopped in their impetuous tracks and took a look at their new "guest."

They were tall girls and slender, but Bea was taller and skinnier, and looked as though someone had thrown her outfit together, the washed-out denims and the T-shirt.

"Hey," Madison said, giving her a smile. "Have you seen your room yet?"

Bea gave her shy upward glance from under her long lashes. "Well, no, I sort of only just got here . . ."

"And Mom's already stuffing you with my banana muffins." Madison laughed. "Come on, then, we'll show you to your room, we'll help you settle in."

"It's the haunted room," Diz called as the girls each took one of Bea's arms and bustled her upstairs, flip-flops banging on the wooden steps.

Bea stopped. She turned and looked at him, bug-eyed. "What do you mean—haunted?"

She looked so scared Diz was sorry he'd said that. "Just teasing," he shrugged it off. "Anyhow it's not serious haunting, just stuff that goes bump in the night. Some guests have said that anyway."

The twins groaned, while Rose laughed.

"He's a terrible tease," Madison told Bea. "Trust me, you'll be okay. It's just my cat, Baby Noir, you have to look out for." But still Bea flung a nervous look over her shoulder at Diz as they ran up the last of the stairs.

The phone was ringing and Rose hurried to answer. It was Harry Jordan.

"I thought you'd be coming with her," she said, without any preliminary "hello, how are you." "She arrived all by herself."

"That's the way she wanted it," Harry explained. "She's an independent young woman."

"Well, my girls are taking care of her, so she'll be fine."

"What about your husband?"

"Wally? Well, of course he's not thrilled but he's willing to allow it, for a week anyway. That is all I agreed to, remember?"

Harry said he remembered. Then, remembering Divon, he said, "Does Roman know Bea from somewhere? I mean, they could have possibly met, walking round the lake . . ."

"Roman? Why, I don't think so, he's never mentioned her, but surely he would have said something now, after all that's happened."

"I guess you're right." Harry wondered again about Divon. Then he said, "I have something to tell you but I don't want to say it on the phone. I should come out there and tell you in person."

"Oh my God, now what?" Rose held the phone closer so Diz would not listen in. That kid was so snoopy he overheard everything and she didn't want her talk monitored, and perhaps repeated to her husband. She didn't know why she was behaving like this about the detective, but her heart beat faster when she heard his voice. And that was that. He had never flirted with her, never indicated any interest. She was behaving the way those blond vacationers behaved with her husband. She was as bad as they were.

"It's better if you don't come right now," she told Harry, "until Bea's settled in a bit. Besides, I almost forgot, we're supposed to be having a dinner party tonight, some of the locals. Really, I don't have time for any more drama today, Detective Jordan."

There was a long silence on the other end of the phone. Then Harry said, "I have no choice then but to tell you now that Lacey Havnel was murdered. I can't say why or how, yet, but we have an investigation going on. Later today my colleague Detective Rossetti and I will be at the lake with a second forensics team, searching for evidence. I would like Bea to know that we'll be there, but please do not yet tell her that it is murder."

"Murder!" Rose said, holding the phone away from her, looking at it as though wondering if what she'd heard could be true. Then, "Hasn't that poor girl gone through enough?" she asked, anguished.

"She has." Harry's tone was gentle. "And I promise we'll do all we can to protect her. But her mother's killer has to be found. We've arrested one person of interest but that's all I can tell you right now."

"I see." Rose really didn't see. She didn't know what was happening suddenly to her quiet household where this evening she was giving her annual dinner party on the terrace for friends of long-standing. Just like normal.

"Please, I'm asking you not to confide in anyone," Harry was saying. "Even your husband."

"Wally?"

"No one, Rose. Please. Can I trust you on that?"

Rose said she supposed he could and Harry said he would see her later. Still stunned, Rose walked back into her kitchen and fixed a quick Nespresso. She thought about Wally sinking his shots of vodka and for the first time she sort of understood why.

She did not see Diz watching from the terrace door, did not know he had overheard.

Rose went back and stood by the phone, looking at it as if expecting it to ring again and Harry to say it was all a mistake . . . "Please forget what I said." Of course it did not ring and Harry did not say it. She was facing a terrible reality and with the murdered woman's daughter in her care, living in her house, she was now involved in it.

"Mom?"

She turned and looked at Diz.

"What's up, Mom?" he asked. In the back of Diz's mind was that scary image of his father rowing back across the lake from that house, from that woman's house.

Rose was so lost in her own thoughts, she hadn't known he was there. "It's nothing, hon. Just someone calling to let me know about . . . about something."

Her son looked so troubled, she went and put her arms round him in a hug. Suddenly it didn't seem fair to be a part of this, it wasn't fair to her family. She would forget about it, tell no one, get on with her own life. Bea Havnel would be gone in a week, then surely things would get back to normal.

Anyhow, she had guests coming for dinner, and it was getting late.

22

It was already 6 P.M. when Rose finally made it out onto the terrace and began to set up her table. She'd had to dash to the supermarket in town to pick up "the necessary" for her dinner. Wanting to make it quick and easy she decided on melon with prosciutto to start, then good old-fashioned beef stroganoff, which no one ever made anymore and which was so dead easy, served with buttered fettucini and a wonderful green salad full of all the best the local smallholder could provide, with, of course, her own homemade balsamic dressing and slivers of good Parmesan cheese. Then raspberries and strawberries with fresh thick cream for those who wanted, and orange sorbet for those who didn't, with the wafer-thin almond tuile biscuits Madison would make.

She had not been able to ask Wally about the wines, since he was still out "fishing," so she raided his cellar and the hell with him, brought up three bottles of the good French with pictures of grand chateaux and the year stamped on them. Might as well drink the friggin' good stuff while she could, she thought, then wondered exactly why she had thought that. Was it that she thought

Wally was going to leave her? What was up with Wally anyway? Why was he so on edge, so nervy? And why oh why had she lost him? Because somehow, she knew she had.

But. Right now. Life had to go on. Dinner parties had to go on. Looking after lost souls like Bea Havnel had to go on. Bringing up four kids had to go on. And maybe everything would work out.

She glanced across the lake to the Havnel house. The scene of a murder. She could see yellow police tape cordoning it off from would-be sightseers, and men in dark blue jackets with POLICE in big letters on them still bending over lumps of blackened beams and charred remains. Not exactly a perfect view for her guests.

Sighing, Rose turned to look at her own house. Her beloved lake house, the best place in the world: a square, simple white house with dormer windows above and a row of French doors below; a chimney of course—didn't all fairy-tale houses have chimneys? And this house was her fairy tale. There was the flagstone terrace with its white painted fence with the little lights slung between the posts; and the wooden jetty where a yellow dinghy bobbed, and the rickety boathouse that looked ready to be torn down and replaced. And of course their own small sandy cove, with the silver birches crowding in the back, and always the lake . . . sometimes blue as the sky, sometimes silently silver, and sometimes when the winds and the storms came, inky and tossing with whitecaps, foaming onto their little shore in sudden anger, leaving behind a trail of greenish weed that later they would rake clear.

How many times, she wondered, had she dived off that jetty? Did Wally remember the first time? Her in the white one-piece bathing suit that fit her like a second skin, breasts spilling out the top? Did he remember diving in after her, sliding down the bathing suit straps, holding her against his chest until their heartbeats sounded as one?

Rose pulled herself back from those memories. She had work to do. Shaking out the linen cloth she smoothed it over the battered redwood table that had been on the terrace forever and that could and often did seat twenty at a pinch. And there had been a lot of "pinches" over the years. Tonight, though, they would be fourteen. No, fifteen now, with Bea. She had almost forgotten the girl. Where was she anyhow?

As if in answer to her unspoken question, Bea came out from the kitchen bearing a heavy three-pronged silver candelabra. "Look," Bea said, placing it at one end of the table. "I cleaned it for you. It was so badly tarnished, from this damp lake air I suppose."

Rose, who liked her silver tarnished almost black because it looked more "casual" that way, forced a smile and said enthusiastically, "Well, my love, that's so good of you. I can't believe how . . . how nice it looks now."

"Oh, I did both. I'll go fetch the other." Beaming, Bea disappeared back into the kitchen.

Rose thought at least she looked happy. In fact that was the first time she had seen her really smile, not just that upward tilt of eyes and the shy hint of a curve to her lips. The girl had smiled. Harry Jordan might be right, perhaps she had done the right thing after all. If only Wally would agree, but Wally had not put in an appearance since Bea got here. And their guests were expected at seven.

The twins arrived bearing piles of the plain white plates Rose always used at the lake. Rose went and got the cutlery and set Bea to work tying knives, forks, and spoons together with strips of green raffia and placing them on top of the green linen napkins. Frazer and Madison were sticking stubby green candles into the silver holders and scattering green glass votives. Bea disappeared inside for a few minutes then came out holding a tray.

"I made these for the table," she said, putting the tray down carefully. On it were eight short green water glasses, in each of which she had placed a small fern from the garden, and a single white rose. They looked beautiful, Rose thought, astonished. And perfect for her table. She had bought those roses at the market herself, intending to quickly shove them in a vase and put it in the center. Now Madison and Frazer were exclaiming with delight at their beauty. "How clever of you, Bea, they're just lovely," they were saying, as Bea set a flower glass between each place.

Rose said, "Thank you, thank all of you, no doubt I'll be needing you in the kitchen later. Time to get changed now." She remembered the Target bags and wondered if Bea had anything to change into. Looking at her uncertain face, she guessed she did not.

Catching on, Madison said quickly, "Don't worry, we'll lend you something, it's not that fancy anyway, just locals, but parents do like to see us in dresses occasionally. Don't know why, it's just the way parents are." Then, remembering about Bea's mother, she shut her mouth quickly and said, "Oh, sorry, Bea. Come on then, let's hurry."

Rose took one last look at her table. A couple of leaves fluttered down onto her white cloth and she glanced up at the fig tree, frowning. Could the wind be getting up? Please God don't let there be a storm coming. But the evening sky was clear. All she had to do now was quickly shower and change into the loose blue and white caftan that felt like gossamer against her skin and hid, she hoped, smiling ruefully, a multitude of sins.

23

Diz crawled back along his branch and was back in his room when Rose knocked, then stuck her head in the door.

"Shower, Diz Osborne. Clean pair of shorts, a polo shirt—there're clean ones in your closet, and don't forget the shoes."

"Sneakers," Dix muttered unwillingly.

"Just no flip-flops," Rose said, closing the door and striding off to her own room, already pulling her shirt over her head. Time was of the essence. She still had the melon to cut, as well as the filet mignon for the stroganoff. She would get the girls to arrange the prosciutto on the plates. Oh, and she mustn't forget the bowls of almonds for the drinks, as well as the special pigs-in-blankets Madison had made. Funny how old-fashioned bits of sausage wrapped in pastry was the most popular item at any drinks party. Men adored them, memories of their childhood, she supposed.

She could hear the girls down the hall talking to Bea, exclaiming how lovely she looked in something they had dressed her in; heard her eldest son's shower go on; God if she didn't hurry there'd be no hot water left, it was always a bit short here at the lake with the small boiler.

Five minutes later she was in the blue and white caftan, sitting at her vanity, brushing her unruly dammit hair and deciding simply to tie it back; powdering her sunburned nose—she should use more sunscreen—a flick of pink lip gloss—Dolce & Gabbana's Beauty—and a spritz of Tom Ford's Neroli Portofino, a little exotic for a woman as down-to-earth as herself but it was a Christmas present from the children.

Oh, God, she wailed inwardly, where is Wally . . . oh God, please let him show up . . . let everything be all right . . .

"Mom!" Diz had stuck his head out in the hallway and was yelling for her. "I can't find my sneakers."

"On the kitchen table," Rose answered automatically; her children always believed she knew where everything was, and mostly she did, except where her husband was.

But a few minutes later, down in her kitchen again, she could not find the knife she needed to cut the melon. It was her favorite old Wüsthof, she used it for almost everything from melon to filet mignon.

"Frazer, where is it?" she demanded as the twin appeared, looking cute in a little white skirt and a red off-the-shoulder jersey top.

"Where is what?"

"My good knife, the German one I always use for cutting."

"That's what a knife is for." Frazer waltzed over to the corner where the knife holder was and took out another. "Here, Mom, use this. It'll all be the same in the end."

Grumbling, Rose began to slice the beef and the onions while Madison went to set up the music. "Leonard Cohen, a bit much?" she called to her mother.

Rose groaned. "Something happy, please," she said; though she loved Leonard Cohen it wasn't exactly upbeat cocktail hour background music.

Frazer put on Neil Young, who was singing quietly about pretty much the same things Leonard was, then set up background stuff for the rest of the evening.

Roman came down. Rose had not seen him all day. He'd been at his books. But Roman had always been remote, even as a child; now he was still in his own world, up there in his room under the eaves. Half the time Rose didn't even know if he was there. And maybe sometimes he was not, and sneaking out, doing what kids his age did, party and look at girls. But Roman wanted to be a doctor and was starting premed in a few weeks' time. Rose knew she was going to lose him too; everyone said once your child left for college, that was the end of life as you knew it. You were on your own from then on.

"Handsome devil," she said, eyeing him. "Better watch out for those girls tonight, I invited two especially for you, nieces of the Elliots, they're staying for a few days."

Roman groaned. Diz came in and stood next to him. He spread his arms and did a twirl. "So?" he asked, looking at his mom.

Rose laughed; he really was cute with his sandy hair still wet and combed flat to his head, and his ears sticking out. He looked like an alien from *Dr. Who.* "You'll do," she told him with a wink.

And then suddenly Wally was there, rounding the corner of the terrace pushing a wheelbarrow filled with ice. He waved at them. "For the champagne," he called. "I'll leave it out here, then I'll go and get the wine."

Rose's heart was pounding . . . he had come back . . . he was here . . . he was coming to the party . . . fetching champagne . . . everything was all right after all. She wanted to run to him, to kiss him, to have him hold her and tell her everything was all right between them, that he still loved her . . . but all she could say was, "I already took out some wine. It looks pretty good. You might want to open it, my love, let it breathe . . . I suppose."

"I suppose you're right." Wally came and stood next to her, he dropped a kiss on her hair. "I'll do that, then a quick shower and we'll be ready for the onslaught." He was smiling as he turned to leave. And then Bea walked in. And Wally's smile froze.

She was wearing a pink cotton dress with a scoop neck and a short flared skirt with a thin gold belt fastened around her waist. Her blond hair was pinned up at the sides with gold barrettes, accentuating the slope of her cheekbones. She wore mascara and pale lip gloss and small gold earrings in the shape of a leaf and gold strappy flat sandals.

"Well," Rose said, looking up from her chopping duties, at her husband and her eldest son. "I must say you clean up good. You look lovely, Bea."

Bea hung her head, sneaking a glance at Roman though. "Thanks to the twins," she said. "They put me together. I wouldn't have known how, myself."

"Why ever not?" Wally snapped. "How old are you? Twenty-one, I heard. The twins are only sixteen."

There was a sudden awkward silence. Rose turned horrified from her chopping board. "I think Bea meant she had no clothes with her, she lost everything in the fire, the girls had to lend her an outfit." Always the mediator, she smiled at her husband. "Of course you haven't met Bea yet. Well now, Bea, this is Wally, my husband."

Bea's head was down. "I know who you are," she said in a small voice. "You're very famous."

"Hmm." Wally's reply was noncommittal. He did not welcome the girl into his home. He simply turned to Rose and told her he would put the champagne on ice. Ignoring Bea, Roman followed him.

"I could use a glass now," Rose said, checking the ingredients for her stroganoff: the beef fillet was already cut into strips, onions already chopped, mushrooms, sliced. If she sautéed the onions now, it would take her only ten minutes to finish off the dish, which meant quickly browning the beef strips in butter, then adding the mushrooms and the onions, stir until heated through with a little beef broth, add sour cream and stir again. *Et voila*. Served with buttered fettucini, also straight out of the pan, it would be heaven, she knew.

"I can help you do that."

Bea was at her side. She took the spatula from Rose's hand. "All I have to do is stir the onions right, so they don't dry up."

Rose watched her approvingly for a few seconds, and said she must have done some cooking before.

"Not much," Bea told her. "I liked to cook, but Mom . . . well, she didn't enjoy good food. We pretty much lived on cold cuts and canned soup."

No wonder the girl was so thin. Rose spotted Wally, back on the terrace, already opening wine. She went over to him and said, "I missed you today."

He lifted his head from the wheelbarrow full of ice, now crammed with chilling bottles. "Caught a couple of little 'uns, threw 'em back in," he said, not directly replying to her unspoken question as to where he had been all day.

He opened a bottle of champagne, precisely, as with everything Wally did, twisting the bottle so the cork slipped out with a mere wisp of smoke. He poured Rose a glass and she nodded her thanks and walked away.

Things were so wrong between them that she did not know what to say, or what to do.

Now, she had to think about Bea. Earlier that afternoon, she had telephoned each of her guests to tell them that they had taken in the daughter of the woman who had died in the fire across the lake. "We're giving her shelter," she'd said, "just until things get sorted." When she'd put down the phone she'd wondered what she meant. How could things get "sorted" for Bea? They were talking murder now.

"Mom?" Diz was at her side and she gave him a smile and put an arm round his shoulders.

"Mom, if I knew something—a secret, let's say—but it was something I didn't think I should tell because it might upset people, what do you think I should do?"

"Do?" Rose asked. "Why, Diz, my boy, I think you are better off keeping your secrets to yourself. We don't want to go around upsetting our friends, now, do we?"

Diz, still unsure, was silent. Then "Maybe," he said guardedly.

Rose went to greet her neighbors, who arrived all at once, along with the girls she was hoping to set Roman up with, but they hung back shyly until the twins pulled them out onto the terrace with tall glasses of something they called virgin margaritas. Then Bea came out from the kitchen, politely offering round the bowl of almonds and the pigs-in-blankets that she had rescued from the oven because Rose had completely forgotten about them.

Rose saw Roman go quickly over to help Bea. She stood back, looking at her "party," the same one with the same people she gave every year, only this time it was different. The atmosphere was different. Evening Lake had changed. The women, as always, Rose thought with a sigh, had gathered in a small group at one end of the terrace, sipping their champagne served by Wally, who was busy filling up glasses and offering no small talk, while the men grouped together at the other end.

Rose wondered why it was that, until she sat them down at the table, her guests inevitably gravitated to their own sex. She went over and joined the women.

Of course they were talking about the fire. "Just like something from one of Wally's books," someone said. "And that poor child, losing her mother, the entire house gone . . . I never saw anything like that blaze . . . that explosion . . . I thought we were all going to be blown to heaven." Good old Rose, they said admiringly, if privately a little doubtful she had done the right thing, taking on such a burden with that girl. Such a tragedy.

Sipping their champagne they looked out of the corners of their eyes at Bea, wondering what was to become of "that girl" when she left Rose.

Rose excused herself and went and stood by the deck rail with its festive fairy lights, staring across the rippling dark lake at what used to be a house. A home. Only she knew there had been a murder. Someone here, in Evening Lake, had killed that woman. Maybe even someone she knew.

24

Divon Formentor was in jail and Jemima Forester felt like a traitor. Guilt-ridden, she paced her apartment, inasmuch as she could "pace" a mere six hundred square feet while dodging the blue sofa and the white IKEA coffee table, while tripping over the shag rug that had been the latest thing for young people a year ago and which she guessed was probably already out of style. She gave the rug a vicious kick, tripping herself up again in the process.

Sinking onto the rug, she stared blankly around her small home. The walls were lacquer-red. She had painted them herself over the course of several weekends and several coats. Now, though, she wondered about it; a redhead could get lost among all this red. And the mouse-color shag rug was wrong too; somehow she'd expected it to set off all the color, the indigo blue sofa, the red walls, but all it did was look like it belonged somewhere else. Besides, her heels always caught in it. If she could have gotten rid of it she would but she could not afford another right now.

Her parents had donated the forty-six-inch TV

clamped to the wall opposite the sofa, which she kept permanently on because it gave the illusion of company. "Other voices, other rooms"—hadn't someone once said that? Capote, she thought. Anyhow, the sound of voices was company when she was up at 2 A.M. watching old movies, or "working."

Working at what? she asked herself, still plumped on the shag rug, staring into space. She was a twenty-eight-year-old actress. At least she had told herself for twenty years she was an actress, starting out as a child doing juice commercials, graduating to appearances on children's TV, then teenage shows, then in a well-known exercise and fitness video that brought her some kind of temporary acclaim and a fair bit of money, enough anyhow to get her own small apartment, fix it up, and begin to think of another life because acting jobs were not coming her way. She was too "unusual," the casting directors said, too distinctive with that fiery red hair, alabaster skin, and pale eyes. "We'll think of you when we have something more 'Goth,' " was what had put the final knell of doom into Jemima's actress ambitions. She had contemplated going blond but realized it would not work, said thanks but no thanks and quit on the spot.

That was a year ago. Having watched too much TV, she told herself it was easy, she would become a private detective. She would start at the bottom with cheating husbands and anxious wives, to make a bit of quick money, then move on to "the good stuff." Real income. She told herself she was now a grown-up and had immediately taken an advanced computer course where she had learned a few "special" tricks from fellow students, like for instance how to hack, which she thought might be illegal but if she had to use it to catch a criminal, in her new career as a private eye, it probably didn't count. She'd put an ad on Craigslist and in the local newspapers touting her services, so far with no results. She was, in fact, an unemployed private detective, with not even a wife wanting to keep tabs on a cheating husband. Now, she sat in front of her sixteen-inch MacBook Air trying to figure out what to do next with her life, while checking out other people's. Which was why she was involved with Divon really.

Because of her friendship with Divon, she had been doing a bit of investigating into where the drugs were coming from—not on Divon's level, but beyond that—and had come up with some interesting, though scary findings. Divon had admitted to her he'd been involved with Lacey Havnel, the lake house woman, and intimated he knew who she was involved with, "higher up." Divon had not actually told her that last bit but Jemima knew he knew. And if she asked herself why he wasn't telling, she knew the answer to that too. Because he was scared shitless.

She untangled herself from the rug, kicked it back under the coffee table, and began to pace again. What she really needed to pace properly, though, was a dog she could take for a brisk walk, with the dog tugging on the lead and her bracing herself, stepping fast after it. A dog like Squeeze, she thought. Which brought her back to Harry Jordan again.

She went back to her MacBook and Googled Jordan. There he was, a simple one-liner, if you wanted any more go to his Facebook. She couldn't do that, couldn't just sign on to his Facebook, then he'd know she was into him. Sighing, she typed in "Havnel." There were a lot of Havnels listed and she typed in "Lacey." To her surprise there she was. Or rather an obituary. No picture, just a short bio . . . a seemingly blameless life, apart, that is, from three dead husbands and no children. And that she had died several years ago.

What!

Jemima went quickly to another search engine and came up with the same result. Oh my God. If Lacey Havnel was dead and had no children, then who was the Bea Havnel who claimed to be her daughter? In fact, who was the dead woman, burned up in the fire, who claimed to be Lacey Havnel?

Her cell phone was lying on the coffee table. Detective Jordan had put his number in there the other night. "Just in case you need to call about Divon," he'd said. They had looked at each other for a few seconds. Jemima had been embarrassed because she'd half hoped he would ask to see her again, if only for supper at Ruby's, but he had not, so she'd said a quick goodnight and turned and hurried away.

"Wait," he had called after her. She'd spun on her heel, smiling hopefully. But "I'll get a squad car to drop you off," was all he had said.

She had forgotten that was the way she had arrived, in the back of a squad car. "My mother would have a fit if she saw me in a police car," she'd told him. "I'll call a cab." And that had been that. But now . . . she pushed Harry's number. "Jordan."

He answered on the first ring, taking Jemima by surprise; in her bravado at making the call she'd hardly given herself time to think what she was going to say, and now she stumbled over her words. "Er, er, it's something important."

"You just can't remember what. Is that it? Fact is, Jemima Puddleduck, I was just about to call you." Harry wanted to ask her a few questions.

She sank down onto the hated mousey shag rug. "Was it . . . I mean I guess it was something important, about the Havnel woman and the daughter."

"Actually," Harry said, "I was going to ask you if you

felt like meeting for a drink. I thought at least if I asked you out you wouldn't think I was about to arrest you as an accessory to a murder," he added. But Jemima did not laugh.

"Lacey Havnel might not be who you think she is," she said quickly, without stopping to think.

Silence hung for seconds between them. Then Harry said, "I'll pick you up in ten. Okay?"

Jemima ran a hand over the old cashmere sweater she was wearing, the one she'd had since she was seventeen and would never, ever throw away, and the baggy black pants she wore when she was alone because they were comfortable.

"Okay?" Harry said again.

"I'll be downstairs waiting," she promised, already grabbing her newest skinny jeans from the floor where she had stepped out of them earlier, a clean white tee, the black leather jacket—it was what she always wore . . . he'd seen her in it before, the only other time he had seen her, she remembered. Two minutes later she was in the jeans though how she ever got her legs into them, they were so narrow, she couldn't imagine; the white tee; jacket slung casually over her shoulders, high suede ankle boots, a quick spray of Gaultier Femme; the Dior ruby lipstick that had somehow become her trademark. She took a step back from the mirror, eyeing herself critically, combing her long red bangs with her fingers where they fell into her pale blue eyes causing foggy vision but it looked good. Jewelry? Keep it simple, she told herself, fastening pearl studs in her ears. A pearl necklace, one strand, medium sized . . . where on earth had she gotten them? They struck just the right note between the ruby-lipped black leather hedonist and a lady. A deep breath. Oh my God she had a date with Harry Jordan. Well—almost a date.

She was downstairs waiting when he drove up in his classic dark green Jag with the goddamn dog with its head sticking out the window. She waited while Harry got out. He went and opened the door for the dog then sent it to sit in the back. He turned to smile at Jemima.

"You'll have to hope Squeeze forgives you for that," he said. "The front seat is his place."

"Old dog, new tricks," she said, inserting herself into the low car.

Harry closed her door then went round and got behind the wheel. "Any objection to Blake's?" he asked.

"You can take me anywhere you like," Jemima replied. And she meant it.

25

I did not hear about Detective Jordan's intriguing little encounter at Blake's with the Jemima he calls Puddleduck until later and then I thought it might—only might—as they say, "put a spanner in the works." I do not need this woman snooping around—doing her amateur "investigative reporting." My stage is getting a little crowded. I need no one. Of course I could shrug this girl off. (I call any woman under the age of thirty a girl and I know she's twenty-eight—in fact I know everything about her, I made it my business to find out because of her acquaintance with Harry Jordan.)

Anyhow, the detective might as well forget her sexual appeal, after all he already has a couple of female interests, to say nothing of the fiancée, the famous Mal Malone, TV star incarnate, who absconded to Paris ne'er to be seen again. Or will she?

Still, I'll take care of Miss Nosey Parker, my potential "spanner in the works." Curiosity can lead to confrontation and to my being exposed. You cannot allow that. It's time to get closer to my objective, the sweet sympathetic Rose and her family, who I'd hate with all my heart if I had one. Yes, I know, I confessed earlier to having a real heart, but you see it's not like yours.

Mine is a killer's heart, it guides me differently, sends me on devious paths. If you met me you would never know it, but my whole being is concentrated on killing. With the Osbornes it's a kind of revenge. I want the whole family to suffer as they make me suffer, admittedly indirectly, but suffering is suffering. If others have to fall by the wayside in pursuit of my goal of destroying the Osbornes, then so be it. What did they do to make me feel this vengeful? You might well ask.

You see, I never had a "family." I was always the outsider. All my life I never counted. The thing that makes a child a bully is what made me a killer, that instinct to go for the weak spot, the chink in the armor. At first you do it to save yourself from those bullies, those killers-in-the-making, then you become them. It's that simple.

And you start to like it. You enjoy it. It's the ultimate power.

First though, you have to get yourself into the power position. I never had trouble with that so of course it made my life easier, and I always got what I wanted. Which was? As well as the power, you could add money to the list. With power and money you can have anything you want, people will rush to do your bidding. Even without a lot of money I managed to charm, wheedle, frighten, if you will, people into doing my bidding. Sounds old-fashioned, in this fast electronic world we live in, but let me tell you when it gets down to it basics are just basics. Same old same it's always been. Fear. Power. Money. Sex. Life. Death.

Being attractive and knowing how to use sex is part of the deal, part of learning the trade of a novice killer.

You have to want the pleasure of killing more than the pleasure of sex, or it won't work. You'll get involved and then where would you be? Broke and alone, I'd bet on that.

26

Jemima and Harry sat, side by side, on a plastic banquette in a dim little local bar and grill where he was obviously well known, since they'd greeted him by name. Harry had a bottle of Perrier in front of him, Jemima a vodka martini. She felt badly now about ordering liquor when he was not drinking, but she'd thought she would look foolish changing at the last minute. True to his name, the dog squeezed under the small table leaving his rear end sticking out under Jemima's feet. She decided she'd better not move or he would have her ankle.

"He doesn't bite," Harry said.

She turned her head to look at him. "How did you know what I was thinking?"

"It's what everybody thinks when they first meet Squeeze. Truth is he's a softy. Unless he's provoked of course."

Jemima surely hoped she didn't provoke him. "Well," she said, suddenly not certain she had got her facts about the Havnels right. Online information was not always to be trusted. "How do you know the burned woman was Lacey Havnel?" she asked.

"We don't, not for sure, until we trace the dental records."

"What about the daughter?"

Harry raised his brows. "I don't know that I should be discussing this with you."

"What if I told you Lacey Havnel died ten years ago and that she had no children. That there was no daughter."

There was the slightest pause before Harry said, "And how, exactly, would you know that?"

"You mean, if the police don't know, how do I?" Jemima shrugged. "I don't, not for sure, only what I found online. It's quite simple you know, you can access almost anyone you want, get their personal information, know about their private lives, their past as well as their present."

Harry stared intently at her. "And why would you want to know that?"

Jemima shifted uncomfortably under his gaze. "Okay, truth is, I was thinking about you, which led me to think about the fire at the lake and the burned woman and the poor young daughter . . . I was just wondering." She let her words hang in the air. "I mean, like, I thought it would help."

"Jemima," Harry said, sighing, "you get under my skin, y'know that? And I'm asking myself why the fuck—excuse me—why I didn't think of that? Or why Rossetti didn't think of that? Or anyone else for that matter."

"Why would you?" Jemima said practically. "I mean it's only that I'm a computer freak and have a terminal case of curiosity."

"Nosiness."

"That would be about right."

Harry swigged his Perrier. She sipped her martini. Under the table the dog rested his big head on her foot. Justin Timberlake was singing something in the background. She glanced sideways at Harry again. He was staring straight in front of him, at nothing—or at his inner thoughts anyway. Certainly nothing to do with her. She heard his phone buzz. He took it from the pocket of his jacket.

"Rossetti," he answered.

Jemima tried hard to appear as though she were not listening. She looked down at the dog instead of at Harry. Squeeze looked steadily back up at her. She could swear the goddamn dog knew what she was thinking. It was unnerving. Anyway, what was she thinking? Only that she—Jemima Puddleduck—had told the big detective something he had not known, something he had not "detected."

"I'll meet you at the lake house," Harry was saying, already on his feet. The dog was up in an instant, next to him. "Sorry, gotta go, something came up," he said to Jemima. He waved goodnight to the guy behind the bar, and, with his hand on Jemima's back, walked her quickly outside, where he turned to look at her.

Jemima hoped the harsh light from the flickering bar sign had not changed her skin to green and her hair orange.

"Come on," Harry said abruptly, his mind obviously elsewhere. "I'll take you home."

It was, Jemima decidedly gloomily, a dud end to a dud date. Though of course it had not really been a date anyway.

A few minutes later they were outside her place. Harry jumped hastily out of the car to open the door for her, but she beat him to it.

"Thanks," she said icily. "I hope I was of help."

Harry was really looking at her now. "Your eyes are the same color as Squeeze's," he said.

Jemima rolled her pale blue eyes back at him. "Thanks."

"No, thank you. You gave me valuable information. I appreciate it."

"And you didn't even have to arrest me," she said.

"There's always a next time. I'll have the cuffs ready."

Suddenly clutched with guilt, Jemima remembered Divon. "He didn't do it, you know," she said. "I'll swear to it."

"I know. In court."

"And I don't believe that woman is the real Lacey Havnel from Miami, who was dead anyway."

Harry gave her a long, intense look. "You know what, Jemima. Nor do I." Then he waved good-bye, climbed back into his car, and was gone. Squeeze hung his head out the window, gazing back at her until the car rounded the corner.

That dog must be in love with her, Jemima decided. Misquoting the Meat Loaf song, she thought, oh well, one out of two ain't bad.

She wondered why Harry was going to the lake house. Curiosity had always been her downfall and in her new role as investigator, she thought she should find out. She thought about the story she would put on her Facebook. The decision took only seconds, then she went to get her car and took off for the lake.

27

There was one immediate way to stab Rose Osborne in the heart, though to prolong the torture I had chosen a circuitous route. Diz of course was the obvious solution. The last born, the "baby" of the family, the child who made Rose still feel young, kept her laughing in the tough times. Rose is the faithful sort, the kind of woman who never so much as looks at another man. At least not wondering how he might be naked. I don't believe Rose is a prude, it's simply years of indoctrination by men.

So. How to get to Rose via Diz. A plan must be made. Should he be killed? The body found at the foot of a cliff? Down some gulch? Floating, green and bloated in the lake? Perhaps he should quite simply disappear? Kidnapped, they would think. But who would kidnap him? A predator. A pedophile. A nut. Kids disappear from their bedrooms all the time, through open windows, without a trace. Mostly, they are never seen again. But I need Diz to be seen. Dead or alive? "That," as it was for Hamlet, Prince of Denmark, "is the question." I should decide the answer later.

28

Rose thought the dinner party was going as well as could be expected, considering the tension between her and Wally. She didn't believe in placement, preferring to let her guests choose to sit where they wanted. She did not fail to notice, though, that Wally went and sat at the far end of the table, about as far from her as he could get. And next to him, surprisingly, was Bea, looking like a sad angel, her long straight blond hair falling over her eyes as she picked delicately at the plate of prosciutto and melon, artfully arranged by Madison. Roman was on her other side. They looked, Rose thought, admiringly, like the perfect young couple.

It was a perfect night, the black lake unruffled by so much as a ripple, the tiny white terrace lights giving the soft Christmasy glow that Rose loved year-round. There was fresh bread in white-linen-draped baskets, tiny flat pots of golden French butter, each stamped with the imprint of a cow and a tiny leaf of parsley, a small touch but typical of Rose's attention to detail. They had moved on from champagne to a rosé from Provence, standing the bottles along the length of the table so everybody could help themselves. The only thing that marred the perfection of the night, of the scene Rose had so artfully set so that it looked effortless, was the faint acrid odor of burned house and the lights across the lake where the police forensic detail was still sifting through the wreckage. No one looked over there, no one mentioned it, everyone kept on talking as though it had never happened, and as though the young woman sitting at the table had not just lost her mother in a horrifying fire.

Which was, Rose suddenly decided, looking at Bea, not normal. Conversation and laughter flowed around the girl but she said nothing. She seemed to feel Rose's eyes on her, looked quickly up and gave her a smile. Heartwarming, Rose thought. She looked at Wally, leaning back in his chair, staring at the activity across the lake, not contributing to the conversation about some proposed local redevelopment with which normally he would have become deeply involved. Now, he simply sat, drinking—vodka, not wine, Rose realized—and saying absolutely nothing.

Rose excused herself to go to her kitchen. "Prepare yourselves for a treat," she warned her guests. "My beef stroganoff. It'll only take a few minutes. Wally," she called. He lifted his head and looked at her. "I could use your help," she said. She had to ask him what was going on. She had to know now.

But it was Diz who followed her into the kitchen, not her husband. "I can help you, Mom," he said, sending her heart lurching with love for him. How, she wondered, looking at him, had she and Wally produced a kid that looked like this?

"It's a nice party, Mom." Diz came to stand next to

her at the stove where she began browning the strips of beef, heating up the onions and mushrooms. The water for the fettucini boiled and she slid the pasta in, glancing at the wall clock to time it.

"Just get me the butter, sweetheart," she said to Diz, who did as he was asked, then stood anxiously next to her again.

"Mom, I have to tell you something," he said. "I don't want to tell you, but I have to, because, well because . . . I heard you on the phone, you said it was murder. And now I'm scared."

Rose turned to look at him. Her son's face was scrunched tight with the seriousness of what he needed to say. She turned out the gas under the beef and put her arms around him. "What can be so bad you can't tell me?"

"I saw Dad that night, in his boat, rowing back from that woman's house. Bea's mom's house." He looked up at her. "Dad was there just before it exploded. I saw him. And I saw Bea, running into the lake . . . and Roman was in the woods too . . . Dad was there, Mom, when it happened . . . and Roman . . . and now the woman is dead . . . and I don't know what else to say."

Rose glanced round her kitchen, at the fettucini simmering gently, at the warmed plates ready for serving. Her life had just fallen apart but she pulled herself together and did what she must do, for the sake of her son who was staring anxiously up at her, and for the sake of her family, and for Wally because she would never, ever believe he had done anything wrong.

"Well," she said, smiling at Diz, "I'll tell you what, I'll ask Dad about it later. He'll explain everything. And I'm sure Roman just happened to be taking a walk. Now remember, we have a party going on. You can help the girls carry the plates. And don't worry, everything will be all right."

As she watched her boy walk slowly out of the kitchen, she hoped she was right.

29

Harry parked at the precinct and saw Rossetti sitting in his BMW, waiting for him. Rossetti opened the door for the dog, who jumped into the backseat, giving his neck an affectionate slurp before settling happily down.

"So what's up?" Harry climbed in, just managing to slam the door before Rossetti took off.

"You are sitting on the evidence," Rossetti said. "In the file under your ass."

Harry pulled out the plastic file. In it were some photos.

Rossetti said, "We were checking the Havnel woman's bank account—which, by the way, is more than substantial—close to nine hundred K—in a checking account, for God's sake, not to mention what she might have in safe deposit boxes, which we have not yet been able to get a look at. Anyway, that's almost not the point. We got hold of the bank security videos, just checkin' . . . and there she is, our murdered Lacey Havnel standing in line, waiting her turn for the teller—and who do you think is right behind her? Perhaps even with her?"

Harry took a long look at the photos printed up from the video. "Jesus! Wally Osborne!"

"The lovely Rose's famous husband."

Harry studied the pictures. Something about Wally's body language told him that here was a man trying to look as though he was not with the woman he was with. "You think he was cheating on Rose, with her?" he asked, looking up at Rossetti.

"That's what we're gonna find out."

Harry shuffled through the photos again. Lacey Havnel was wearing crotch-high white shorts and a dangerously low-cut tank top.

"Hardly appropriate clothing for a visit to the bank," he commented. "In fact I'd say it was more appropriate for a little come-on rendezvous with a man she had her sights on, like the famous writer, her neighbor."

"I'd guess she was not the kind of woman to respect marriage. Or another woman's husband." Rossetti shrugged. "All's fair in love and war was probably Ms. Havnel's motto." He handed Harry another photograph. "There's more. This was taken outside the bank, on the security video."

There were three pictures. In the first, Wally and Lacey were standing outside the bank. In the second Wally was handing her an envelope. In the third, she was kissing Wally full on the mouth.

"Rossetti," Harry said, "are we looking at blackmail?"

"Sure looks that way to me, buddy."

"So what do we suppose Wally Osborne got himself into, that this woman had the power to blackmail him?"

Rossetti shrugged again, unsure. "The guy has everything: success, fame, money, a good wife . . ."

Harry was thinking about that good wife, thinking that Rose Osborne had no idea of what was about to hit her. "You thinking what I'm thinking?" he asked Rossetti, who glanced at him out of the corner of his eye.

"I think we have a motive," Rossetti said.

"Which doesn't necessarily mean Wally killed her. The man's intelligent, clever, he could have come to the police, talked to us about blackmail."

"But he didn't," Rossetti said. "There's another reason, Harry, and I'll bet it involves his family. With a guy like that, it always does. He might be protecting someone. Aw, shit, man, I hate to be talking like this. That's a nice family there, they don't deserve what's gonna happen to them . . ."

Harry held up a hand to stop him. "All that's gonna happen right now are some questions," he said. "And who would he be protecting anyway? Wait a minute, you don't mean the son? Roman?"

Rossetti shrugged. "Why not?"

"Because he's a simple, quiet kid and she's an experienced 'woman of the world,' and I mean the kind of world he knows nothing about."

"Sounds like temptation, to me," Rossetti said. And Harry had to agree maybe it did.

"Yeah. Well. Roman. He's kind of a ghost kid around there, don't y'think. Like, he's there, but he's not there at the same time, if you see what I mean."

Harry did. "A teenager," he said, trying to come up with an explanation and coming up instead with the same tired cliché.

Rossetti gave him a long disbelieving stare. "Were you like that when you were a teenager?"

Harry thought about it for a while. "I think I was into wine, women, and song, as the saying goes."

Rossetti laughed. "As the saying goes, so did you. Myself I was all for hanging with the guys, looking at the girls and hoping . . ."

"Hope springs eternal," Harry added, another cliché, and they both grinned. "Still, I know exactly what you mean. What gives with this kid? He's got the world on a plate, an adoring mother, a great family, a good future."

"It's got to be a woman," Rossetti said.

Harry gave him another of those searching glances. "That's why I work with you, Rossetti. You always come up with the answer."

"Wanna bet this is the right answer?"

"Who do you have in mind?"

"There's only one woman round the lake who fits the bill . . ."

"Jesus, you think he was romancing Bea?"

"They don't call it 'romancing' these days, my friend. And let's also not forget Bea's mother, the lovely Lacey. Older woman, all that young guy temptation stuff. A woman who is now well and truly dead. Murdered, if you recall."

"Jesus!" Harry was truly stunned, and, thinking of Lacey, repelled. "If you're right, we have another problem on our hands," he said.

"And another suspect," Rossetti said.

Harry didn't want to believe it, but he knew Rossetti was right and he had better look further into young Roman Osborne's life. And who would know more about that than his mother.

Harry put that on the back burner for now, though. He thought Roman Osborne was only an also-ran in this case.

"And before that I have something else I want us to think about. Ask yourself, Rossetti," he said, "do we really know who Lacey Havnel is? Do we know for sure the woman in the morgue is in fact the woman she claimed to be? Let me tell you," he added, "I have it on good authority"—he thought Jemima would have enjoyed the definition—"that Lacey Havnel of Miami, Florida, died some years ago. Childless."

Rossetti drew in a deep breath. "Then who the fuck is she?"

"That's exactly what we have to find out. And also, let's not forget, buddy, who exactly is Bea Havnel."

"The daughter."

"The young woman who calls herself her 'daughter.'"

They were on the lake road now. Squeeze scrambled to his feet as they approached Harry's house, thinking he was going home. He gave an annoyed little whine when they did not stop.

"Okay, dog," Rossetti called over his shoulder. "We have work to do first."

Harry saw the fairy lights strung across the Osbornes' terrace, the lamplit room behind. It looked so peaceful, so welcoming. He hated to do what he was going to have to do, but Lacey Havnel had been murdered and it was his job to find out who had killed her, and why. Even a man like Wally Osborne would have to take his chances in the court and the justice system, like any other citizen.

The charming image of Bea Havnel came into his mind. He wondered how involved she was, whether it was true that the real Lacey Havnel was already dead and buried and the body in the morgue was an impostor? Or was Jemima wrong and this really was her daughter? Thinking of Bea, of her quiet demeanor, her simplicity, he could not see how she could be party to such a fraud. And then, thinking of Rose Osborne, he said, "I'm praying I got it wrong, Rossetti."

Approaching the Osbornes' turnoff, he spotted a car pulled over to the side. A small silver Honda Accord. "Looks like we're not the first here," he commented, opening the back door for Squeeze, then walking with Rossetti up to the house.

Jemima had gotten there before them, just as the dinner guests were leaving. Now, she crouched behind her car, watching the two detectives. She had no idea what was going to happen, if anything, but at least she was there. If somebody got arrested she could report what happened on her crime blog. She was right on the scene of the action.

Skulking after the detectives, through the birch trees, she saw the front door open, saw the kid who opened it stare bug-eyed at the two men, then disappear quickly inside, heard him yelling "Mom." Then the detectives followed him inside and closed the door.

Something rustled the leaves in back of her. A footstep. She half turned, with an "oh" of recognition, saw the hand holding the bloody knife as the weapon came at her.

30

Rose saw the two detectives in the hall, heard them ask Diz where his father was.

Pretty in her silky caftan, her cloud of hair tamped in a bow at the back of her long neck, as she came toward them her eyes were a golden-brown question mark.

"Mrs. Osborne." Harry acknowledged her with a small polite bow.

"It's Rose. Remember?"

"This is Detective Rossetti." Harry waved in the detective's direction.

"You both look very official. Somehow I get the feeling you're not here for my dinner party, though you'd be a bit late for that anyway."

"Mom? What's going on?" Her daughters came to stand next to her, staring inquiringly at the two strangers. Roman joined them. He stood quietly behind. He was wearing glasses that hid his expression.

"Sorry to interrupt your evening, Mrs. Osborne." Rossetti was doing the talking since Harry had fallen silent, mouth shut tight as a trap into which he had no wish to fall. "In fact it's your husband we would like to talk to."

"Wally?" "Dad?" The girls and their mother spoke as one.

Then Diz said, "I saw him go outside a couple of minutes ago. He's probably taking a walk by the lake."

"Walking off the vodka," Roman said. His father was drinking too much.

Harry looked at Rose, who seemed to pull herself together, take control.

"I know where he'll be," she said. "I'll go get him for you."

Rossetti held up a hand. "No need, Ms. Osborne, the detective and I will find him. You said he won't have gone far."

"No, no, of course he won't, he never does."

"Unless he takes the boat out," Diz blurted, then immediately wished he had not. "I mean, like, just sometimes he does that. But not like now. Not usually at night anyhow."

A muffled whine came from the direction of the BMW. Harry looked outside and saw Squeeze with his head out the back window, kicking up a racket. Harry's eyes met Rossetti's, and they excused themselves and went to check what was going on. The dog was staring intently toward the birch woods by the lake shore.

Harry let him out and the dog ran immediately into the trees. They could hear him snarling as they threaded their way after him, saw he had a man backed up against a tree. The man held his hands protectively out in front. Slumped at his feet was the body of a young woman. Harry would have recognized that flame-colored hair anywhere.

His heart fused into lead as he took in the chilling

scene. That same heart was telling him to get the bastard, to kill as he must have killed. Adrenaline surged. Then his brain reminded him that he was a detective, that his job was to catch killers, not to kill them. No matter who the victim was.

His hands shook as he called off the dog, who came immediately to his side, never once removing its eyes from the man who still stood, too terrified even to move.

Rossetti swung his flashlight over Jemima Forester's body, then up into the man's face. It was Wally Osborne.

Out of the corner of his eyes he caught a glimpse of something else. A movement. Rossetti saw it too. The Sig Sauer was already in Harry's hand, safety off. He yelled, "Stop or I'll shoot."

The person stopped for a split second, then took off, fast, into the night. The rat-tat-tat of gunshots ripped into the trees, echoing across the lake, black under the moonless sky. Harry was running hard, the dog ahead of him, while Rossetti cuffed Wally, calling for medics and reinforcements.

"Stop or you're dead," Harry was yelling. "Arms over your head, down on the ground. Now!"

The person stopped suddenly, did as he was told, flung himself onto the gritty path, arms and legs splayed, hands flat. Snarling, the dog stood guard.

Gun in hand, Harry walked carefully toward his prisoner. "Bastard," he groaned softly, almost to himself, thinking of Jemima Forester lying back there and this killer . . . on the ground in front of him . . .

He walked closer, knelt, went to check for weapons, saw his prisoner was a woman. Blazing, he grabbed her hair, lifted her head to face him.

"Jesus Christ," he said, stunned.

"I'm so sorry, I'm so sorry," Bea said so loudly Harry thought the shots must have deafened her. "I didn't mean anything, I just came out for some air, I saw her there, I wanted to see what was wrong, see if I could help . . . I don't know who she is . . . I don't know why she's there . . . I don't know why she's dead . . . oh God, oh God . . ."

Harry let go of her hair and Bea put her face in her hands, muttering to herself about not knowing what she should do.

Harry noticed she did not ask who the girl was, did not ask what had happened, did not ask if she was hurt or dead. Did not ask what the girl was doing there. Bea did not ask one thing about the victim.

Squeeze stood guard while he went back and checked Jemima, turned her onto her back, pressed his hand hard on her chest, felt nothing. Blood from a throat wound mixed rustily with her long red hair. Small pearls were scattered across the ground, remnants of the necklace she was wearing, part of which still lay across her white neck.

He went back to Bea. "Get up," he told her, keeping his voice deliberately neutral. "Hands behind you."

Bea did as she was told. Harry snapped the cuffs on. She stared at him, stunned. "You can't do this," she said. "Why are you doing this? What have I done? Why don't you speak to me, let me tell you what happened . . ."

"So? Tell me." Harry stood in front of her, his face unreadable. Behind him Rossetti was on the phone to Medical Emergency, explaining the situation.

Bea's blue eyes widened in panic, words spilled out of her as though she couldn't wait to tell. "I saw him." She was talking quickly now. "I saw him do it. I did. I saw him . . . oh God I don't know why he did it, there had to be a reason . . . the poor girl was just . . . here . . . maybe she was his girlfriend . . . or one of them anyway . . . maybe she was jealous . . . angry . . ."

Those wide blue eyes met Harry's pleadingly. "It was Wally."

Rose had come quietly up to them and now Bea turned her gaze on her. A sob caught in her throat. She moved her cuffed wrists behind her. "Look," she cried, showing Rose, "look what Wally has done to me. I saw him, Rose, I saw him with her." She stopped and hung her head, as though in shame. "Oh, God, you were so good to me, you are an angel, you are the mother I should have had, you are everything I want to be. I am so sorry, Rose. I'm just so sorry, about Wally, but you knew what he was like with women. You must have known."

Bea stopped talking and Rose stood for a long silent minute looking at her. Her blue and white silk caftan made a soft swishing noise as she turned and, without a word, walked away.

31

Harry looked at Wally Osborne standing silently under the birch trees, his hands cuffed behind his back, the dog at his feet. He said nothing when Rossetti reminded him of his rights, did not look at either detective, nor at the dead woman on the ground. Nor did he look at Bea Havnel, whose sobbing rent the night air, a low moaning that Harry had not heard previously, not even when he'd fished her out of the lake with her house exploding in flames behind her, not when he had confirmed her mother was dead, not when he had suggested social services would help her.

Harry had come to the conclusion then that Bea Havnel was a very independent young woman with a kind of inner strength gained through adversity. She had survived life with a drug-addicted "mother" who very probably was not her real mother, survived near-death by fire, seemingly with her innocence intact. Now, though, he was skeptical.

He was aware that Rose was standing next to him. The twins, Roman, and the nosey-parker kid were all standing silent and stunned, looking back at him, at their father, at Bea.

The wail of sirens broke the silence of the night, blue and red lights flickered through the blackness; squad cars; an ambulance, crunching over the sandy lane, squealing to a stop; medics hurrying toward them, dropping to their knees next to Jemima, rolling back her eyelids, a shot of epinephrine, for the heart, tubes, fast, into her arm, an oxygen mask. Harry knew it was too late.

The sheriff's cars were there now, three of them. The officers stood silently, waiting while the medics did their work. When they had Jemima zipped in the body bag and placed on the stretcher and in the ambulance, they came forward, hands on their guns, looking at the wailing, handcuffed Bea, slumped on her knees, her blond head resting on the hard ground in front of her; at the handcuffed man they all recognized as the famous author; at his family standing in stunned silence.

"So, okay," one of them said, "let's get this show on the road." He glanced at Harry, who nodded. The officer hauled Bea up. She was limp, unresisting. As he walked her to the squad car she turned to look at Harry.

"You've got it all wrong," she called. "I told you what I saw, I told you the truth." She turned her head and looked directly at Roman. "You'd better get me out of this," she said, but Roman looked away.

The officer held on to her arm, getting her into the back of the car. "Save all that," he said. "You can tell us the truth later."

Watching Bea looking back at him out of the police car window as they drove away, Harry wondered about that.

He turned to Wally. Rose was standing in front of her husband as though to protect him. The twins held on to each other, terrified. Diz stood by himself, staring blankly at his father. Roman was expressionless behind his glasses.

After a moment Diz ran over to Rose. Harry heard him saying over and over, as he ran, "I'm sorry, Mom, I didn't mean it, it wasn't true what I said I saw . . . I'm so sorry, Mom . . ."

It seemed to Harry that suddenly everybody wanted to tell their version of the truth. He wondered what Diz's was.

Wally was being put in the second squad car. Harry noticed that Roman did not make a move to help him. Harry went over to Rose. He didn't know what you were supposed to say to a woman you had come to think of as a friend, and whose husband you had just arrested on suspicion of murder. Her head was bent, her gleaming hair pulled to one side. She gave him a long tired glance from eyes no longer golden brown, but dark with anguish.

"He didn't do that," she said quietly. "He didn't kill that girl. Wally writes those things. He would never, never hurt anyone. He doesn't even really know her, he was here with us, we had a dinner party . . . everything was normal . . ."

"Rose." Harry was about to say the hardest thing he ever had to say in his life, because he cared about this woman. "Your husband has been taken in for questioning in the death of Lacey Havnel." He remembered Jemima's face as she lay on the ground, alabaster pale, her brave ruby lipstick, her fiery hair and feisty personality. "And also on suspicion of the murder of Jemima Forester."

32

Bea Havnel slumped in her chair, pushed back from the table in the small interrogation room. Her clothing was disheveled, her hair straggled over her downturned face, and she held her wrists out in front of her, rubbing the red marks where the cuffs had been. Harry almost did not recognize her as the fresh, young blonde he knew. Bea was a hot mess and her eyes were filled with anger at him.

"Why am I here?" she asked, in a very small voice, like she was a pitiful creature being held against her will.

"You know why you are here, Bea. Because you were caught at the scene of a murder. In fact two murders. You have to admit that's not something that occurs often."

Harry kept his tone reasonable, though the truth was he was bewildered as to how Bea had gotten to this point. He could swear she was an innocent who just happened to be in the wrong place at the wrong time. The only argument against that was that it had happened twice and one of the victims was her mother.

"What do you know about knives?" he asked. Bea said nothing. Behind him Harry heard the door open and Rossetti enter with the almost obligatory cups of coffee.

Harry watched Rossetti set a mug in front of Bea. She did not acknowledge him.

"Coffee, hon," Rossetti said loudly. Harry knew he did not like the girl, and thought maybe now he had reason.

He said, "I have to inform you, if you do not already know this, that your mother was stabbed in the eye with a kitchen knife, the ordinary kind you'd find in almost anybody's home."

Bea did not raise her head.

"You told us earlier," Harry rustled the papers detailing her version of what happened in the fire, "that—and I am quoting here, 'her hair went up in flames and then she was running and then the whole place exploded and my own hair was on fire.' "

Bea looked up at him. "That is what I saw happen."

Harry glanced at Rossetti, who was leaning in his usual nonchalant stance, against the wall, arms folded over his chest, eyes boring into the girl, who, Harry knew, he did not trust. Not one inch. So? Why did *he* trust her? Instinct, he guessed. Pure instinct told him Bea could not have killed.

"The fact is," Harry said, gently now, because he did not want simply to trust his instinct where this young woman was concerned, because all the facts were against what she was saying. "The fact is, the autopsy confirmed your mother was stabbed before she was burned."

Bea remained silent.

"Can you offer any explanation for that? Anything that differs from what you already told us?"

Again, Bea remained silent, seeming, Harry thought, to be thinking about what he had just said. Finally she looked up at him.

"My mother was on fire, the whole place exploded. I was on fire. I ran for my life as she was running for hers. Whoever stuck that knife into her eye did it after I ran from her. Not before. I am not capable of stabbing anyone, especially my mother, even though things between us were not what I wanted. She did things I did not believe in. She led her own life. I was just—" She stopped, then lifted a shoulder in a shrug. "I was just along for the ride. She never wanted me. I knew it but I had no choice. She had all the money, she paid for me. And I did that. I looked after her all these years, because even though I despised her, despised who and what she was, I had an obligation to her. I did my duty," she said, her tone serene now, looking at the two detectives as though to say "those are the facts now do with me what you will," but with an undertone of confidence that Harry knew meant she'd bet there was nothing they could do. They had no evidence.

"And what explanation do you have for being at the scene of the murder of Jemima Forester?" Harry's tone was cold now. The image of Jemima was engraved in his memory.

"I told you, the dinner party was over, I needed some air, I went out there—just to take a walk—a normal thing like that. And there she was. I practically fell over her. I had no idea who she was. I still don't know who she is and why you think I have any connection, any reason even, to kill the poor young woman. My God, she can't have been much older than me. Why, why, why would someone do this?" Bea put her head down and began to weep.

Harry and Rossetti looked at each other. Bea was

right; they had no direct connection between her and Jemima, no reason to think she might have wanted her dead, no reason to believe she might be a killer. Except the coincidence of that knife in her mother's eye. And the knife that had slit Jemima's throat.

"I think I should get a lawyer now," Bea said.

For a second Harry thought she was going to add, "Before I verbally hang myself," but she merely looked at him, awaiting an answer.

"Of course," Rossetti agreed. "And you are aware that this entire interview was videoed and can be replayed for your attorney." He wanted it clear that they had not overstepped the bounds or broken my regulations.

"I understand," Bea said. Despite everything, Harry felt sorry for her. He had no doubt when her attorney arrived she would be out of there fast. This time, though, he did not ask where she would go, where she would stay. It was none of his business.

33

Interrogating Wally Osborne was quite another matter. First, he came complete with family, Rose Osborne leading the way, determined, it seemed, not to allow him out of her sight.

"You can't just take my husband and lock him up," she told Harry. "He did nothing wrong."

Clinging on to his mother's hand, Diz said, "My dad did nothing. He only went to visit that Havnel woman that one time when I saw him."

Harry saw Rose give him a quick sideways "keep your mouth shut" glare. He would not interrogate a child but Diz had just confirmed what he had blurted out earlier; that Wally knew Lacey Havnel, or Bea Havnel, or both, and that Diz had seen him rowing back from their house right before it exploded into flames.

The fact that Wally certainly knew Lacey Havnel and was seen on the lake when her house exploded, and that he was found standing over Jemima Forester's body, seemed not to have penetrated this family's armor. They believed in Wally. It was that simple.

"Don't worry," he said to Rose. "I'm not going to ask

Diz anything, though he will be interviewed by a member of child protective services later, as well as a child therapist. We don't want any harm to come to him, emotionally. He might think he is responsible," he added, quietly, so that Diz could not hear him.

The two daughters stood in back of their mother. The elder son, Roman, was next to her. Always the observer, Rossetti would have said.

"I think we need to call my dad's attorney," Roman said. Harry nodded, of course.

Meanwhile Wally had been taken off to an interrogation room and there was no doubt in Harry's mind he was going to end up in jail. For how long, he didn't know. That would depend on Wally's story, and any evidence they could produce, and on a clever attorney. He thought it ironic that the man who wrote novels about evil should end up being involved in evil. Perhaps it was true that the apple did not fall far from the tree—a writer of killers turning into a killer. The question was why.

It did not take long to find out. Wally was no match for Bea in the quiet confidence department. He seemed, to Harry, to be a broken man.

He sat in the same place Bea had, behind the same table, ignoring Rossetti's coffee, his handsome face haggard. Even his tan seemed bleached-out, toned down, unreal. Had Wally Osborne been living out one of his own stories? Had he wanted to kill Jemima for the pure thrill he got when he wrote those books? It was unheard of, but Harry knew from experience there was always a first for everything.

"What explanation can you give for Jemima Forester being at Evening Lake?" Harry started out.

Wally looked at him, bewildered. "I don't even know who she is."

"I might remind you, sir," Rossetti said, "she no longer is. She was."

Wally shook his head. "I'm sorry."

"Her throat was cut," Harry added, glancing at the video screen to make sure it was taping. Wally looked dumbly back at him.

"Lacey Havnel, who you knew, was also stabbed."

Wally shook his head. "It was the fire."

Harry said, "The fire burned her. The knife killed her first."

Wally stared down at his hands.

"How did you know Lacey Havnel?" Rossetti asked this one and Wally turned his head to look at him.

"She was a neighbor," he said. "She'd come to live on the lake, like us . . . my family I mean. I didn't really know her."

Harry's eyes met Rossetti's. This time his gut instinct told him Wally was lying. It did not tell him why, though.

"Were you having an affair with Lacey?" Rossetti asked, casually, looking Wally in the eye. "Y'know, man-to-man, these things happen, you both living on the lake and like that . . . proximity is always a big factor in sexual affairs."

"I didn't know the woman."

"Then why were you at her house? Why were you seen rowing back from there that night, right before the explosion?"

"I wasn't rowing from there. I was tired, worried about my writing, I just went out for a row around the lake. I often do when things get tough, stressful. Things were wrong between me and my wife, there wasn't anyone else. It was all my fault," he said, looking directly at Harry.

There was a knock on the door and a uniformed cop told them Mr. Osborne's attorney was there. Behind him, Harry saw Roman, still watching, still waiting. Was it only concern for his dad? Or was he watching out for himself, and maybe for Bea?

When he came into the room Harry told him they were holding Wally on suspicion of two murders. Wally was going to jail and there was nothing his attorney, or his family, could do about it. Right now.

34

Unhappiness made Mal cry. Boredom made her want her job back. She had given it all up—and for what? To look at paintings in the Museé d'Orsay? Lovely paintings but she was in no mind to take them in, absorb them into her soul, so to speak. She was alone again. She had drunk a glass of champagne last night in the café with the charming Frenchman who had helped her dry her tears, but she'd refused his offer of dinner and . . . And what? She wasn't in the mood for romance, a flirt, sex. She wanted that from Harry and he wasn't giving it to her because he was up to his neck in the lake with Lacey Havnel and the twenty-one-year-old beautiful blond daughter.

Mal was strolling down the crowded rue de Buci. It was market day but she was indifferent to the fragrant displays of cheeses, the polished piles of fruits, the colorful baskets of flowers, and the bright-eyed silvery fishes. Mal's thoughts were firmly on the Havnels. She got the feeling Harry was getting nowhere fast in his investigation, stalled, she'd bet, by the innocence of the girl he felt needed his protection. And maybe she did, but, woman-to-woman, Mal needed to find out a bit more about the Havnel family.

Mal might have left her job in a huff but her office still functioned, as did her assistant, Lulu, who was always at the end of a phone and always on the job.

Lulu answered immediately. "I knew you'd be calling," she said. "You just can't keep away, can you?"

"Not without a man to wrap myself around, I can't," Mal agreed, then proceeded to give Lulu a quick breakdown of her and Harry's current situation, or lack of it.

"I mean, what's wrong with me, Lulu?" She glanced critically at her reflection in a shop window: black pencil skirt, high suede boots, winter-white jacket, and a new blue cashmere scarf tied exactly the way the French tied theirs; there was definitely an art to French scarf-tying. Her earrings were small gold hoops, the dark glasses hiding her swollen eyes were Dior, her perfume Hermès. "I mean, I'm the kind of girl a guy can take anywhere."

"Yeah," Lulu said, practical as ever. "Except this man doesn't want to. Not right now anyway. So, what else is up?"

"I want you to check on someone. Name of Lacey Havnel. Also her twenty-one-year-old daughter, name of Beatrice. They were involved in a fire at Evening Lake."

"Harry's Evening Lake?" Lulu asked, surprised.

"The very same. He saw their house burn down with the mother in it, rescued the beautiful blond young daughter from the waves, and has not been seen by me since. I'm just curious about the girl, Lulu, you know how it is."

"I do," Lulu agreed. Men were men and women were women and jealousy usually reared its head at some point in that game.

"Anyway," Mal said briskly, "supposedly they're

from Florida, Miami area . . . leads one to wonder how they could afford a big house that just burned down. One might question the insurance on it, for instance, and exactly where they got the money to buy it in the first place."

"Mafia?" Lulu asked.

"Drugs?" Mal answered, thinking either might be true. "Oh, and if, just by chance, Harry calls and asks, tell him nothing."

"Will do," Lulu said, ready to get to work.

Satisfied, Mal rang off. She would go and sit in the movies, watch a French film in un-understandable French, just to torture herself in her aloneness; after that she would drown her sorrows in some more champagne. Or maybe she would just drive out into that lovely countryside where they didn't issue so many parking tickets, and no dogs lifted their legs on your tires, and the coffee was just as good anyway. Actually, she was getting to like France.

It wasn't until much later that she heard from Lulu of the murder of Jemima Forester, and Wally Osborne's arrest.

35

For once, Harry was at home, in his apartment in the converted brownstone with its stainless-steel-equipped chef's kitchen, barely used now except for the micro because he never had the time; the bathroom with its oversized shower with five jets and plain white subway tiles; the living room with its dark wood floors and the ebony baby grand in the bow window and the faded antique silk rug that Squeeze, as a puppy, had chewed at the corners; the plain leather chesterfield and the red leather wing chair, set next to the original marble fireplace, where a damp log currently burned in a desultory fashion, and where a bottle of Jim Beam stood on the chrome side table next to that red leather chair, next to Harry's hand, so he might replenish his glass without the effort of getting up and going to the bar counter to fetch it. Because tonight Harry was drinking.

It was not the first time Harry had seen a murdered woman. But it was the first time it was a woman he knew. Gutsy, feisty, daredevil Jemima Puddleduck was no more, and Harry was remembering her wild red hair, her ruby-red mouth, her joy of life. His heart was not broken; it was a lump inside his chest, a meaningless organ because the life he was leading was meaningless.

He had been thinking of quitting the force, thinking of coming to terms with a new life, considering seriously settling down with Mal, the love of his life. But not for this reason. Not because he could stomach it no longer.

Without even glancing at the bottle on the table, he reached out blindly and refilled his glass. A couple of ice cubes would have been good but he couldn't make the effort to get up and get them. Tonight, booze was meant to numb him, take away his feelings, remove his despair in the knowledge that he had probably been the cause of Jemima's death. If it were not for him, Jemima would not have been involved in the Havnel mystery. She would never have gone to the lake house. Though why she had done so was also a mystery. He remembered Jemima saying she had a bad case of curiosity. "Nosiness" Harry had called it. He recalled that she'd overheard him say to Rossetti he would meet him and they would go to the lake. He had no doubt Jemima had followed. In fact, she had gotten there first, because Harry had to make a detour to the precinct to collect Rossetti. It was Jemima's small silver Honda he'd noticed parked to one side, and Jemima's pearls—the ones he remembered gleaming on her slender alabaster neck—that lay scattered, like the trail of crumbs in the woods in that fairy tale, that lay on the ground around her bled-out body.

As he poured another glass the dog nudged urgently at his knee, wanting his attention. Harry patted him absently. His thoughts turned to Mal, to Paris, where she had run after their fallout. What if he had just gotten on that plane? Gone to meet her? Would any of this have happened? Would any of it have happened if he had kept his promise to himself to quit the force, to turn his life around, to give himself and the love of his life the time together they needed if they were to remain together?

Regret is a terrible emotion; it erodes the soul with its "what if's" and "might have been's" and "if only's." The truth was there was only the present, and currently Harry had had enough of that.

He lifted his hand and glanced at his watch. Unlike his gift to Rossetti, his was plain, serviceable, inexpensive. He was not a man who needed that pricey kind of glamour, not a hot guy on the loose, like Rossetti, who he'd bet right now was in some club doing his best to forget the earlier events, dancing with some cute chick who would definitely fancy him and with whom he might end up spending the night. Lucky Rossetti, to find forgetfulness, even temporarily.

Jemima's face floated in front of Harry's closed eyes: her flame-red bangs shaggy over her pale blue eyes; her eagerness to grasp at life and become a detective when she had no knowledge of what she was doing; her ruby mouth and pale skin, her aliveness, for God's sake.

Harry checked his watch again. It was exactly five minutes later than the last time he'd checked. It was probably midday in Paris. Where Mal was. Alone. Or last time they'd spoken she had been alone. Anything might have happened since then.

The love of his life was a very attractive, sometimes he would say even a beautiful, woman. On her "good days" was how Mal qualified being beautiful—when her hair was just right and she'd slept properly and wasn't made up for the TV cameras. How she hated that makeup, she so preferred bare skin and lip gloss and her special perfume, Hermès 24 Faubourg, which Harry believed only Mal wore because nobody else seemed ever to have heard of it, and the name of which, Mal had explained, was in fact the address of Hermès in Paris. Its soft spiciness hung like her own aura around her, leaving a hint behind when she left a room.

Harry not only knew Mal's perfume, he knew the very scent of her skin, of her womanliness, the texture of her, the supple smoothness, her gold-painted toenails and her pink fingernails, her laugh that began like a silly little-girl snort in her nose and which always embarrassed her. He knew the sound of her TV voice, the different sound of her voice on the phone, the sexy sound of her when they made love. He knew, he decided, everything about Mal. Except exactly where she was right now and whether she would even talk to him again.

He looked at his cell phone, lying right there next to the bottle of Jim Beam and the half-filled glass—one of the glasses Mal had bought him as a gift because she said his supermarket ones were undrinkable from. "When you're having the good stuff, that is," she'd added with a wicked smile. Of course Harry's wineglasses were Riedel because he would never pour a good wine into a thick glass, when the fragility of the glass against your lips enhanced the flavors and pleasure of the wine . . . What was he thinking! Fuckin' call her, find her, talk to her, tell her you are dying here alone, tell her you can't go on . . .

He picked up the phone, pressed speed dial, heard it ringing, once, twice, three—

"What now?" Mal answered, sounding aloof.

"I can't go on," Harry said simply. "I'm quitting. Somebody I knew, a young woman, was murdered tonight and I was the one who found her. I might be responsible. She was young, Mal, she was so alive, so eager for her future. I almost think she must have been the way you were at her age, wanting to be like you, a TV detective. And now she's dead and I'm supposed to find who killed her. Rose Osborne's husband is a suspect, the blond girl is a suspect. I can't do it, Mal. I'm guilty."

He heard her deep intake of breath, then she said, "I understand. I'm not sure you are quitting for the right reasons, but I understand. I never thought I'd say this, but I want you to think about it first, Harry. And if you want to talk to me, then get on the next flight. Okay?"

"Okay," Harry said. And this time he meant it.

36

Rossetti was not surprised when Harry called him in the middle of the night. He was used, anyhow, to odd-hour telephone calls. He was surprised, though, by what Harry wanted.

"Come get the dog" was exactly what Harry said.

Rossetti, the cool guy who always had an answer, was taken aback. "You mean, like come and get Squeeze? What the fuck for? What am I gonna do with him?"

"Look after him for a few days while I'm in Paris," Harry said.

Rossetti took in the sound of him. "You're slurring your words," he said. "That's booze talking, Detective, not common sense."

Harry's sigh was magnified in Rossetti's ear and he held the cell phone away, staring amazed at it. This was so not Harry.

"It's my heart talking, Rossetti," Harry was saying. "I can't take sitting here alone, except for my dog, remembering that poor murdered girl bleeding out with her broken pearls strewn around. I can't bear to think I might be responsible. I don't want to be the man who has to speak to her family, to attend her funeral, to nail the guy that killed her. I'm cracking, Rossetti, and I need you to take Squeeze because I'm off to Paris to see Mal. See if she can put me back together again."

Rossetti understood. His friend's life was at crisis point. "If anybody can help you, it's Mal," he reassured him. "Go to her, my friend. I'll come round now and collect the dog. Don't worry, I'll care for him like he's my own kid."

"I know it," Harry said. "And thanks. For everything."

Harry rang off and Rossetti thought, panicked, it was as though he had said final goodbyes. Jesus, he said to himself, climbing into the BMW and setting off for Beacon Hill. I hope he's gonna be all right. I just hope he's gonna be all right.

Harry had not even mentioned the two suspects and he seemed to have forgotten all about the fact that they were holding Bea Havnel for questioning and Wally Osborne for suspected murder. Harry's own life had overtaken him and he was not coping. It was up to Rossetti to set him straight, remind him of his duty, of his respect to the dead girl's family. They were cops. This is what they did.

Harry had obviously heard the car pull up and was standing on the steps to greet Rossetti. They held each other in a hug for a long minute. Rossetti could smell the alcohol on his friend's breath. Squeeze whined softly, wagging his tail.

"Don't worry, Squeeze, he'll take good care of you." Harry spoke to his dog, urging Rossetti indoors.

In the living room, he indicated the bottle of Jim Beam, lifted a glass questioningly. Rossetti shook his head. "It's better if only one of us is drunk, my friend," he said, taking a seat opposite Harry, who sank into his red leather chair, gazing back at him, as though, Rossetti thought, he had all the cares of the world on his shoulders.

"You didn't do it, you know," Rossetti said, deciding to get straight to the point.

Harry raised his brows, but said nothing.

"Jemima died because of her own foolishness, not your misguidance of her. You did not encourage her. You had no idea she would take matters into her own hands. Jemima was young but she was obviously very much her own woman. She was reckless and got herself into a game that was bigger than she knew how to play."

Rossetti leaned forward, shoulders stooped, hands clasped between his knees, his handsome face worried. "Harry, the girl got herself into a situation she shouldn't have, and suffered the unfortunate consequences. Unfortunately, 'consequences' is a word few of us ever think about when we lose our heads, whether in sex, marriage. Or murder. She put herself in the wrong place at the wrong time. That's all."

Harry's eyes met his over his glass of Jim Beam. "Did you see the look on her face?" he asked, as though suddenly remembering it himself.

All Rossetti could think of was the amount of blood and those pearls like from a little girl's necklace . . . they had grieved his heart, those pearls.

"Jemima was surprised when it happened," Harry said, recalling her expression. "Not just that somebody was gonna strike her, but as though she recognized the person who did it. I think she knew him, Detective."

Rossetti said nothing. He went to the bar and found some Perrier in the refrigerator. He drank it out of the bottle, went back and sat again in his chair opposite Harry, who, Rossetti thought, seemed to be coming to his senses. At least Harry was thinking again. Constructively thinking about Jemima's killing, not simply hiding from it.

Rossetti said, "I have it from forensics that from the angle of the entry, the assailant was pretty much the same size as Jemima. Not more than an inch in it."

"Then that would eliminate Wally Osborne, who's well over six feet," Harry said, surprised because he clearly recalled Wally standing over Jemima.

"It doesn't eliminate Bea Havnel though," Rossetti said, noting Harry's startled expression as he took in what he'd just heard.

"That kid." Harry got up and began to stride around the room, as far as the ebony baby grand in the window, then back again, and then again with the dog tagging at his heels, hoping for a walk. "She wouldn't harm a fly. Christ, have you forgotten, man, she almost died in the fire that killed the mother, and she might have drowned if I didn't get there in time."

"But she didn't," Rossetti said, taking another slug of his Perrier. "Besides, let's not forget we have some identity issues here. The woman was not Lacey Havnel. That woman died years ago, in Miami, Florida. The young woman who calls herself her daughter might be anyone. Anyone at all. One thing's for sure, her name is not Bea Havnel. Besides, we need to think again about Roman. I'm willing to bet that kid was lovesick for Bea. And let's not forget all we know about his movements that night to what he told us. Never forget, he's the one who could come and go from that house, via his private outdoor staircase, with no one the wiser."

Harry thought about it. A young man crazy in love? Did that description fit the silent, watchful Roman? He sighed. You just never knew, but for Rose's sake he hoped not.

"Jesus." Harry sat down again in the red leather chair.

Squeeze went and stood in front of him, ears pricked, eyes pleading, still hoping for that walk. "So," Harry said, after thinking for a while. "We have two dead people. At least, two that we know about. We know the woman was a drug dealer, how major we don't yet know, nor who in that line of business might have wanted to eliminate her. We have Divon, who worked for her and claims to know nothing. And a young woman who shall be nameless and who is not who she claims to be."

"I think you and I have some questions to ask her," Rossetti said, getting to his feet.

"No time like the present," Harry said, also getting up, but Rossetti shook his head.

"In the morning, my friend," he said. "You've gotta sleep it off first. Besides, you have to call Mal, tell her you'll be on the afternoon flight."

"Oh, God." Harry's face fell. He thought for a minute, then, "I'll call her tomorrow," he said. "Squeeze and I need a walk."

Rossetti accompanied his friend and the dog twice around the block, saw him back into his red chair, put away the Jim Beam and the glass, put his friend's feet up on the ottoman and a cushion behind his head; found the dog food in the kitchen cupboard and fed the grateful Squeeze, gave his friend a long final look, and he and the dog took their leave.

Tomorrow was another day. Hadn't somebody famous said that? Scarlett O'Hara maybe? All Rossetti knew was that whoever it was, was right. For him, and for Harry, and for Mallory Malone in Paris, and for Bea Havnel, and Rose Osborne and her family, tomorrow would indeed be another day.

37

After he left Harry, Rossetti went directly to the precinct, with the dog on the leash drawing comments from the usual bunch of overworked uniforms and detectives, in that hive of activity, with men hunched over computers or on the phone and where crime never stopped.

He requested to speak to the captain, told him Harry's story, about his state of mind, that overwork and no time off and stress had finally gotten to him.

"Everybody knows this dog," Rossetti said, smoothing a hand over Squeeze's soft head. The dog laid back his ears and gazed adoringly at him.

The captain said, "So, now you've got to take on Harry's work—meaning the Jemima Forester/Wally Osborne/Bea Havnel case. As well as his dog."

He was a big man in a blue shirt, sleeves rolled, twiddling a pen between his fingers, a frown plastered permanently on his wide brow where his hair had receded years ago into a kind of Donald Trump rusty fringe. "What's his real problem, anyway?"

Rossetti thought about it for a second, then he said,

"His future. Here, as a cop. And elsewhere with a woman."

"Malone?" The captain knew about her, everybody did. Personally he thought Jordan was a lucky guy to have her in his camp, whatever that might mean. "He marryin' her, then?"

Rossetti shrugged. "I couldn't say, but I surely hope so."

"Put us all out of our misery," the captain said, stopping his twiddling. "A man can't do his job right when he has woman trouble on his mind."

"You bet," Rossetti agreed. "Anyhow, Harry's worked his butt off without stopping for the past year. Now he's exhausted, as well as troubled about Mallory Malone. He needs time to himself."

The captain leaned back in his chair, crossed his arms over his big chest, and sighed. "Just when we could use his expertise," he said. "But then nothing ever seems to happen at a convenient time. He's friggin' earned it, though," he added, suddenly coming round to Rossetti's point of view. "No man works harder than Jordan, or does a better job. He's got a mind like a steel trap, it'll fasten onto the smallest detail and lead him into pastures new."

"Pastures new?" Rossetti said.

"By that, I mean Harry sees stuff from a different point of view from the rest of us, sometimes several points of view at the same time, and he follows them all up until he sorts out the one that means something."

Rossetti was remembering what Harry had said the previous night about Wally being too tall to be Jemima's attacker, about Bea Havnel being the right height, about Lacey and maybe Bea not being who they said they were. And his worries about Roman. "I think I'd better fill you in on Harry's thoughts, then, sir," he said, and proceeded to do just that.

The captain listened, nodding occasionally in agreement, then he said, "Forget Roman. But we can't hold Wally Osborne any longer. We'll let him go immediately. But it still doesn't take him out of the equation. The man was caught standing over Jemima's body with blood all around. And Bea Havnel was caught running through the woods."

"Maybe she was running for her life—from Wally?" Rossetti suggested, because suddenly it seemed logical.

"Anyhow, there's no way we can hold her either." The captain leaned over his desk, looking into Rossetti's eyes. "She's got the best lawyers in town, she'll get more if she has to. This young woman has money to burn and she's prepared to burn it."

"Just like she burned the house," Rossetti said, as though to himself. "The mother dies in the fire, the mother has money, the girl inherits the money."

"The house was expensive, and it was insured," the captain said.

"Jesus." Rossetti looked back at him.

"But . . ." The captain leaned back in his chair again and recommenced twiddling his pen. "But can we prove anything? All we have is theory. And that's why we need Harry, because he's the one that finds the links in these cases. Harry's a bit of a genius like that."

"Not in this case." Rossetti got to his feet and so did the dog, whining, ears down, missing his master and friend. "Harry thinks the sun shines out of that girl. Innocence in a blond package, that's what he believes, Captain." Rossetti made for the door. He turned and looked at his superior officer. "And you know what? He could still be right."

He walked through the precinct, stopping to check on

work in progress only to find he had been abruptly removed from Jemima Forester's murder and assigned to a case involving a series of armed holdups, mostly small shopkeepers bashed over the head, cash registers lifted bodily from the counter, nobody killed. The captain had demoted him. Rossetti thought at least it would take his mind off Harry and Mal, and off Jemima and the rest of the bloody fiasco.

First, though, he'd go to see Bea Havnel before she got off scot-free. Just to test his instincts about her. He'd find out who she really was. Murder for gain was common and Bea stood to inherit Lacey's money, plus two insurance policies that he'd bet amounted to another couple of million. The motive was there all right. And if Roman was in fact involved with her, he'd be the first to show up. A man in love could be guaranteed to be there for his woman. Poor Rose Osborne, as if she didn't have enough to cope with already.

38

Bea Havnel and her lawyer, whose name was Mike Leverage and who was known to be a legal killer and cost more than a yacht to run, were sitting at the table in the interview room at the precinct when Rossetti walked in. He glanced quickly at the young woman, who managed to be as demure and innocent as always, even in an orange prison jumpsuit. She had a way of looking up, under her lashes, chin down, a timid half smile on her lips as though asking for approbation, or maybe, Rossetti thought, for forgiveness for something he was certain she was going to call her "foolishness."

He was correct. Mike Leverage shook his hand across the table, leading off immediately with an account of his client, Bea Havnel's "silly behavior," which he claimed to be quite understandable "under the circumstances."

Rossetti sat quietly, listening. He gave Bea a long look and she looked back, directly into his eyes. Hers were wide and very blue and innocent. His were brown and cold and skeptical.

"The circumstances?" he asked, folding his hands on the table in front of him and not asking if they wanted coffee, something he knew would get under the collar of the lawyer, who expected due deference whether he wanted the coffee or not. That was who he was, and how powerful he was.

"No thanks, Detective," Leverage said, allowing irony to permeate his voice. "I don't want coffee. Meanwhile the special 'circumstances,' as you well know, are that my client, Ms. Havnel, was running because shots were being fired at her. Ms. Havnel was afraid for her life, Detective. I call that a very 'reasonable circumstance,' as I am sure you will too. Now you know the truth."

"The truth is still debatable, sir." Rossetti was careful to be polite, though he hated this fuckin' lawyer and did not trust his client one bit, and knew he would not be able to hold her in jail any longer.

Mike Leverage shuffled some papers on the table, clipped them together, and pushed them across to Rossetti. "Here is a copy of my client's sworn statement of the events of that night," he said. "You may read it at your leisure, Detective, when Ms. Havnel has been released and the charges against her erased from the record."

"Those charges are 'being present at a murder,' as you well know," Rossetti said. "I assume Ms. Havnel is not disputing that?" He looked at Bea, who looked him straight in the eye again. Rossetti thought of Harry, of how he saw innocence personified in this young, lovely blond woman. He wondered for a quick moment whether Harry could be right and he was wrong, but dismissed it immediately. She had been present at two major disasters, two suspicious deaths, he was hoping there would not be a third but he knew she knew he could not keep her there. The questioning was over.

"Ms. Havnel was indeed at the scene, but as you will

see from her sworn statement that was because the young woman, Jemima Forester, was following her. In some sort of charade as a detective, I believe. I think you can confirm that with your colleague, Detective Jordan," Leverage added with a smugly confident smile.

Rossetti nodded, keeping his eyes on Bea. A smile lifted the corners of her mouth.

"Thank you, Detective Rossetti," she said in her low, sweet voice. "I don't know where Harry is but please, would you thank him for me, for all the help he gave me. For his trust," she added.

At that moment even Rossetti was inclined to believe her; after all, he had no concrete evidence. But he needed to find more about who she really was, and who the woman who called herself Lacey Havnel—and also called herself Bea's mother—truly was. Meanwhile, he would ask her no questions about her identity; see where she took it. He'd bet the insurance would have no choice but to pay up. And meanwhile also, the burned woman could not yet be buried, not until it was found who had put that knife in her right eye. And also why.

Half an hour later, when Bea had changed from her prison overalls into her usual jeans and the new black sweater her lawyer had thoughtfully bought for her because the weather had turned cold, she told him she wanted to go back to the lake. "I need to stay out there," she said. "Somehow, there, I will feel closer to my mother. Until they find out who did this to her. To me." She put a hand gently on his arm as he held the car door for her.

Mike Leverage looked at her, surprised. "But your house is gone. Where will you stay?"

"Why, with the Osbornes of course." Bea looked surprised he had even asked. "You must take me there right away. I have to apologize to Rose, explain my mistake in thinking it was Wally because I saw him there too. I mean, it was exactly the same thing that happened to me. Wally and I were put in the same position. Somebody killed that poor girl and we were just there and we got the blame. Somebody with a motive, somebody who hated her, did it, then ran off, drove off, escaped . . . and I want to know who that person was. And so, I am sure, do Rose and Wally Osborne."

Mike rolled his eyes. He did not see a chance in hell of Bea getting what she wanted from the Osbornes, but he would drive her there, try to open negotiations, see what happened.

Wally had not come home, though Rose knew he'd been reprieved, albeit temporarily. Therefore she was astonished when she saw the lawyer's car pull up in front of her house and Bea get out. She opened her front door, stood, arms folded, waiting for them to speak.

Mike Leverage went first, standing at the bottom of the low flight of steps leading into the house. "Ms. Havnel has come to apologize, ma'am," he said, holding his arms wide as though it was he who was apologizing. "Ms. Havnel is innocent of any wrongdoing, ma'am. As innocent as your husband. They were both caught in a bad position, the wrong place at the wrong time. Ms. Havnel entreats you to let her speak, to please see her, allow her to apologize to you and your husband. Indeed, to all your family. Her life has fallen down around her ears, so to speak. She has nowhere to turn. No one to listen to her."

"No one to take her in. Again," Rose said, in a voice so cold it almost made Mike shiver.

Bea was staring at Rose out of the open car window. She looked young, terrified, and alone.

"Please tell your client," Rose said to Mike, "that if she cares to cast her mind back, she might remember that not only did she accuse my husband of murder, but that she caused infinite distress to my entire family, that my husband's reputation is clearly ruined, and that she has her own property across the lake. Burned down, of course, and with her mother in it. Murdered, they say, though Bea, who was with her when it happened, seems not to know anything about that. Nor does she know anything about the death of young Jemima, though she was also at that scene. I do not think it advisable to take in a woman with those suspicions hanging over her. Not only that, you might want to remind Bea, since she appears to have also forgotten, there is a small guest house on her own property which was not burned in that fire. I suggest she goes there, makes of it what she will. She is not welcome in my home."

Bea heard everything. She got out of the car and went and stood next to her attorney at the bottom of the steps. Her face was pale, her mouth tight.

"Please, Rose," she said, almost in a whisper, she was so close to tears. "Let me apologize. I came here to you when all was lost. You took me in. I'd always admired you from afar, when I would see you walking round the lake, you and your family. I wanted a family so bad and all I had . . ." She stopped herself, and clasped her hands together, staring down at them. "I never accused Wally," she said. "All I said was that he was there, and so was I. We were both caught in the same trap. Both innocent. I was put in prison, Rose, just like Wally. Please, please, can you forgive me? I will not beg you to take me in, I know that's too much to ask, but please, speak to me again, Rose. Allow me to be the person you believed I was, the person I really am."

It was tempting. The girl seemed so truly hurt, so

completely alone. All she had was a lawyer and money in the bank and a room at the Ritz. Rose thought of her own family, of her girls, of Diz who saw everything; and Wally who was going through his own hell. She found she had no emotion to spare for Bea Havnel.

"I'm sorry, Bea, but you must find your own future," she said, and she walked back inside and shut the door.

Mike looked at his client. Her face was unreadable, completely lacking in emotion, though he guessed she had just received a serious blow to her future.

Bea caught his glance, looked away, and said, "Rose is right, I had completely forgotten the guest house. It's on the other side of the lake. You can see it from here, next to the burned ruins where my mother died. And," she added, "I am going to make sure whoever did that pays the final price."

39

Later that day, Wally came home. He just walked in, said "hi" as if he'd been off on some book-signing jaunt, while they stood silently, gaping. Then he went upstairs to change.

Rose was trying to act normal, as though everything was the same as it used to be. She went into her usual kitchen bustle, attacking the stove with rashers of bacon sizzling madly in the pan, even though it was suppertime, whipping eggs into a frenzy for omelets all round, slicing leftover chicken, heating up frozen gravy in the micro, boiling water for some kind of vegetable she knew she must have in the fridge, she just hadn't had the heart to look right now. In fact she didn't want to be doing any of this; she wanted to be alone with her husband, to ask him what the truth was. Not that it mattered because she knew Wally would not tell her anyway.

Everyone but Wally was sitting around the table. Bottles of wine had been opened, Cokes dispensed in cans her sons crackled in their hands after they'd drained them. Seemingly unable to bear the lack of conversation Roman got up and put on FM radio, playing contemporary classics: Rod singing oldies, Bublé singing something else. At least, Rose thought, it covered the silent hole in their lives. Temporarily. Roman sat back down staring at his can of Coke, remote as always. It was as though life was being played out in front of him and he chose not to notice.

"I hate that stuff." Diz glared at his brother, who shrugged an uncaring shoulder and answered, "Whatever."

Rose slammed down her spatula, strode across the room, and turned off the music. "He's right," she told Roman. "At least put on something decent."

Without waiting for him to do so she slipped in a disc of Chopin piano études being played by someone with ethereally delicate fingers, which somehow in their nerve-ridden kitchen sounded totally out of place.

All eyes swiveled to Wally when he walked into the room. He'd changed from what Rose now thought of as his "prison garb," meaning the clothes he'd been wearing when he was caught at the murder scene, into baggy tan shorts and a white tee. His hair was plastered to his head, still wet from the shower. He nodded acknowledgement to his family and took a seat at the table.

No one spoke; the only sound was of the bacon still sputtering. Everyone was eyeing Wally out of the corners of their eyes, afraid to be the first to ask the questions that were on the tips of their tongues.

After a minute Wally got up. He went to the freezer, took out a bottle of vodka and a glass, frosted-white, then poured the vodka into it. He drank it straight down, standing by the still-open freezer door, then turned and surveyed his bug-eyed family.

"I never expected to have to tell you this." He slammed the freezer door shut and stood tall, blondly handsome, the man any woman would want, the man any kid would be proud to call Dad. "I am a drug addict," he said. "I fell into the situation I have tried all my life to keep you out of. I became trapped by it. Drugs are insidious, they steal into your life while you, poor sucker, feel you have the world by the balls. Only you don't. The person who first turned you on—turned me on when I was at a low point, wondering if I could ever write again, wondering about where my life was going, falling into a depression so deep the bottom of the lake looked like a valid answer. This person saw me, saved me, found the answer to all my problems. That's what I thought, as all addicts do I guess, until very quickly I found I still had all my problems, plus now another even bigger one. One I had to pay handsomely for. And did."

Diz got up and went to stand next to his father. "It'll be okay, Dad, we know you didn't kill Jemima, we'll help you with the drugs."

Wally stroked his boy's hair. "Thank you, son."

Rose put down her spatula and left the bacon to burn. She stood in front of her husband, her hands on his shoulders, gazing into his eyes as though searching for something he might be hiding.

"I had nothing to do with Jemima," he told her. "I never even met her, but for the police I remain 'a person of interest.'" Wally frowned, as if thinking of the dead young woman becoming simply a police case. His voice trembled as he added, "I mean, in her murder. I don't know who did it, though I have to believe it has something to do with drugs. I'd just left the dinner party, Rose, I simply went outside for a while because I needed to be alone, to ask myself what I thought I was doing, where I imagined I was going to end. And that's when I heard Bea screaming. I saw her run through the trees, went after her and found Jemima lying there." Wally put his head in his hands. "Dear God, I hope never to have to see anything like that again. I write about this! I know exactly how it's done, exactly what knife to use. I write how that knife feels as it slits open a throat, the way the blood spurts then oozes, I write about blood matting the hair, the broken necklaces . . ."

He lifted his head and looked at his stunned and silent family. "I am telling you the truth and I'm thinking I deserve to be suspected of this horror, a man like me, who makes money from it."

Rose slid her arms around her husband and he bent his head into her smooth throat, the kind of throat Rose knew Wally knew how to slit, knew exactly where the jugular was, knew where the muscle was that paralyzed. "I believe you," she told him, though an uneasy weight seemed to have gripped her heart. "I believe you, Wally," she repeated, looking round, collecting her children's eyes with her own.

"We believe you, Dad," Frazer and Madison chorused staunchly.

"What about Bea?" Roman said.

Everyone turned to look at him.

"Were you having an affair with her?" Roman asked.

"Jesus!" Wally was shocked. "Don't be ridiculous," Wally replied, quickly. "I certainly was not."

Diz thought Roman looked relieved as he turned away, and he guessed the reason why. It was *Roman* who was enamored of Bea, not his dad. Bea had Roman in her clutches and he'd do anything for her . . . But *murder*? No, no, he didn't think so. Roman could *not* do that, not with a mother like *Rose* . . . he would not hurt *her,* though he might be out to get Bea if she was stringing him along. Oh God, what was happening to his family?

Diz looked at his mother holding tightly to his father

as though if she let go the whole family might sink into Evening Lake. As though, without Wally, they would all be gone forever.

With an arm around Rose's waist, Wally walked back to the table where he poured her a glass of wine. He glanced at the label. It was a good French chateau and a prime year. "You always know best," he said to Rose, who hurried, too late, to try to save the burning bacon.

"Dad?" Diz said, and his father glanced up at him. "Exactly where is Bea?"

The name dropped like a stone into a pool, with ever-widening circles until it entrapped them all.

"I asked you never to say that name again," Rose said too quickly, because she was nervous and quite possibly afraid of the answer.

But Wally replied, "I believe she has her own place, back across the lake. I imagine that's where she will live."

"You mean—near us?" Diz was stunned.

"Either there or at the Ritz," Rose said, making a joke of it and scraping the burned bacon into the garbage disposal.

Diz was kind of wishing she could have done the same with Bea, but he simply shrugged and took himself off upstairs, where he climbed out on his branch and focused his binoculars on the Havnel property.

There were no lights. Even Forensics must have called it quits for the night. A woman had been murdered there; a second woman killed right here in their woods. His father had been implicated. Bea had been implicated. Diz needed to know the truth and he meant to find out that truth by watching, waiting for the one wrong move that would give Bea's game away. Because he was certain now, it must be her. Tomorrow, he could go over there, spy on her, he could follow her, find out what she was up to.

She was sure to make a mistake, criminals on TV always did, and Diz desperately needed to prove his father's innocence.

40

Harry was sleeping off the booze. In his dream he was in some cold, dark, labyrinthine hole, a place filled with inky water where no sound could be heard except a muffled ringing. It rang and rang. Try as he might, Harry could not get away from it. And then he woke up and it was still there. God almighty, it was his doorbell. Somebody had their finger on it and was not letting go.

Filled with sudden anger, he hurled himself out of the red leather chair and went to open the door, ready to give whoever it was a choice piece of his mind.

"What the fuck . . ." he said, then stopped. Rose Osborne was standing on his doorstep, wrapped in a big orange shawl over gray sweatpants and a jacket that said HARVARD in crimson letters across the front. Her thick dark hair was dragged into a bun, she wore no makeup, and her eyes were huge angry brown daggers looking at him.

"It's three in the morning," Harry said, knowing it must be at least somewhere near that.

"So what?" She pushed past him and stood in his hallway, looking round. "Where's the dog?"

"Gone. Er . . . my friend—er, Rossetti, took him while I'm gone."

"You are not 'gone,' " Rose pointed out. Coldly.

"Well, yes, that is no, but I will be gone, tomorrow. That is," he glanced at his watch one more time. "That is, I mean—today."

She turned on him then, eyes not "blazing" as he might have described them, but hard, inimical. She looked, Harry thought, ready to kill him.

"Rose," he said, trying to recapture the picture he'd first had of her in the white gypsy blouse with her bare brown shoulders and flying free hair and that lovely aura of womanliness that so attracted him. Now, she was a virago. Now, he knew, she was here to protect her man.

"Bea came to tell me she was innocent," Rose said. "Begged me to believe her. I think she even wanted me to take her back, look after her. Again." She shook her head at such madness. "You arrested Wally," she said, in a voice of ice. "You accused my husband of murdering that young woman, Jemima. I told you Wally would never have done that, he could not have done such a terrible thing." She took a step closer, her face in Harry's. "I know now what he was doing," she said. "He won't admit it because of his children, he believes his innocence will be proven and there will be nothing to besmirch his reputation, his family's reputation, Wally's children mean everything to him. Except . . ."

Harry took Rose's arm and led her into the living room. He sat her down on his red leather chair He hunched on the footstool opposite her.

"Except?"

Rose took a deep breath. "It was drugs. Wally was doing drugs, Detective Jordan."

It flashed through Harry's mind that he was no longer "Harry," chummy over cups of coffee at her long pine table in that peaceful kitchen with the good smell of soup on the stove and the freshness that was Rose. He thought how far they had come in just a few days.

"I'm willing to bet I know who was supplying them," he said.

Rose shook her head. "Then you know more than I do. I only know what he told me. Perhaps he's told his lawyers more, they were with him for hours, I don't know what will happen next."

"Your husband was being blackmailed. The 'good family man,' the 'famous writer,' 'the upholder of clean living,' 'the charmed life.' I'm afraid, Rose, Wally's ego could not tolerate being exposed as a liar and an addict, it would mean ruin and he knew it."

She was looking at him, her big dark eyes stunned into blankness. He got up, went to the bar, opened a bottle of wine, actually a decent California Syrah he thought substantial enough to calm shattered nerves, a little bit anyway. He poured her a glass, took it over and put it in her hand, closing her fingers around it so she would not drop it.

Rose glanced down at it, surprised, and, always well mannered, thanked him. She took a gulp, then another. She wiped the back of her hand across her mouth and said, "What do you mean, Harry Jordan, my husband is a drug addict?"

"That's not the important issue right now. What's important is that I believe—I know—your husband is not a murderer. He did not kill Jemima Forester. I'd bet my own life on that."

Rose began to cry, huge tears running unheeded down her cheeks, over her chin, into her neck. Harry went and got the box of Kleenex from the bar.

"It's okay," he said gently. "It'll be okay now, you'll see. I'll make sure Rossetti gets everything right, he'll take care of it for you."

"But what about you?" She stared, panicked, at him. "Why don't you take care of everything? After all, it was you who started it."

Harry sat for a moment, on the footstool, looking up at the lovely distraught woman who needed his help, whose husband needed his help, whose very lives had been touched by evil. Of course he was the man who should be taking care of her. Of them all.

"Trust me," he said to Rose. "I want to. But I'm leaving tomorrow—today that is, for Paris. It's something I can't put off."

He got to his feet, and so did she. He took the empty glass from her hand, wrapped her orange shawl around her, smoothed the fringes over the edges. It was soft under his touch, cashmere, he knew. Soft as the woman in front of him, whose arms now came and wrapped around him. He held her close, breathing in that fresh-air scent of her, loving her gently.

"It'll be okay," he whispered in her ear. "You'll see, everything will be okay. I know it."

She moved away, looked at him. "Promise?" she asked.

"I promise," Harry said.

Then he called a taxi to take Rose home. Next he called the airline to confirm his flight to Paris the following—or rather that afternoon. Then he called Rossetti.

"I want you to speak to Wally's attorneys," he said. "He's not our man, I'm sure of it."

"I know, I already spoke to the captain," Rossetti said. "Anyway, why the fuck aren't you on the flight?"

"I am," Harry said. "I just need to shower, pack a bag, and I'm off."

"You sure you're off to Paris?"

Harry smiled at the skepticism in his colleague's voice.

"This time I'm sure," he said. "You are gonna work it all out, Rossetti. All by yourself."

41

When she met Harry at Charles de Gaulle Airport, Mal thought he looked just the same as always: same unruly dark hair; same keen gray eyes searching her out in the crowd; same loping stride, like "a panther on the loose," as she had once told him, only half joking. Lean, lithe, and sexy, that was her Harry. And also, she could see as he came closer, a very tired Harry.

He felt her eyes on him, spotted her, smiled, and then they were in each other's arms, his face in her hair, his hands firm against her back, pulling her closer.

"You don't know how good it is to see you," he murmured.

Smiling, she said, "I've always tried to get you to Paris."

"And now you've succeeded. And I'm glad to be here."

"You'll be even gladder," she said, inserting herself closer to him, not caring what the rest of the world hurrying by burdened with hand baggage and fatigue thought about them. They were lovers. So what? This was Paris.

She glanced searchingly over his shoulder. "I'm looking for the dog," she explained, glad when she made Harry laugh.

All he carried was his old duffel in which Mal would bet would be one clean pair of Jockeys; maybe a pair of socks if he was wearing socks right now, most often he did not; one clean white shirt, an old cashmere jacket he sometimes wore when they were going somewhere "posh," as he termed a good restaurant, which meant to him anything other than Ruby's; definitely no tie, he never wore one. There would be the old leather bag with his toothbrush, etc, and a copy of *War and Peace.* Harry always took *War and Peace* on his travels. He never finished it; said he always had to start again, at the beginning, because he couldn't remember who was who, the names had him so confused. "Good training for a detective," he told Mal when she laughed. Harry was definitely not a Kindle man; he still wanted that old book, the feel of paper in his hand, pages he could turn, the end he could read first to catch up. Harry always needed to know the ending first, and now, with this Havnel case and the death of the young woman, Mal realized he did not know the ending and that it grieved him.

She had, naturally, parked her car on a red line. There was another parking ticket and an irate warden who, when she tried a few tears and in garbled French explained that her passenger was Homicide Detective Harry Jordan, famous in the USA, let her off with a warning.

"You haven't changed one bit," Harry said, folding himself into the Fiat. "You get away with murder."

Under the circumstances, Mal thought it an unfortunate choice of words. "Wanna go to my place first? Or would you like to go all Parisian, and sip a glass of wine, in a particular sidewalk café I like?"

"Definitely the wine." Harry put his hand on her knee and gave it a squeeze. "And the sidewalk café you like so much. I need to know where you've been spending your time, alone in Paris."

Mal thought it was better not to mention the young man in the tweed jacket with whom she had shared champagne the previous night. After all, she had been crying over Harry, which was the reason they had met.

She drove rapidly and confidently through the rush-hour traffic, through the unending grim suburbs and into what Mal termed "the light," when the famous skyline, marked by the Eiffel Tower, appeared.

"Cities are all mere cities until you find their heart," she explained to Harry, jostling her way into Saint-Germain and parking, illegally one more time, on the narrow rue Jacob, a few paces from her tiny hotel room, where she had been so lonely, listening to nursery school children singing, and longing for Harry. And now here he was.

"Then cities are like women," Harry said. "You have to wait to find their heart, just like I waited for yours." He leaned toward her and slid his arms around her as their mouths met in a long kiss.

When she pulled away he said, "Sure about that wine, right now?"

Mal grinned. "I heard that anticipation was the best part of sex."

"I'm not sure I ever found it that way."

"I'm parked illegally," she said. "This might turn out to be the most expensive glass of wine you ever had." But Harry took a blue tag from his duffel and stuck it on the car window.

"Police," Mal read, astonished.

"An international code," Harry told her, more jaunty

now than when he'd gotten off the plane. "Gets a guy anywhere, any time."

"It sure does with me," she said, linking his arm and striding round the corner into the Café Deux Magots, where a waiter, who had gotten to know her from her lonely evening sojourns, greeted her with a smile. He raised his eyebrows, though, when he saw her with a partner.

"La meme chose, madame?" he asked, pulling back her chair, while Harry attempted to fit his legs under the tiny table, hemmed in by other tiny tables filled with people who seemed completely into their own conversations and their own worlds, except, that is, for the tourists like him who were there to take-in-everything-they-possibly-could-and-happy-for-it, and who threw welcoming smiles of the "we're all in this together" variety at them.

"Oui, s'il vous plait, le champagne, mais, je crois, deux café aussi."

"Avec du lait, madame? Du lait chaud, peut-être."

The waiter obviously knew Mal's usual order and she impressed Harry by her command of the language.

"Pas moment," Mal said, showing off and smirking at Harry to see if he had noticed.

"You've been here too long," he said. "You speak the language."

"What you heard was about it. I can order stuff, buy a baguette—actually a *ficelle*—that's the long thin one with two points at the end instead of one. Don't know why, but it just tastes better somehow."

"Glad to know you haven't been starving."

The waiter came back with two glasses of champagne.

"Maybe we should have gotten a bottle," Harry said, as they raised their glasses to each other.

"We might not be here long enough for that." Mal gave him a meaningful smile that meant everything to Harry's wounded soul.

"This—coming here to be with you—is the best thing I've ever done," he said softly, leaning closer. "Except . . ."

He paused and Mal waited.

"Except for when I got Squeeze," he added, making her groan.

"Remember, that dog saved your life," he reminded her.

She nodded. She would never forget. But that was another story. "You know how much I love him." She sipped her champagne, looking at him over the rim of her glass. "So, what went wrong, Harry? I know you are in pain, I know you're at a crisis in your career. Perhaps even with me? I just want to help you work it out."

Harry took a deep breath, thinking of the thousands of miles between him and Evening Lake and the dead girl with her throat cut and the pearls from her broken necklace littering the bloodstained ground like white spring flowers pushing their way through the dead earth.

"I didn't really know the young woman," he said. "Not well, that is. Only for a few days. But she was so alive, Mal. Her name was Jemima. Puddleduck, of course," he added, remembering that night at Ruby's. "I guess in a way, she reminded me of you, or at least of the way you must have been before you became the famous TV investigator. Young, curious, nosy in fact, getting into situations, places you shouldn't."

"That was me," Mal agreed.

"She came to me because she knew the young drug runner, Divon, was involved with the woman at Evening Lake. He was working with her, getting and selling hard stuff. He was at high school with Jemima, she said she would swear in court that he would never kill. And I believe her."

"So then he—Divon—did not kill Jemima?"

"He couldn't have, he was already in jail. But he was at the Havnel woman's house at the lake the night it burned. I didn't tell you before, but she'd also been stabbed. A kitchen knife in her right eye. We assume she was running from whomever it was who wanted to kill her, right before the house went up in flames. The odd thing is, though, the daughter, who told us the whole story of how the inferno happened and who was with her mother at the time, never mentioned a kitchen knife."

"She didn't see a knife in her mother's eye?"

"All the daughter said was she saw her mother go up in flames after spraying her hair too lavishly with lacquer then lighting a cigarette." Harry shrugged. "It's been known to happen. The girl ran when the house caught fire, I saw her fling herself in the lake to stop her hair burning . . ."

"When you rescued her," Mal said.

Harry looked at her. "The flaming hair was a wig."

Their eyes linked across the tiny table, their knees touched beneath it. Mal clasped Harry's hand in hers. "Now I have something to tell you," she said. "The woman's name was not Lacey Havnel. That woman died ten years ago."

Harry said, "I believe Rossetti found that out."

"What none of us has found out though, is who, exactly, is the young woman who calls herself Lacey Havnel's daughter?"

"I left that to Rossetti," Harry said, weary now that it was all being brought back to him.

"Leave it to me, too," Mal said. "I'm here to help you."

"And I'm here because I love you," Harry said.

She gave him a long look and waved a hand to the waiter for the bill.

"I'm taking you home to bed," she said, sliding her knees out from under the table and getting to her feet. "I just want to love you, Harry Jordan."

In the too-small bed, France's famous "lit matrimonial," never meant for sturdy U.S. citizens, Mal lay on top of Harry. Both were naked.

"We fit," she whispered, "like a pair of old gloves."

"Socks," Harry corrected her.

Mal raised her head from his chest and met his gaze. "Gloves. On hands. Sort of like that."

"Or socks. On feet."

"There's two feet and two socks," she insisted. "One glove, one hand, if you get my meaning."

"Jeez," Harry groaned. "Why are we talking in euphemisms? My cock is in you and it fits perfectly. At least it did a few moments ago before we got into semantics, and I lost . . ."

"Lost your 'glow,'" Mal said, giving Harry's bum a pinch that made him yelp in pain but did nothing for his erection.

"It's my turn to say 'Jeez,'" she told him indignantly. "I saved myself for you, here, in Paris." She remembered the cute French guy at Deux Magots and added for good measure, "All alone."

Harry raised his head from the pillow, looking over her shoulder at the naked length of her. "You are beautiful," he murmured.

"I know," she said. "I'm beautiful when I'm here, like this, with you. I'm beautiful when you have your arms around me. When you taste me and make me cry out in either agony or joy, I'm never quite sure which, and when you are inside me and I'm empowered by that great surge I feel as you come, and I find myself crying out again, and again, and I want more."

She felt Harry's chest moving and glanced indignantly at him. He was laughing. "What's so friggin' funny about that?" she snapped.

"You are insatiable," Harry said, running his hand the length of her back, along the indent before the curve of her behind, which reminded him, he was forced to say out loud, of twin melons.

"Cavaillons? Or watermelons?" Mal asked.

"One of each," he replied. So she hit him.

"What about the tits?" She pushed him away, clasping her hands under the twin rounds whose nipples now stood out like laser pointers.

Harry groaned. "Please, please—they are breasts," he said. "And they are beautiful. And you are beautiful, even first thing in the morning with bed hair and faded perfume and the scent of last night's sex on you."

"You've forgotten morning breath," she reminded him.

"I think I'd rather forget that," he admitted.

Mal sighed. "I always knew you were not a true romantic."

Harry rolled over. He pulled her hair back with one hand and gazed at her unmadeup face, still rosy with recent lovemaking, eyes still brilliant with excitement. "Oh, yes, I am a romantic," he said. "And regardless of what might happen, don't you ever forget it."

Mal stared at him, surprised. What could he mean—what might happen?

42

Rossetti obtained the details of the death of the real Lacey Havnel ten years ago in Miami, primarily through social security, which allowed access not only to her identity but to her bank account, both of which had been taken over by the woman they now believed was Carrie Murphy, aged fifty-two, originally from Gainesville, Florida. The real Lacey Havnel had never been married, had no children, and had died in a hit-and-run in the parking lot of the bar where she worked as a waitress. It was not known whether Carrie Murphy, the woman who had stolen her identity, the "new" Lacey Havnel, had any children, though it was clear that prior to becoming Lacey, she'd had three husbands, all of whom "died on me" as she was quoted as saying at an inquest of the third. The first husband's saw had slipped when he was cutting wood in the garden; the second suffered a heart attack, though there had been no autopsy; and the third had simply disappeared at sea. "Out fishing," Lacey had told the court.

Then Rossetti read the rest of the text:

> Our Drug Enforcement Department had Murphy (Havnel) under surveillance in Miami for some months before she left the area. We had been given information to the effect that she was expediting the shipment of cocaine and possibly heroin out of Mexico, where she went frequently "on vacation." Efforts were made to locate her, the thinking being that she had been "eliminated." She was a risk to those higher up in the drug cartel. No further activity was registered with those with whom she had had previous contact, though there was some evidence that she might have been working with a partner.

Rossetti sat back in his chair, taking in what he had just read. The woman was a drug runner on a high level. She had gone to Evening Lake to hide from whomever was after her, a prominent Mexican cartel, he suspected, and they were probably after her in the first place because she had either cheated them, stolen the money, or the drugs, or both. Money, drugs, and sex were the factors in most crimes. Lacey Havnel, aka Carrie Murphy, qualified on two of those counts.

So, where did that leave Bea Havnel? Of whose existence there was no mention? The lovely, gentle, so blondly innocent "daughter"? Or accomplice.

Troubled, Rossetti needed to think. He called the dog, clipped on the leash, and went out for a walk. His footsteps took him, as they always did when he was troubled, to Ruby's Diner, where Squeeze was greeted as a long-lost comrade, though in fact he'd been there just the other night with Harry.

"Sorry about your young friend," Rossetti said when Doris came over with a biscuit for the dog and a Diet Coke for him.

Doris took out her iPad, ready for his order. "She was my niece," she said shortly, and Rossetti caught the glitter of unshed tears. "Innocence comes in many forms," Doris added, "and my Jemima was a true innocent. Which is why she was killed. She never saw the danger, the truth, until it was too late."

Remembering what Harry had said, Rossetti asked, "You think it was somebody she knew?"

"Nobody who really knew Jemima would have done that," Doris replied. "Nobody that knew her well, knew what a lovely girl she was. Sometimes I think 'trust' is a bad thing, these days," she added. "And Jemima was too trusting."

Rossetti thought she was probably right.

He lifted his cuff and checked his Rolex Oyster Perpetual, for once getting no pleasure from the sight of it adorning his wrist. Then he thought fuck it, it didn't matter what the time was in Paris, he needed to speak to Harry. He got up, went outside with the dog, got out his phone, and speed dialed Harry's. It was Mal who answered, though.

"Why are you calling him?" she asked in a stern whisper. "The poor man is sleeping. In fact that's all he's done since he got here. Except for a glass of champagne, that is. He fell into my bed with not even a bite to eat, nor . . . well . . . anything," Mal added, making Rossetti smile. He didn't believe her for a minute.

"Wake him up, Mal, this is urgent," he said. Then realizing he was behaving like a rude cop added, "Please."

There was a pause, then Mal said a reluctant okay.

Harry, though, sounded alert and not at all sleepy a second later when he got on the phone.

"So? How's Paris?" Rossetti asked, because it was all

he could think of for openers having just gotten a man out of his lover's bed.

"Paris makes a better man out of me," Harry replied, with what Rossetti thought, astonished, was his old carefree man-of-the-world aplomb. "At least it did until you called," Harry added.

"I know you're fearing the worst." Rossetti wished he didn't have to tell him, wished he had not called him, had left him there in his Paris dreamworld away from the reality of the woman stabbed in the eye then burned; away from Doris's niece, Jemima, with her throat cut.

"I was in Ruby's," he said. "Squeeze got his usual bounty," he added, to lighten things up a bit.

"Glad to hear it, and thanks, for Squeeze." Harry glanced over his shoulder as, hearing the dog's name, Mal groaned. "Best dog in the world," he added, just to get at her. "Remember how he saved Mal's life, that time."

"How could I forget," Rossetti replied, hearing Harry laugh. Mal had thrown a pillow at him.

"So? What's up?" Harry sank back onto the bed, putting an arm round Mal's shoulders. She flung a leg over and lay smoothly against him. It was almost too much to bear as well as talk sensibly on the telephone, but there was an urgency in Rossetti's voice. Harry knew he was not calling simply to ask if he was having a good time in France.

Rossetti quickly brought him up to date.

"Interesting," Harry said, alert now.

"I also spoke with the waitress, Doris," Rossetti said. "Jemima was her niece. Remember?"

Harry remembered only too well. Jemima's image floated suddenly in front of his closed eyes, her wild red hair, her pale eyes, her blood. "I know Doris," he said.

"Well, Doris said something I thought interesting. She said, and I quote, 'My Jemima was a true innocent. Which is why she was killed. She never saw the danger, the truth, until it was too late.'" Harry was silent. Rossetti cleared his throat. "And what that means to me, Harry, and I believe you will agree, is that Jemima knew whoever it was who killed her."

"Right," Harry said. "I'll be on the next flight out," he added, consulting the watch which he had not taken off; even in bed he needed to know the time. "Expect me tomorrow. You are on the right track, Rossetti."

He clicked off the phone and heard a groan from behind him. He turned and met Mal's eyes.

"I knew it was too good to be true," she said.

43

It was, Diz thought, a good idea to keep an eye on things. By which he meant through his binoculars. He'd seen some pretty strange stuff out at Evening Lake. Every now and again, for instance, he would spot old Len Doutzer rambling in his quick mountain-man stride, up the hillside opposite, shotgun slung over his shoulder and looking, Diz thought, very creepy. Sinister, in fact. He would make sure not to go to that side of the lake alone, not with a crazy guy like that around.

He saw his father quite a lot too, now that he was back home, rowing around the lake looking lonely as hell, but hey, he'd brought it on himself. Currently, Diz was not a fan of his father. He did not know exactly what had happened, but Wally had hurt his mom and nobody should be able to do that. He wasn't even sure his mom and dad were speaking. How could his father ever have gotten himself arrested in connection with the murder of nice Jemima Forester. And horrendous Lacey Havnel. How could those two women even be spoken of in the same breath? Young as he was, Diz recognized the

Havnel woman was bad news, which made her daughter's sweetness and simplicity even more astonishing.

With a mother like her you wouldn't have thought Bea stood a chance, which was why it wasn't a surprise when she was arrested along with his father. The police had soon dropped that, though, but now his mom was having nothing to do with her. Bea was forbidden from their house. Diz hoped Rose was doing the right thing. He thought maybe he should ask her about that.

He went down to the kitchen, where Rose stood over the ancient AGA stove that generated a load of heat in the winter as well as kept its ovens and hot plates always on the go. It was Rose's pride and joy and she claimed it had made a good cook of her. Perhaps it had.

Diz hovered in the doorway, worried he might say the wrong thing. His mother looked up, saw him, and smiled.

"Your old favorite for supper," she said. "Spaghetti Bolognese." She heaved a great sigh. "Truthfully, it's all I could think of, right at the moment. My mind seems to be on other things."

"We could always do the burger joint." Diz stuck his hands in his shorts pockets, staring worriedly at her as she stirred the sauce. "You know Bea is back. I saw her across the lake. She's at the small house behind the wreck."

"Pity it didn't burn down too," Rose said, astonishing Diz, who had never before heard his mother say anything nasty about anyone.

"Mom?" She glanced up again. "Like, well, I mean . . . is everything okay with Dad now?"

Rose stopped what she was doing. She put down her spoon and folded her arms, leaning back against the stove and regarding him with the new eyes of a mother who has just seen her son grow up quite a lot.

"I never thought I would need to say this, but your father acted like a fool. He got involved with bad people. It's over with now, thank God, and we should say no more about it."

"What about Jemima?" Diz was going to say "what about Jemima's murder" but couldn't quite bring himself to articulate that word.

"The homicide detectives are investigating that." Rose looked closely at him. She walked over, put her arms round him in a bear hug. "Listen, kiddo," she said gently, "your dad is okay. He did nothing wrong. Seriously wrong, I mean, and I don't want you ever to think that. Okay?"

"Jemima was murdered, Mom. Even I heard that," Diz said. "On the TV news," he added.

"We didn't know Jemima. Your father didn't know Jemima. The poor young woman foolishly got herself involved in the investigations of the fire and Mrs. Havnel's death."

"Murder," Diz corrected his mother, who heaved another great sigh.

"Look, Diz, Harry Jordan is in charge of the investigation, he and Detective Rossetti. I have complete faith in both of them. They are the best. Whatever happened, whatever the truth is, they will find out, and the person, or persons, responsible will be arrested."

"Like Dad, you mean," Diz persisted. "And Bea."

Rose turned back to the stove, took up the spoon, and began stirring again. She tasted it on a finger, added a touch more salt. "I do not want to talk about her," she said in the quiet voice Diz knew meant trouble. "Please do not mention her name to me again."

Diz went and stood next to her. "Can I have a taste?"

"May I," Rose corrected him again. That's what

mothers did, corrected, Diz thought, dipping a spoon into the bubbling red sauce and burning his mouth.

"It's too hot," Rose told him, too late.

"Thanks, Mom." Diz wandered back out of the kitchen, en route to his room. "It's great."

It always was, Rose thought, wondering whether if she made a salad they would eat it. Nobody seemed much into food these days. Especially Wally.

Out on the porch Diz spotted his father in the small boat, rowing toward the house. He walked out onto the jetty, waiting for him.

"Hey, Dad," he said, as Wally pulled alongside. "How about we go fishing." He thought his father needed a little friendly company.

44

Harry said goodbye to Mal at the airport and was back on what Rossetti jokingly called terra-cotta, meaning terra firma, "home ground."

"How come you always go away at the wrong moment?" he demanded, when Harry walked into the precinct. "Shit, man, what's with Paris, anyway?"

Harry leveled a look at him that spoke volumes. "Go there," he said. "Try it and see." He appeared to think for a moment, then added, "Just take a woman with you, that's all I have to say about that."

"I heard the food's not too great." Rossetti grinned at him. He was glad to have him back. "Stuff's goin' on here," he said. "Lacey Havnel, aka Carrie Murphy, was quite the dealer. Poor Divon was small stuff to her, simply the one who hand-delivered the shit. He's still in custody, by the way. Still haven't let him off the hook, for Jemima."

"We don't actually believe Divon did it?" Harry asked, surprised.

"Of course not. We're just letting him think we believe he did it." Rossetti grinned. "Keeps a guy on his toes, thinking he might be indicted for murder. Might put him in a frame of mind to tell all he knows about whatever he knows. To a good cop, of course," he added. Smugly, Harry thought.

"What about Fairy Formentor?"

"Divon's mom was definitely murdered by a person or persons unknown, as they say. No one ever arrested. Therefore no prosecution."

"And Divon was never a suspect."

"Jeez, Harry, he was a kid . . ."

"It's been known."

Rossetti said, "The question is why was Jemima killed?"

"My guess, and yours, is Jemima saw something, or someone she shouldn't have. Wrong place, wrong time, for her. Fact is, Rossetti, we have no conclusive forensic evidence, which means we have to pursue the intangible."

"There you go," Rossetti sighed. "What's intangible?"

"Intangible, as you well know, means nothing we can see or touch. In fact it means, my good buddy, we have not a fuckin' clue."

"I can only agree with that." Rossetti put his feet up on Harry's desk, took the emery board from his pocket, and began on his nails. It helped him think.

Harry said, "What happened to the wig?"

Rossetti looked up, raised his brows. "Bea's wig? Never turned up."

"Did we drag the lake?"

"Evening Lake? You gotta be kidding. Know how many square blocks that thing would cover?"

Harry did.

Rossetti took his feet off the desk, sat back, arms folded. "Oh, something I forgot to tell you." He waited for Harry to ask "what?" Harry waited too.

Rossetti gave in first. "So it's like this. Forensics found prints on the knife."

Harry said, "I'll bet they're Rose Osborne's."

"Not only that, her son Roman's. Now the boy probably used it to cut an apple, maybe, but I'd have bet good odds Wally was not the chef in that family. So why are *his* prints also on the knife found sticking out of a woman's eye?"

"Oh, fuck," Harry said, thinking of Rose.

"Catching on," Rossetti added. "Of course Rose's prints were on the knife too, I mean that would be expected, it was her kitchen."

"His kitchen too. A man might cut an onion to go on his burger, a tomato for his ham sandwich . . ."

"A throat for his fun."

Silenced, Harry gave up trying to defend Rose's husband.

"The question, though," Rossetti said, "is why. We know, despite his books about murder and weirdos, Wally is not a psycho. He's not a man who might simply kill for pleasure. And he's up to his eyes in pricey lawyers all protesting his innocence."

"Which I happen to believe," Harry said.

Rossetti said, "There's probably a dozen or more folks out there who might have been happy to see Lacey Havnel dead. She was dealing pretty big-time, cocaine and heroin. Cartels don't like it when you cheat on them."

"You think that's what it was?"

Rossetti shrugged. "If you stayed away from Paris and spent more time at your desk like I do, you would have figured that out for yourself. As well as asking yourself who the fuck else would want Lacey Havnel dead? Her daughter, maybe?"

Harry frowned at Rossetti. "You off on that tack again?"

"Mom had nine hundred thou stashed in the bank. In a checking account! Plus the house on the lake, and Lord knows what else in safe deposits that we haven't found yet, and maybe never will."

Harry was silent, thinking, Rossetti guessed, about Bea.

Harry said, "Rose Osborne came to see me, she told me Bea had gone to her house to beg her forgiveness. Bea asked to be taken back into the family. 'The family I never had' was how Rose said she put it."

Rossetti stopped fooling with the emery board. He sat up. "And?"

Harry shrugged. "In effect, Rose told her to get lost."

"How about that! I thought softhearted Rose would have fallen for the 'poor little me' spiel and taken her back 'into the bosom of,' so to speak."

"Meanwhile, what about Wally's prints on that knife?"

Rossetti shrugged. "And the son's. It's normal enough not to count as forensic evidence. We can go nowhere on that. Anyhow, why are you asking?"

"Wally's behavior is too erratic to be dismissed. Drugs can get a hold of your mind, especially meth. It can change a person. We'd better keep an eye on him."

"But he's right there, living at home, with his wife. The lovely Rose."

"Right," Harry said, feeling the twinge of danger as he said it. "The lovely Rose."

45

There was a knock on Harry's door. Usually it was kept open but today he needed to be alone, to think. Something was troubling him, something he'd heard, seen perhaps, and couldn't quite put his finger on. He called to come in and a uniformed cop put his head around the door.

"The Forester family is here, sir, they'd like to see you."

Harry was surprised. The Foresters were a nice middle-class couple, he a bit country club in golf shirt and loafers; she in a St. John pants suit with big clip-on gold earrings and low heels; nothing like their exotic daughter, Jemima.

He stood by the door to welcome them, shook their hands, pulled out chairs, sat opposite, looking expectantly at them.

Mrs. Forester, in the black pantsuit and a white shirt of enviable crispness, with her gold earrings in place, managed to smile at him. Harry caught a glimpse of Jemima in her smile.

Mr. Forester opened the dialogue. "We need to know exactly what's going on," he said, though not in a demanding tone.

"You see, we'll never be able to sleep until we know who killed our daughter." Mrs. Forester kept her tone low too, but Harry could see she was fighting for self-control. The woman wanted to weep, as she had probably wept ever since her daughter's murder; you had only to look into her eyes, the same pale eyes as Jemima's, to see how swollen they were, see the look of helplessness that meant, Harry knew from experience, that Mrs. Forester felt she had failed in her duty as a mother, failed to protect her daughter. It was obvious the father felt the same. Murder rendered families helpless, ineffectual, feeling they should have been there, done more, saved her. The Foresters were living every parent's nightmare and wanted someone in the dock and a judge sentencing him to life, or death, for what he'd done to their child. Harry did not blame them but right now he had no answers.

"We've come to you for news on the investigation," Mr. Forester said.

Harry told him they were following up on leads, mentioning, as delicately as he could, that they had "the weapon"—he refrained from saying "the knife"—and explained again about questioning Wally and Bea, which of course they already knew. What they wanted was reassurance; they wanted to know the cops were still on the job, that their daughter had not become simply another statistic, another unsolved killing.

"She's my daughter," Mrs. Forester reminded Harry. Unclipping the latch on her black patent leather handbag she took out a photograph and passed it over to him. "This is a good likeness. I thought you might be able to use it, you know, in the papers, on TV, see if anyone comes forward who saw her that night. I think it captures Jemima perfectly, if you see what I mean."

She was right; Harry remembered Jemima looking exactly like that the night they'd had drinks together in Blake's, even the black leather jacket slung around her shoulders was the same, and the mischievous grin that lit up her eyes.

"Of course, you are right," he said. "That's Jemima."

"Was," the father reminded him, sounding angry. "That was our Jemima until some bastard decided to take her from us. And what are we supposed to do now? Sit around and wait while you guys 'pursue your investigations'? Isn't that how you'd describe what you do, Detective?"

It was never easy dealing with the distraught family, Harry knew it never would be; he also knew that he would be doing this again with some other family, some other time. For a split second he wondered again about his work; where he was at; whether he should quit. Experiences like this took an emotional toll, especially where he had known the victim.

"Sir," he began, though he was still searching his mind for exactly what to say, how to calm the father, comfort the mother. "I'm asking you to trust me. I am personally tracking down what happened here, I personally am determined to find out why this happened, and I promise to do everything I can to apprehend the perpetrator."

Jemima's dad gave a derisive snort. "Apprehend? Perpetrator? Sounds like cop talk to me."

"You are right. Cop shorthand you might call it, Mr. Forester, but what it means is we are on the trail of your daughter's killer and we are determined to get the person who did it and put that person in jail and then on trial to suffer the judicial consequences."

Forester leaned his elbows on the table, he put his head in his hands and said, "And I voted against the death penalty."

His wife patted him gently on the back. "Don't go there. His fate will not be in your hands. Right now it's in Detective Jordan's." She looked at Harry with swollen, red-rimmed eyes. "I'm sorry we bothered you, it was really, in a way, I suppose, simply to reassure ourselves something was being done about Jemima, and to tell you now that the body has been released, her funeral will take place on Friday, at noon. Of course, there's no need for you to attend," she added. "I just wanted you to know that Jemima was finally being taken care of."

Harry nodded his thanks and told them he would be there. They shook hands and he went to the door with them and watched them walk away. Was it his imagination, or did they look smaller, more stooped than when they came in? As though, he thought, they had lost their spirit along with their daughter.

Of course it rained Friday. Hard, slanting rain that hit viciously under umbrellas and filled the plastic sheeting in the coffin-size hole with muddy water. Harry thought it was a terrible way to say goodbye to a young woman filled with sparkle and life and the promise of a future.

He recalled finding her body, the almost execution-style killing and the fact that there was no apparent psychological motive, no logical motive. Standing at the back of the small crowd he remembered Jemima's brave ruby lipstick, the wild red of her hair, her pearls scattered on the earth.

Rossetti was with him and the two detectives eyed the mourners carefully for "strangers," meaning anyone not obviously family or friends or in some way affiliated. It was a shock to recognize Bea, dressed head to toe in black, standing in front with the family. A black scarf was wrapped over her blond hair and she wore rose-tinted glasses that hid her eyes.

Rossetti said in Harry's ear, "I thought she said she didn't know Jemima."

"The only connection Bea had to Jemima, according to her, was when she was arrested on suspicion of her murder."

"Which Mike Leverage got her off faster than it took to spin a roulette wheel. So, why is she here?"

"Let's ask her," Harry said.

They stood respectfully to one side as the coffin, borne by Jemima's father and several strong young cousins and friends, was placed at the side of the rain-soaked gap in the earth that was to be her final resting place. The priest intoned a blessing while Harry kept his eyes on Bea, who simply stood, as though transfixed, gazing through her rose-colored glasses as the young woman she claimed never to have known was buried. Only then did she look up at the detectives observing her. She walked over to them immediately and stood, her head wrapped in the black scarf, searching Harry's eyes.

"You are wondering, of course, what I'm doing here when I didn't even know her," she said very quietly. "You might have forgotten, Detectives, that I was questioned about this girl's murder. When you did that you involved me in her spirit." She shrugged. "Whatever that is. Anyhow, I couldn't let it just be, I had to come, I wanted to know who had done this to her. I don't quite understand why I thought I would find the answer here, all I can tell you is I have not." She shrugged a slender, black-clothed shoulder again. "I'm hoping you have."

And with that she stalked away, her black ballet flats squishing through the mud. She reached the gravel path and strode off, like, Harry thought watching her, an awkward long-legged heron about to take flight.

"Y'know what?" Rossetti sank his chin into the collar of his Burberry, which in his estimation had gotten far too wet for a really good trench coat. "That young woman is fuckin' crazy."

Harry was watching as Bea stopped at a long black limo pulled to the side of the road. A uniformed chauffeur got quickly out and held the door for her. She disappeared inside, the door slammed, the chauffeur got back in and edged into the traffic.

"Y'know what," Harry repeated thoughtfully to Rossetti. "You might be right. Only now she's rich and crazy."

They thought it best not to intrude on the family and drove back in Rossetti's car to the precinct.

46

Rose was alone in her bedroom, curled up on the love seat by the window, a glass of wine in one hand and the TV clicker in the other. She stopped when she got to the news channel which was showing the funeral of the "murdered young woman," as Jemima Forester had now become known. As if, Rose thought sadly, she had lost her identity along with her life. On the newscast the rain was coming down in sheets, as it was outside her own window, obscuring any view of the lake and leaving the porch awash like the deck of a ship in a storm.

On TV, somberly clad mourners were shown filing into the church, then standing by the grave to which the coffin, awash in wet flowers, was borne by sturdy-looking young men who did not flinch from their task, nor from the terrible weather. Rose's heart went out to them, to the parents following their daughter to her final resting place, eyes cast down, putting one slow foot in front of the other. In the quick intrusive shot of the mourners standing by the hollowed-out grave, she caught sight of Harry Jordan in the back, with Detective Rossetti. Both men were bareheaded out of respect, despite the torrential downpour. With rain streaming down his face, Rose thought for a minute Harry looked as if he were crying. Then she remembered that he had known the dead girl and thought perhaps he really was crying. Harry, as she had found out, was a man with a heart under his tough cop exterior.

She sat up, shocked, though, slopping wine onto the sofa, when she spotted Bea among the mourners. She wondered if it could really be her. Surely not. But yes, she would recognize those long skinny legs anywhere, now in black tights with black flats, and that slender body now encased in a sober black coat, even though her blond hair was covered by a scarf and she was wearing tinted glasses.

Rose thought the coat looked expensive, then remembered Harry saying Bea would inherit her mother's money, as well as the house, the burned-down one in which the mother had died, and on which no doubt Bea had claimed the insurance.

Remembering the horror of the night Jemima had been murdered right out there at the lake, and Wally and Bea being arrested, Rose wished she had the magic ability to erase time, to remove herself, remove all her family, return to the place they had been before Bea Havnel came into their lives.

She had a guilty feeling of responsibility. Even though, after she had "come to her senses" and told Bea to stay out of the Osbornes' lives, it was she who had at first accepted her, who had become like a mother to her, without questioning what Bea might really want. Now it came to Rose like a revelation, an epiphany almost, exactly what Bea had wanted. She had wanted to be her. To be the woman who had it all: the husband, the family, the position in life, the house on the lake filled with friends. Rose understood Bea's envy, but not her jealousy. It was too crazy.

With a little stab of worry, she took a gulp of the wine; she didn't even taste it, her mind was so occupied with the new worry about Bea, about what she might do next. In fact, Rose suddenly knew that what she felt was fear.

She grabbed her cell phone and punched in Jordan's number, at the same time wondering if he was still at the funeral. But this was on the six o'clock news, of course it would have been over hours ago. She heard the phone ring and ring, then the request to leave a message. Actually, that's all Harry said. No name, no chat, simply "Leave a message." So Rose did the same: simply her name and number, then she sat back, listening to the drumming of the rain on the porch.

Down the hall, she could hear Diz talking on his phone with a friend. The two girls had gone off for a visit with their aunt, in New York, escaping from the new chaos of their lives. Roman had gone to the movies in Boston and would stay the night with friends. Rose thought it was as if suddenly her entire family wanted to escape. Only Wally was left and he was downstairs, in the room she optimistically called the "library" because of the two tall bookcases holding the many foreign editions of Wally's works, as well as the English-language ones, and where he sat at his computer, writing, Rose hoped, the next.

She wasn't sure about that, though. There was a silence between Wally and herself; admittedly it had been there before the fire, before Bea came to share their lives, before Wally was arrested on suspicion of murder. Mike Leverage had told Rose not to worry; he said "a scandal" was all it was; Wally was no murderer, this would only sell more books. Right now, Rose did not care about that. She wanted her life back. Real life, the way it had been before Bea, the newly rich young woman in the expensive black coat riding in a limo to the funeral of a young woman she did not know. Again Rose asked herself why. You might have thought someone arrested on suspicion of her killing would not have shown up at her funeral.

She punched in Harry's number again. This time he answered.

"I saw Bea," Rose said. "At Jemima Forester's funeral, and I asked myself why she was there."

"The drama queen always wants to be where it's happening," Harry said. "I guess she misses the media attention she got when she was arrested for Jemima's murder, probably thought they'd be interested in her again. Bea enjoys the limelight, knows how to milk it, in case you haven't noticed that."

"I've noticed now," Rose said. "What I didn't know was that she knew Jemima."

"And we don't know that she did," Harry said. "Other than being at the scene of the murder."

"There's something about her that scares me," Rose admitted. "I mean, seeing her there, all dressed up in expensive black like she was the sister or something, then stepping grandly into the waiting limo, just the way she did when she first came here, to stay with us."

"I remember, you said 'only for a week.' "

"It's turned out to be a life sentence."

Harry said, "I asked you to trust me before, Rose. Now I'm asking you again. I can't talk about it but I want you to know we are investigating Bea and her mother. You will be the first to know if we find she's into something she should not be."

Rose's first thought was drugs, and she said so.

"We'll see," was all Harry said, before he rang off.

47

As yet, Lacey Havnel had had no funeral; what was left of her was still wrapped in plastic in a drawer in the morgue. Now, though, it was decided she could be released.

"I guess we should call the daughter," Rossetti said to Harry.

"She hasn't called us, to inquire."

"True." Rossetti thought about that. "What kinda daughter is that, anyway, who doesn't call to ask when she might be able to bury her mom."

"I'd call that a bad daughter. Or maybe no daughter at all."

"You still think maybe Bea is not Havnel's kid?"

Harry sighed, thinking about it. "None of it makes sense," he said, after a while. "She's clearly daughter enough on paper to claim the bank accounts and the insurance. So Lacey Havnel's proper daughter I guess she is."

"Then who is the father? And where is the father?"

Harry shrugged. "Perhaps he'll pop out of the

woodwork now that money is involved. That's usually the way things happen."

"Odd, though," Rossetti continued on his theme. "Bea goes to the funeral of a young woman she does not know, yet never even asks about her own mom." He looked for Harry's reaction. Harry had always been soft on Bea and he thought he would make another excuse for her, but this time Harry did not.

"Since she hasn't called us, I'll call her," Harry said. "Tell her she can send whatever funeral home personnel she chooses to pick up the body, and that she can bury her mother anytime she wishes."

He took his cell phone and punched in Bea's number. She answered on the first ring.

"Harry," she said.

He was surprised; the last time they had met it had been "Detective Jordan." "I'm calling to tell you that your mother's body can now be released. I suggest you have the funeral home of your choice deal with it. I'll make sure the necessary papers are available immediately." There was a long silence. Harry raised his brows at Rossetti. "Are you there, Bea?" he asked, and was answered by a sob. This time he rolled his eyes.

"We are talking about my mother." Bea spoke through tears. Harry thought Bea cried well.

He said, "I am sorry to sound so harsh but you are now free to take care of your mother. As I said I'll make sure everything is dealt with at this end."

"But I don't know any funeral homes, I don't know anything about funerals," Bea said, sounding desperate.

Harry recalled seeing her just a day ago at a funeral at which she seemed very composed and to know exactly what was going on. "I'm e-mailing you the names of several in the area, all of which are more than competent and reliable."

"But where shall I bury her? We didn't live here, I don't have a church."

Rossetti, who was listening to the conversation on the speakerphone, was now the one to roll his eyes in a "who's she kidding" look. They all knew that basically there was little left of the mother after the fire. And "Bea" and "church" were two words that did not fit together.

"I'm sure you'll work it out," Harry was saying, already summoning up the names of funeral homes in the area on his computer and clicking the Send button that delivered them to Bea's iPhone. "Good luck, Bea," he said and heard her say "But—" as he clicked off.

"Now let's see what happens," he said to Rossetti.

"Now she's got her hands on the money, y'mean."

"I remember, at the beginning, you asked whether I thought she wanted to get rid of the mother," Harry said.

"And?" Rossetti asked.

"I think you called it right, Detective."

"So what do we do now?"

"We still have the knife the coroner removed from her eye, the one that belonged to Rose. As well as to Wally," Harry added, a little more thoughtfully because Wally seemed too involved in this whole scenario for his comfort. "I think Bea killed her mother to get her hands on the money, she thought she would get away with it because of the fire."

"You mean she thought her mom would simply burn up, no visible knife wounds."

"Mom didn't go away so fast, though. Bea should have pulled that knife out before she set her alight." Harry heaved a regretful sigh. "All this is pure speculation, a stringing together of events that might or might not be true. Bea could be innocent and we are bad guys for even thinking badly of her."

"I mean a girl who looks like that . . ." Rossetti added, remembering Bea's cool blond young beauty.

Harry remembered only too well the scene at the hospital: Bea in the oversized flowered gown, her childish eagerness to please, to tell him what happened. He had fallen for it big-time, and he still was not convinced she was guilty of killing her mom.

"At least with the mom, there was a motive," Rossetti said, thinking of the nine hundred thou in the bank account. "But what about Jemima?"

"That, we may never know," Harry said.

48

As usual, Diz was keeping an eye on things, though this time he was not up in his tree, and this time he had a purpose. He was stalking Len Doutzer and he was doing it because he was worried about his mother, who, as Wally and the family had left for Boston, was now alone at the lake house with only him to protect her.

He'd noticed Len lurking around; somehow he always seemed to be where Rose was, up on the hill, or moored in a small boat on the opposite shore, unmoving. Of course Len made like he was fishing but Diz knew the lake well, knew there were no fish to be found where the man was because the water was too shallow and the sun glinted off it, sending the fish diving for darker, deeper waters. A serious fisherman would be at the far end of the lake where the hills sloped steeply and trees dipped branches into the steely water, chilled by a rippling underground stream, which probably also fed the various wells dotted around the hills, most of them now contaminated and long disused or dried up.

Today, though, Len was not even pretending to fish. He simply sat, allowing his old boat to drift, all fifteen feet of worn fiberglass, and certainly not the glamorous and expensive old wooden craft Diz longed for and might put on his Christmas list. If, that is, the Osbornes had Christmas this year. The way things were going the family might not even be together by then. Anyhow, Len was allowing his boat to drift with the current that took him past the burned wreckage of the old Havnel property when suddenly, to Diz's surprise, he began sculling toward the shore, sliding the small boat into the shade of an overhanging tree where Diz could no longer see him.

Diz sat for an hour or more, watching, waiting, until he heard his mother calling his name and the clang of the old brass handbell that announced supper. He would have stayed longer, anxious to see what Len was up to, but he could smell burgers on the grill and his mom made the best. Served on a seeded roll, slathered with a dollop of her homemade mayo, ketchup, lettuce, tomato, and a slice of dill pickle, it resembled the one in the Burger King TV ad with the sexy girl, though Diz bet Rose's tasted better.

He sped down to the kitchen. "Smells great," he said, concentrating on the first juicy bite. If the great chefs of the world combined to provide any eleven-year-old with a meal, in Diz's opinion they would never equal this.

"I don't know whether I like your Bolognese more, though," he said, just to tease Rose, but for once she was unresponsive.

He waited a few minutes then added, "Mom, why does that mountain man keep rowing around the lake near us? I mean, like, I see him over at the Havnel place but sometimes he's right here."

Rose was pouring a glass of red wine. She looked up, alarmed. "Who are you talking about?"

"Len Doutzer. He keeps rowing too close to our

house. I mean, he's trying to look like he's fishing but there's no good fish to be caught right here. Dad took me where the fish are."

Rose was concerned. These days she did not like to hear of anyone lurking around the place. Still it was probably nothing. She took a sip of the wine then went and got a bowl of small green olives from the sideboard. "They have pits," she warned, popping one into her mouth.

Diz said, "You should get the other kind, the black ones."

"I like these more. So, how do you know Len?"

Diz shrugged. "I've seen him around in the store or coming out of Red Sails, or Tweedies coffee shop. Anyhow I remember thinking he looked like a mountain man, kind of grizzly long iron-gray hair, scruffy, like he lived in a cave or somethin'."

"Some*thing*," Rose corrected his speech and Diz groaned.

"Not the point." He finished off his burger in one gigantic bite, making Rose groan about his manners. "Look, Mom," he said, still chewing, "I have to protect you. I'm all you've got so I'm keeping my eye out."

"As usual," Rose said. "And anyhow, Len is the local character. He's lived here as long as anyone can remember, up the hill across the lake. He carves benches and tables for people like us, with houses here. I've never heard he caused any trouble."

Diz took in what his mother said but his gut feeling was telling him otherwise. Later in the afternoon, he was lying on his bed, playing a video game and feeling pretty lonesome without his dad and the rest of the family.

The house seemed to have settled into silence. It wasn't the kind of silence Diz had noticed before; this was a deeper kind of quiet, where, he thought, recalling some old poem from his younger days, “never a mouse stirred.” It was so quiet Diz’s scalp crawled and he wished the mice *would* stir. Then the barn owl that lived a half mile downstream hooty-tooted mournfully and life returned to normal.

Diz went to look out the window. Clouds had slung in, darkening the sky, and the lake slid like gray silk under the breeze. He heard the ripple of oars and quickly climbed out onto his branch to take a look.

Bea Havnel was rowing, expertly as always, toward the island. Diz couldn’t quite make it out, he wasn’t sure, but he thought someone was there, waiting for her. He got down from the branch and walked as quietly as he could through the trees toward the lake.

Though he watched for over an hour, he did not see her row back again. He was telling himself he must have been wrong about her, he’d been so tired he’d missed her return, when he heard a noise. He turned to look, just as Bea swung the oar at his head.

49

Diz played right into my hands. I'd noticed him, creeping along the shore road, binoculars focused on me, watching as always. I saw my opportunity and I took it. The single blow felled him and I got him into my small lightweight boat that I liked especially because of its ability to cut soundlessly through the water, sleek as a water moccasin only without the deadly fangs. I, of course, had those.

How to do it though? That was the question and as I pulled to the shore and sat in my little craft, I pondered the answer. I was a sincere believer in the old saying "curiosity killed the cat"; after all, remember Jemima? I'd wondered exactly how long it would take an eleven-year-old spy to try to find out exactly what I was up to.

I know the meaning of the word "compulsion" only too well; there have been times when I have had to resist it, others when unfortunately I succumbed. I say "unfortunate" because those times—two in fact—turned out to be dangerous for me. The first was in Florida where Lacey—I could never call her "Mom" though in fact she was my mother—botched up a drug deal. She got greedy, took the goods and did not pay, which, being a drug deal meant immediate death. Of course we went on the run, changing identities, or looks, and I took care of the would-be "exterminator" in my own way, not because I wanted to save Lacey from the consequences of her actions, but because at the time I was only thirteen, she was all I had and I needed her.

The second mistake was killing Jemima. I knew she had seen me with Wally, that she suspected the drug situation, knew she was friends with the famous, or perhaps "notorious" is a better word, member of the police, Detective Jordan, who by the way, if he were not so smart and full of himself, I might easily have seduced. Even I can recognize "danger" when it stands in front of me in jeans and a leather jacket, concern in his grave blue eyes as he looks at poor little me in my oversized hospital robe, saved from death only hours before. What man could resist? I gave him a small flirt, just to ensure he was on my side, but nothing more. I needed Harry Jordan, just as I needed Rose.

Rose is my ultimate target. You can have no idea how long, from my so-called "home" across Evening Lake, I have watched that family coming and going. Several months at least. Of course my first target was Lacey. I needed to get my hands on that cartel money before the cartel took it back, which they would since even I knew Lacey was cheating them. She was a big-enough dealer to count, money-wise, and I must admit, clever at it. Lacey had found her métier, you might say, after years of scrambling and poverty and selling anything she could, including herself, though never, I repeat never, me.

Do not give Lacey credit for this. It was I who took the stand against it. I always had a sense of my own worth, and an idea of how to go about realizing that, and it wasn't just some cheap hustle in Las Vegas along with all the other harlots feeling lucky if they got five hundred for an hour giving some fat creep head and letting him have his ugly way. Not for me. I was much more into the Harry Jordan mode. In fact if a creep like that had so much as touched me I might have killed him. Instead, I killed my mother. I considered it a much better deal.

And now I was rich, or would be when the insurance paid up on the burned house (accidental, of course) and on my mother's life policy, which was much trickier due to the knife in the eye. I should have resisted that impulse but the bitch was running, hair aflame, polyester dress stuck like hot molten lead on her body, screaming my name, and that I had done it. I had to silence her. Immediately.

Don't you love that word "immediately"? It stops you right in your tracks. "Stop your wife from doing this, immediately," the sour mistress says to her married lover. "Stop doing that immediately," the exhausted mother tells her child. "Stop immediately or I'll shoot." That's what Jordan and the other detective yelled at me when I was running from Jemima's body. It was a pity they caught up so quickly, I had so little time to admire my handiwork, to gloat over the blood sliding silkily from the thin line I had carved on Jemima's throat. Such a lovely red, like no other, really. Of course it's not as pretty when it begins to congeal and gets that rusty look, the color of old plush cinema seats. Same texture too.

By now of course you understand that I love what I do. I live for what I do. And other people must die so that I can live. As I mentioned earlier, I am not a vampire, I simply am in love with the power of the kill. The ultimate control over another person. That moment when I know I have her, is it.

How many, you might be asking, have I killed. Not counting Lacey, I believe it must be five by now. A couple of schoolgirls who got on my nerves; a woman tending bar on a Florida beach who refused to serve me a mojito because I was underage; an older woman in some cheap hotel who tried to get into my bed. She never slept another night in a bed, or with another woman, after that. And the others I've mentioned.

A sordid life, you might say, but my own. All that will change now. Now that I am rich. And now I can take care of the lovely Rose, the woman who has it all, who is every man's ideal, every child's best mom in the world. She rejected me and I can't allow that. Had she only taken me in as she'd said she would, had she only let me be part of her life, a member of her family, she might have saved herself. Not now. I am jealous of Rose and I've never been jealous of anyone. I want to be Rose.

Of course I am not going to kill her yet, that's way too risky right now. No, I'm going for the emotional jugular. Her child. Diz will disappear. "Into thin air," they'll say, puzzled. "Kidnapped," they will add, afraid. All pedophiles in the area will be rounded up, all potential crazies locked up, all past child offenders brought in for questioning.

And I will be the one who brings Diz home. I will find Diz. I will rescue him, return him to his grateful family. To Rose, whose gratitude will be such she will forgive me the past and welcome me into her home. Where, let me tell you now, I will take over. Within months I will be in command. I will have all of them eating out of my gentle hand.

I will be Rose, and then when she is emotionally wrecked I'll think about what to do with her.

I've been keeping my eye on Diz, I know his routine at Evening Lake well by now. He's a curious kid, always with his binoculars, out on his tree at night looking for owls or maybe just spying on his family, who, God knows, had little to hide up to this point other than Wally's descent into drugs. Pity the kid didn't catch on to that earlier, I guess he knows nothing of drug culture other than what he sees on TV or his iPad games, which come to think of it is probably quite a lot. Not enough to see me coming though, and I suspect what he's really looking at through those binoculars is me. Diz is suspicious and so am I, and I have to get him before he gets me.

It's important Diz does not see me, he must not recognize me as the "abductor," because later I am to be his "savior," the one who will return him to his ever-grateful mother, all credit to me.

I know that a few hours after they realize he's gone, the search will be on. We shall all join in, all those Evening Lake regulars who know the kid and the family. It will take a while, maybe a day, perhaps even two before I "find" him, and every clue will point to abduction by a stranger. There are plenty of them, hikers and such, rambling round our lake, our hills. In fact I'd better watch out for them, don't want any of them seeing something they shouldn't. Not that anyone comes this far. Almost no one other than Len Doutzer even knows this place exists, so hidden is it among old growth and matted brambles. No, I'm betting the first place the family, then the police, will search, will be the lake. The boy is always out there on his own. "Drowned kid in lake," will be immediately what they will suspect. And you know what, if things go wrong, they might be correct.

With practice, though in fact it is also my nature, I have become silent as any cat, which enabled me to catch Diz from behind. I struck a blow to his head with the oar. He cried out, put up a hand, then crumpled to the ground. I stood for a second looking down at him: all he was was a bunch of old clothes, grubby old shorts, dusty sneakers, a Grateful Dead T-shirt that was too big and probably belonged to his older brother.

There was no time to be wasted. Despite being small, Diz was too heavy for me to carry and from the bushes I pulled the small handcart, like the little red Radio Flyer only this was old and brown and full of splinters, must have been rescued from some charity garden sale years ago, until I came across it, and it was finally coming in useful. I strapped Diz onto it, knees under his chest, sort of in a fetal position. Then I stood and looked about me. This was my most vulnerable moment. Anyone taking a walk might come round that bend and see me. I had to move fast.

Only I know the pathway through those brambles leading up the hill to the well, not that far really, perhaps five hundred yards, but it's a secret kept for years now. No ordinance map has ever shown the well's location, no local has ever so much as mentioned its existence. There's a small lean-to erected long ago, someone's dream vision of escaping the real world: merely a stunted walled-in mud-brick room, roofed in bamboo, laced with branches and leaves. In one corner I have provided a bucket for the necessary relieving of nature's call. Not that I cared, I just didn't want to have to play the heroic rescuer wading through filth.

I rolled Diz off the cart onto the floor then bound his

hands in front of him with a strong piece of vine I had previously cut from the undergrowth. A second length secured his ankles, more loosely though, so he might make it across to the bucket without having to be carried. I was avoiding carrying him not because of his weight, which was meager, but because he might smell me, recognize me the way an animal does. For good measure, I tied his thighs together. Now I was sure he could not move.

I stepped back, took a look at my handiwork, went to the corner where I had stashed the coil of rope, took it and threaded it around his neck, securing it with one of those seafaring knots Boy Scouts are sometimes taught, to get their badge. This one was better than that though. I had practiced long enough to make certain I knew what I was doing.

So, there I had Diz, on the earthen floor, propped against the mud wall, rope around neck, chin drooping on his chest, tethered arms sticking out in front of him, thighs strapped, ankles bound.

I was in complete control of his future.

50

It was later that Rose realized Diz was not in his room. A hungry eleven-year-old always showed up in time for meals, or anything in between, but not this evening. She went onto the deck and yelled his name, noting that the small boat was still at the jetty. Diz was not allowed to take the boat out alone without first asking permission and telling them exactly where he was going, and why.

She went back inside and got the big brass handbell then stood on the deck, clanging until her ears ached, but still Diz did not appear at his usual fast trot from around the corner, or from the woods, or a walk to the village to get a smoothie. He'd told them Tweedies made the best ever and his father told him they'd been doing it like that since he was a kid and he prayed they would never change the recipe.

Still, Rose felt sure Diz had not gone there today because he would have had to ask her for money since he'd already spent his allowance on fishing lures and a video of punk rockers so loud she'd had to ask him to use his earphones so the rest of the house wouldn't be deafened.

She stopped ringing the bell and had pushed the sleeves of her red T-shirt up her arms, staring, a little worried, at the lake. Then she heard a car crunch up the sandy road and swing to a stop. Thinking it must be Diz, that someone had given him a lift back from the village, and that she was gonna have to give him hell for going there alone, without asking her, she ran round the side of the house and saw Harry's dark green Jag.

Harry was in love with Mal but it didn't stop his heart from giving a little lurch when he spotted Rose, standing forlornly under the trees in her too-large white shorts that drooped to her lovely knees, and her breasts rounded at the V of her red tee, with her long brown curly hair floating sideways in the sudden breeze that rattled boats against jetties and soughed in the treetops like wind in a fairy story. Beyond the white clapboard house, the lake was suddenly all silver sparkle, reminding Harry of Christmas ornaments. The only thing that spoiled this image was the despairing droop to lovely Rose's shoulders.

Squeeze stuck his head out of the car window and Rose went and tickled his ears, though even now she couldn't help thinking it would be nicer to be tickling cute Harry Jordan's ears, set flat against his head, but of course that was an irrelevant thought. She was a married woman and Harry had a gorgeous girlfriend. Rose knew she was gorgeous because she had seen her on TV.

Harry got out of the car and gave her a hug that lingered only fractionally too long. There was, they both knew, a little something between them, that frisson of electricity which, notwithstanding other obligations, other loves, other lives, would always be there. Another time, another place perhaps something could have happened, but, Rose told herself firmly, not now. And with what she had going on with Wally and the family she had other things to think about.

"I don't suppose you spotted Diz on your way through the village?" she asked, stepping back.

"No, I didn't." Harry opened the door for the dog and he bounded out in one long solid leap. "Like a bird in flight," Harry marveled, laughing as Squeeze, freed, ran madly round.

"Kicking up his heels." Rose smiled. "I guess if Diz is out there, Squeeze'll find him."

Any thoughts about Rose as a woman fled from Harry's mind and he became a cop again; he wasn't that worried; boys were boys and Diz might be up to anything, but with proximity to the lake there was always concern.

He'd also caught the flicker of concern beneath Rose's quiet words. "You really don't know where Diz is?"

She lifted a shoulder in a helpless shrug. "Y'know, he just went out for a walk, I guess. He had his binoculars. He hasn't taken the boat—I mean, he wouldn't anyway without asking permission. Wally never lets any of our kids go out on the lake alone." She half smiled, remembering something Diz had said. "Whenever Diz got fed up and threatened to leave, he'd say he'd go and live on the island with the badgers. I told him they didn't have fries or chocolate there so he always reconsidered."

"Where did he pick to run away to instead?"

"Nowhere, actually." Rose frowned, trying to think. "Diz is not the kind of boy to run away. He kind of likes it here at home, even with Wally and . . . well, everything that went down. He was 'supportive.'" Her eyes met Harry's anxious ones. "In fact, just the other night he said to me, it's you and me alone here, Mom, I'm gonna take care of you."

"Obviously you've been calling him, he'd have heard the bell."

"He always comes for that, he knows it means supper time."

"Then I think we'd better go look for him."

Harry called Squeeze, who galloped from the bushes and skidded to a stop, then sat, head tilted, eyes fixed on Harry, awaiting instructions. Squeeze had no official training as a search dog; it was simply a natural instinct in him and he had worked many disaster scenes, sniffing out victims.

Rose went to salvage one of Diz's as yet unwashed T-shirts from the laundry room, then gave it to the dog to sniff. Then she put on sneakers and she and Harry followed the dog as he took them on a narrow trail framed in brambles ripe with berries, dark with juice. Behind them the hill buzzed with cicadas; in front of them the lake gleamed gray as the dusk. The dog stopped here and there but Harry could tell he had no lead. It was getting dark and his concern was rising.

He said, "We'd better go back and get help."

Rose closed her eyes and gave a horrified little gasp. "You don't mean . . . you can't think something might have happened to him?"

Harry put an arm around her shoulders and said as confidently as he could, "I'm not thinking anything yet, Rose, only that your boy should be home and he's not. It's getting dark and we need to get up a search party. He might have fallen, he could have broken a leg, lost his way."

Back at the house Harry got on the phone to the local police station. A search party was hastily organized, firemen arrived in their truck, sheriffs in black-and-whites, surprised neighbors asked what was going on, offering immediate help; another search party was organized from the village. Within an hour the now-dark woods were being systematically combed for any sign of Diz.

Wally came home, and Roman and the twins. Rose was trying to keep the panic out of her voice when she told them what was going on. They immediately went out to help, calling for Diz, searching the sandy shore road, flashlights gleaming into the undergrowth.

Then local TV arrived with a sympathetic young man, and Rose, frantic, went on camera holding up a picture of Diz and asking anyone who might have seen him to contact the sheriff's office.

Wally and the twins stood beside her. "He's just a lost boy," Wally said simply. "Please help us try to find him."

The hearts of those watching went out to them. All except for one. Actually two, because at that moment Diz was unconscious and unaware he had been kidnapped. He was not even able yet to think about where he was. Or what might happen to him.

51

Mal was still jet-lagged, hungover, and exhausted but she was feeling good. When she'd kissed Harry goodbye at Boston's Logan air terminal, she'd watched him climb into the unmarked police car that met him, driven by Detective Rossetti, of course, and in which she, a mere civilian, was not allowed to ride. She regretted leaving Harry but the endless-seeming flight from Paris in economy, because that was the way Harry traveled, had left her creased, cramped, and with freezing feet. Where did all that icy air that swept around one's legs come from when the rest of the plane's air felt like warm mush. They didn't even have those small round buttons you used to be able to twist in your direction anymore; now "air" on a plane was universal: you got what they gave you.

She had not even envied Harry his police car; the limo that had met her felt pretty good. As did the shower later, clothes stripped en route to the bathroom, hair and skin soaking up water like a sponge, even the shampoo that got in her eyes was okay. Dried off, wrapped in her best robe—gray plush, old and baby soft, wet hair flapping round her shoulders, a glass of Napa Sauvignon Blanc in hand, complete with two ice cubes just the way she liked it—not something she would ever do in front of wine purists but Mal liked her beverages with an edge of chill—she slumped on the sofa, opened her iMac, and Googled Bea Havnel.

Instantly, Bea was looking straight at her with those unafraid blue eyes: calm, composed, almost regal in her bearing. Harry was right, this was no shrinking violet; Mal could swear the woman was enjoying the media attention, the notoriety even, which obviously she was confident she would shake off. Her very stance seemed to invite the watcher to dare to accuse her, this lovely gentle young woman, of any crime, other than being present when her mother burned to death with a knife in her eye, and being there when Jemima Forester was found with her throat cut. "Unfortunate circumstances," as Mike Leverage had no doubt said. Mal thought he was right.

Wondering what Rose Osborne felt about all this, she Googled her too, but there was nothing.

She switched on the TV news. And there was Rose with Wally, standing on her porch, telling some young media guy with a microphone that her son had gone missing.

Mal sat up and took notice.

"His name is Diz," Rose was saying, holding up his photograph for the camera. "He went fishing earlier and we have not seen him since. We feared an accident but Diz is an excellent swimmer and he knows Evening Lake well."

"Does that mean you think your son might have been abducted?"

The reporter stuck the mike closer to Rose's face and she took a nervous step back, grabbing her husband's hand. Her white gypsy blouse slid off her shoulder and she pushed her long dark hair impatiently away as she hitched it back up. She had on old paint-stained jeans and flip-flops. Mal thought that it was probably the first time ever that Rose looked her age, as well as very worried. And very "womanly," Mal thought, remembering Harry's closeness to her.

Mal tried to get Harry on the phone but he didn't answer. She left a message. "What else can fate have in store for this lovely woman? Have you tracked down the boy? Please, Harry, let me know."

Harry's response a couple of minutes later was terse. One word. "No."

Mal knew not to push it and went back to her glass of wine, and to watch the news. She had been going to fix a tuna sandwich but suddenly was no longer hungry.

Harry and Rossetti were driving along the shore road with Squeeze in the back of the BMW, head sticking out the window, sniffing and making the yelping noises that, being a malamute, were his personal form of excited communication.

"We could use him as a tracker dog," Rossetti said.

"I think we're gonna need one," Harry said. Rose had called him with the news that Diz was missing. He'd immediately gotten a squad car out there to organize a search.

"You told me to trust you," she'd said. Accusingly, he'd thought.

"And you still must," he said, though he had no idea of what might have happened to Diz. "We'll find him," he promised. "He probably just got lost in the hills, he might have tripped, broken an ankle."

"He had his cell phone."

"There are many places around Evening Lake with

no reception; most likely Diz couldn't use it. I know it's ridiculous to tell you not to worry, Rose, of course your whole family must be worried. A search party is on its way and Rossetti and I will be there as soon as possible."

"Why do you always call him Rossetti?" Rose asked, out of the blue.

"I can't get around to thinking of him as a real person," Harry said, grinning at his friend, who had slipped on the black quilted vest, hand-tailored, over his dark blue custom-made shirt and removed his pink-flowered Liberty silk tie. Now he unbuttoned his shirt at the neck. He was ready to go search the hills for the missing boy.

"We'll be there soon," Harry told Rose. "Just hang on, okay?"

"Better put sneakers on," he told Rossetti, eyeing his shiny brown loafers. "We're going walking."

52

It had not escaped Harry's notice that the man who knew the terrain better than anyone had not shown up to help search for the missing boy.

"Len Doutzer knows this place like the back of his hand." He frowned at Rossetti. "Better, even. He strides these hills like he owns 'em, and it wouldn't surprise me to find out he did, some of them anyway. Len is a mysterious character; I'm willing to bet if we search the land records we'll find his name there."

"Which means?" Rossetti leaned against the white brick wall of Tweedies Coffee Shop, throwing longing glances through its plate-glass window, where tired searchers were being treated to coffee or tea or hot chocolate, take your pick. Everyone was mucking in, showing support for one of their own. This was a small town, scarcely more than a village, perched on the edge of the lake where right now every house showed a light, and where a helicopter still hovered, its searchlight close to the steely water's surface.

Harry said, "Which means Len might know where to hide someone."

Rossetti unraveled himself from the wall. "You mean a body."

Harry thought of Rose, distraught, waiting at her house, looked after by Roman and her girls while everybody else was looking for her young son. He said, "I still want to believe the kid could simply have gotten lost, fallen somewhere in the woods." He glanced at the birch trees crowning the hill, silvery in the moonlight. He knew what he was saying was unlikely; this had all the earmarks of an abduction. He didn't have to spell it out to Rossetti, who knew what he was thinking. "The question is why?" Harry said.

"Why is that always the question in abduction cases, and we know what the usual answer is."

Harry didn't need it spelled out either. He glanced round the lake with its necklace of lights, its small jetties where boats were returning and being moored. The search would restart at dawn. He wondered how Rose and Wally and the family were going to make it through the long night.

"I can't give up now," he said. "There's something out there, some clue we missed. See those clouds?" The two men turned their eyes to where the sky seemed suddenly to have lowered itself over the treetops. "When that rain comes it will wash away any sign of what happened, we'll be clueless and that kid might be dead. We can't allow that."

"No, sir." Rossetti pulled himself upright.

He looked down at his brand-new now dust-covered white sneakers, bought especially for this job. They didn't matter anymore. This was a life they were talking about. "So," he said. "Let's go find Len Doutzer."

Half an hour later they were at the A-frame atop the

hill. It was in darkness and both it and the shed were padlocked.

Back at her house, Rose did not get up from her bed to answer when the doorbell rang; one of her children would get it. She heard voices, wondered who it might be, but so many people had called round with small offerings; a fresh-baked pie, a jug of sweet iced tea, donuts from Tweedies, hot soup, her own specialty. Even now the pot was still sitting on the stove. Cold, though. As was she.

She thought she might never get warm again, huddled under the blue mohair throw, worried that she should not be here, that she should be out with the others, searching for her son.

Madison popped her head round the door and Rose sat up. "Yes."

Her daughter caught what she was thinking and said, hastily, "Oh, no . . . it's not . . . it's well, it's Bea Havnel. She wants to see you."

Rose shook her head, puzzled. "Bea? Of all people!"

"She says she needs to talk to you. I don't know why, after all we've been through with her, but somehow she's just so . . . desperate maybe you should."

"You think she knows something about Diz?"

Madison's young face contorted with sudden tears. "Oh, Mom, I don't know. Why don't you just ask her."

Rose went to her vanity and took a long look at her ravaged face; she brushed back her hair, straightened her old blue sweater—her comfort sweater, so old and soft it was like wearing nothing—collected the box of Kleenex, and went and stood by the window. She hadn't really thought why she needed to stand, but somehow she didn't want to be the one sitting down while Bea towered over her. "Bring her in," she told Madison.

Seconds later, Bea Havnel was at the door. Skinny as the snake Diz had called her; no makeup; eyes swollen into slits from crying, yet still managing to look beautiful. Standing there, at the door to Rose's room, Bea personified innocence.

"Rose," Bea said, but Rose said nothing. "I'm not here to ask forgiveness," Bea went on quickly. "I already did that and I know it's not possible. I've asked people, asked therapists what I should do to make amends." Bea took a hesitant step into the room. "They told me don't ask for forgiveness, what you must ask is for events to be forgotten. To put it behind us, leave it in the past where it belongs. I'm not a good person, Rose, that's obvious, and if you knew my true background you might understand why. But Rose, I do care. I care so much about you. You are everything I aspire to be, and fear I never will be. You are hurting so badly and there is nothing I can do, except maybe . . . well, if only you would let me help search for Diz. I'm used to being alone here, I'm like Diz really, roaming the hills by myself. I know places where he might go. I can't tell you I'll find him, Rose, but please, I'm begging you, pleading with you, let me try."

Desperate, Rose saw the girl's pain, her need to belong, to be counted in. She saw her true desire to help.

"My dear," she said, stepping toward Bea and wrapping her in her arms, the way she had when they first met. "Of course you must help us."

53

It was dark. Diz had something tied over his eyes. Something rough, and he could smell whatever it was. It reminded him vaguely of a dog. Or could it be a horse? He thought idly about that, as though his mind was on a go-slow, almost as if it didn't really matter. No, he decided, it was definitely dog.

He suddenly had the most awful need to pee. Urinate. That was the proper word. His father had told him he had to say that when he had to go when they were out together. Never sounded right to Diz, though. When you had to pee, that's what you had to do and now he was almost beside himself with the need. Bursting, in fact. But he could not move. He could not walk. He could not even unzip because his hands were tied together. Not behind his back the way the cops did it. They stuck out in front of him, bandaged it felt, almost up to his elbows. It was very uncomfortable. As was his bladder. Oh God, what was he to do? He couldn't just go. He moaned in an agony of need, wiggling his bandaged arms to get them nearer to the target area, without success.

He thought about where he might be. He was in a sitting position, his back resting against a wall. A smooth wall. There were no sticking-out bits, and it was cool. His knees were pulled up, there were ties around his thighs and also his ankles. Alert now, because of his urgent need, fear suddenly swept through his body like a gust of wind sucking the heartbeat out of him, pausing life's machinery, sending unbidden tremors the length of his spine. The spine that was propped against a cool wall. In the darkness of he knew not where.

And then he heard footsteps. Almost silent, but in his blinded state his hearing seemed sharper. No shoes, he thought. Naked feet. They stopped next to him. His skin crawled with terror. His skin sweated. His eyes under the blindfold were tight shut. He was going to die.

For a long moment there was only silence, not even the sound of his own breathing. Then someone knelt beside him and unbound his feet. Hauled him up with a hand on the back of his collar. Diz felt the sweat spring up beneath the touch, slippery as a fish on the hook. He stood for a few moments, muscles burning as the blood flowed back, then he was hauled forward. By the neck.

Oh, Jesus, oh Jesus . . . there was a rope around his neck. Somebody was dragging him, jerking that rope cruelly until it bit into his skin, dragging him forward into a blackness that seemed tangible because his eyes no longer functioned. His only senses were hearing and touch. He hurtled blindly on with his executioner. He was a boy on his way to the scaffold. Only he wasn't. He was pushed into another, smaller blackness, his hands unbound, his shorts unzipped, pushed again.

Diz sank thankfully onto the bucket. Urine gushed out of him loud as Niagara Falls. The relief was so intense he wondered why he wasn't more concerned about being stabbed or bludgeoned to death, then realized if that was about to happen they would not have bothered about his need to pee. Urinate.

So. What next. Finished, he was hauled to his feet. Zipped. Dragged again. Back into the cell from which he had hoped he was to be freed.

He leaned his spine against the wall. He thought about blind people, about how sad it was not to see, not to know about color, about the way sunshine looked as well as felt, about the river's silvery-brown sparkle as well as its rushing and gurgling; about enjoying the green of the leaves on his fig tree along the branch from where he spied. The blind could not spy. Diz wanted to cry.

In fact, now he was crying. He stopped though, when he felt something against his leg. He thought about rats. He held his breath. But this was no rat; it was not furry, it made no sound, it simply oozed along his bare calf, slowly, rhythmically. It couldn't be a snake, snakes lived above the earth, hiding in leaves and rustling grasses, creatures of light and shade. He was underground. This could only be a worm.

Nerves throbbing, he monitored its progress up his calf. Every inch of his being longed to sweep it off him. He could not. He had to accept it. He thought about his mother, how she might have laughed at him wanting to sweep a worm off his leg. Worms were good for the environment, she had told him that. But he was not a part of the environment, he was just a scared kid who wanted to get out of here and live. Be alive again. With no worms creeping up his leg.

Think of a story, his mother would have told him. Amuse yourself. Okay, so the worm was called Petronella. He would write, in his mind of course, the story of Petronella the worm, who was sharing the warmth of his leg, to keep away the overpowering chill of always being a worm. He began to cry again. Small tears. No sound. The very air around him was silent.

Oh God, he was being left here, abandoned, to die alone. No one would ever find him. Him and Petronella, who might be only the first of the worms coming to take advantage of his bare leg. Oh God, oh God, he so wanted to scream, the terror wanted to yell out of his throat, to proclaim to someone, anyone, out there, that he was here. Alone.

The darkness seemed so thick he could touch it, taste it even, like earth on his tongue. How long had he been in here? He had no way of knowing, no sense of time . . . he had no way of measuring it. Time had morphed into more of a cloudy texture, a feeling not a look, because after all he could see nothing. Then how did he know it was a cloudy darkness?

He must try to remember everything so he could tell them when they came to get him. Rescue him. Roman, his big brother, would be there. And of course, his mother would be first. And his dad. Logically, though, it would be the detective. Harry Jordan. His idol. Wait, though, now he remembered, Jordan had gone to Paris.

Diz knew for sure then, he was a dead kid.

But who would want to kill him? He meant nothing, except to his family and friends. By "nothing" Diz meant he didn't count enough in this world for anyone to need to kill him.

He sat, thinking about it, remembering the touch on his arm, the hand at his neck, the tug of the rope.

Just as with Petronella the worm, every fiber of his being remembered; every raised hair, every bead of his sweat, every sense in his thin young body had listened, heard, reacted. Suddenly he knew it was a female. The hairs on his arms bristled like a hedgehog.

"I know who you are," he yelled into the darkness, suddenly finding his voice. "I know it's you, Bea."

54

The sharp little fucker had just signed his own death warrant, calling my name, recognizing me the way an animal would sense a predator. Signed, sealed, and delivered, he was mine. I had meant to be the one that "found" him, rescued him, gave him back to Rose, then I'd become the darling of the Osborne family, move into their lives and take over. I would be the "Rose." I would become "the mother." Rose would be my devoted slave and I would own her entire world.

Sounds crazy now, huh? Trust me, it would have worked, such is the human psychology, the makeup of "decent" people. By "finding" the lost boy, Diz, I would have become a celebrity, famous, a heroine. Thereafter I could do no wrong. Now, it would have to be different, or I would be the one to die.

I was always an outsider. All my life, I never counted. I never even had a friend. What about school, you are no doubt asking? Well, what about it? Surely I must have made friends there? Hah. My mother would never have allowed me to ask anyone back to our apartment in one of the lower-end, riskier areas of Miami, where, with my blond hair and pale skin, I stood out, a freak among the golden Cubans with their big families, whole generations of them living so happily together it never ceased to amaze me. I hated my white skin that never turned sweet-girl gold like theirs. I hated their mothers who always met them at school and covered their happy faces with warm kisses. I hated the girls because I was not like them and they felt it and were afraid of me. I was, you might say, an unknown quantity, though I knew from an early age perfectly well of what I was capable.

This was my first mother we're talking about, the real one, I guess.

The only activities she allowed outside the house were to go to school, because she had no choice; and to swim in the local public pool, for which I allowed her no choice. I simply went. And I swam my bitter heart out every morning at six when the pool opened, and later, after school, until it closed.

My mother was always a drug addict. At first she'd dealt, small-time, in pills, faking multiple prescriptions, and also cocaine, small-time too, until she got too confident, too big for her boots you might say, and usually ended up in jail.

In effect, I had no mother. I certainly had no father, at least not then. I had no family. I looked after myself. I stole, a few dollars at a time, to buy packets of ham or baloney and white bread wrapped in plastic that lasted forever without going moldy, as well as ice cream and Cokes. My mother never displayed any curiosity about what I might be eating, or whether in fact I had eaten. It did not take long for me to realize she did not care whether I lived or died. In fact she told me frequently she would be better off without me. I did not doubt that she was right. And that's when I decided to get me a new mother.

The real one "overdosed" on a lethal amount of steroids mixed up in her nightly bottle of gin. Gin was an oddball drink, mostly people like her drank scotch or vodka, but she loved that bitter quinine flavor, which was useful in disguising additives, like steroids. It was to be her undoing.

I was twelve when she departed my life for, as the social workers told me, "a better place." It surely couldn't have been much worse, I told them. And just like that, they found me a new mother.

I did not last long in my new family. They took a dislike to my quiet, "scheming ways" as they called them. And I took a dislike to their sanctimonious condescending attitude, when I knew all they wanted anyway from their new foster child was the money paid over monthly for my keep.

I was out of there and on the run when I was thirteen, and never regretted it for a moment. I was an independent thinker, I could look after myself. I was a girl on the loose and I enjoyed it. I learned lessons even those of good heart would have found useful, and with my own evil heart only made things even clearer. I loved myself. I loved the way I looked. I learned how to use those looks, cleverly, how to play the innocent, to catch at their hearts with my long blue gaze. I learned how to be a killer. And I want to tell you, it came easily.

And then Lacey Havnel, aka Carrie Murphy, found me. Or did I find her? Whatever, we knew we needed each other. It was at a bar, of course, where else? And of course I was underage and she recognized it just as the cops arrived. She got me out of there. We hooked up. I became the "daughter" of a con artist supreme, a bad drug dealer and an alcoholic. It worked for me since I was better at the con game than Lacey. I got her to take out the insurance policy on the house, one and a half mil, and another mil on her life. I wanted two but she wouldn't go for it. I also got her to steal the cash she was meant to hand over to the representative of a drug cartel—a minor one in that world, but still, nobody likes to lose their money.

And then, of course, I needed to get rid of her so I could take the money, become the beautiful little rich girl. That's the way life works out, right? She had nine hundred thou of the stolen money already stashed in the bank after buying the lake house. No mortgage, that would never have been possible. With her dead, it was all mine. I could afford that room at the Ritz.

And then a whole new life opened up for me. I found Rose, the mother I had always wanted, the Osbornes, the family I had always wanted. But because they were not mine and never could be I set out to destroy them. It was the old principle: if I can't have them, no one can.

It was easy to take out this kid, Diz. More. It was a pleasure because I could think of Rose, suffering. I offered to help her, of course, and of course she could not resist my soft pleading, to be counted in, to help find her beloved youngest child. They say the youngest is always the most precious. I had no doubt, in Rose's case, this is true. First I'd dealt with her husband, Wally. Now Diz. A blow to Rose's heart.

I knew exactly where I would take Diz next and what I would do. No one would see Diz Osborne alive or dead again. The thought gave me intense pleasure.

55

Len watched the woman he now believed to be his daughter, on the opposite side of the lake, striding purposefully up the hill behind her house through the birch woods, then out of sight. He guessed he would have known who she was, what she was, if he'd looked properly at her earlier, taken a blind bit of notice instead of dismissing her from his mind as a meaningless grifter, a con artist of the highest order; a drama queen who milked her beauty for gain; who used her demure demeanor, her sad puzzled gaze until the world gave her what she wanted. And what they didn't give, Bea took.

Bea Havnel's name should, in reality, have been Beatrice Doutzer, though Len would never have claimed paternity. Only after her death had Lacey tried to foist that on him, and he was still puzzled about why. He guessed it was because in life, there'd been nothing to gain from a man who had nothing; she'd probably gotten more off whoever the poor bastard was she'd told was the father, until he'd disappeared into the night too. Or into death, the way Lacey had. The way several people who came in close contact with the beautiful Bea had.

Bea certainly did not have Len's dour looks, nor his desire to be alone; nor, he guessed, his taxidermy skills. Not from him had she inherited the desire to torture, because Len was not into torture. That was purely Bea's own desire. And torture was exactly what she was doing now, to Rose Osborne.

Again, Len asked himself why, and immediately understood the answer. Rose was everything Bea was not. Admittedly Bea was the more beautiful, but Rose was also lovely. Rose was warm. Rose was the good wife, and the good mother. Her children adored her. Her friends adored her. Her husband still adored her, though Bea had gotten him off the rails with drugs until he'd almost lost his mind. And then she'd latched on to Roman, who was young enough and dumb enough to be completely taken in by her. Though not dumb enough to be caught up in her evil. Rose had the man, the good husband, the family, the home. Bea wanted everything Rose had and was. She wanted Rose's life, and she had been prepared to do anything to get it. She had succeeded with Wally; she'd known just how to get into his very soul, and now, she had their boy. The perfect element for the final deed of torture.

Just yesterday Len had stood by, right there by the Osbornes' jetty where he could see and hear everything, watching Bea doing her act, leaving Rose's house, apparently beseeching Rose to give permission for her to help search for her missing son.

"If you can't forgive me, at least allow me this," Bea pleaded again, practically on her knees.

Len watched Rose lean in toward Bea, saw her put a hand on her shoulder, heard her say quietly, "I so appreciate your concern, Bea. Let's forget the past. The future is my missing son. We must all help find him." And all the while Len had known that Bea knew exactly where Diz was. He was where she had taken him; where nobody would ever find him. Diz was as good as dead.

A grim smile cracked his face. Bea had forgotten that Len Doutzer was the eyes and ears of the small world of Evening Lake. Forgotten he knew every inch of the land, every hill, every tributary, every dip and rise, every small sandy lane, every thicket and woods and cave. No place at Evening Lake was a secret to Len. What he needed now, though, was to find in which of those secret places Bea had hidden Diz. And whether the boy was still alive, or if Bea was planning on being the one to "come across his body"; the woman who would comfort Rose and the family on the death of their boy, the woman who would move into their lives again as silently and stealthily as a snake, so gently and easily they would never know she had taken them over until it was too late. Rose was the doyenne of the Osborne house, but the whole family would be beholden to Bea for finding their dead son.

Len stood outside his shed, staring into the stand of trees halfway up the opposite hill. Unlike Diz he needed no binoculars to sharpen his vision. He was as clear-eyed as the red-tailed hawks circling above in search of prey. He knew now exactly where Bea Havnel had gone.

He went back inside and stood for a minute under the eviscerated carcass of the German shepherd, still swinging by its legs on cables strung from the slatted ceiling beams. He studied the array of knives arranged neatly in front of his workbench, selected a ten-inch, very thin surgical blade that he particularly liked, fitted it into a scabbard, hitched up his worn cord pants, tightened his belt, and stuck the sheathed knife in over his right hip. He pulled himself up straight; took a deep breath; looked for a long time at his place of work, at the pelts of the badger and the coyote, at the dog swinging overhead. This time would be different.

He jogged down the hill, taking the route through undergrowth only he knew, emerging lakeside. He pulled his small boat from its hiding place, dragged it into the water, climbed in, and began sculling rapidly across the lake toward the wreckage of the Havnel house, which, with his powerful arms, took only a few minutes. He stepped out into the shallow water, dragged the boat after him, and left it partially hidden in the copse of birches. Then he took the same route as Bea up the hill in back of the burned house.

It took a little longer than he'd thought. Ten minutes. This disturbed Len because he knew time was of the essence, and he increased his pace, careless of any sound he made: the crackling of leaves and small branches underfoot; the startled bird calling the alarm; the pair of hawks hovering, outstretched wings completely still as they floated on an air current, seeming to watch events below with a coldly calculating eye, almost as cold and calculating, Len thought, as his own.

He found Bea exactly where he'd anticipated he would find her, standing at the rim of the old well, pumped dry a hundred or more years before, leaving a great rift in the ground and where, Len was sure, Bea now had Diz Osborne.

The well was a perfect burial ground. Nobody had been here for donkey's years, no one would ever come here because no one except Len, and Bea, remembered it existed. And the bitch knew only because she had followed Len when he'd gone on one of his taxidermy expeditions, when he'd hoped to find something new to add to his collection, a snake perhaps. He'd thought a snake would be exciting. He knew that several pythons had been abandoned by owners of "curiosity" pets. They quickly had proliferated, the way they had also in the Florida Everglades, but not here in such big numbers, the winters were too cold for them. As yet he had not found one.

He stopped, stood silent when he saw Bea with the boy. She held him by a rope around his neck. His hands were tied in front of him, his ankles loosely bound together, leaving just enough leeway for him to walk while rendering him unable to escape.

Bea was so intent on what she was doing, so secure in the absolute privacy of the location, that despite Len's heavy-footed progress through the trees, she seemed not to have heard him. Len could hear her, though. She was talking to the boy.

"So, young Diz, you watched me often enough through those binoculars of yours. Took note of every move I made, didn't you?"

The boy hung his head, made no answer. Len saw that his shorts and T-shirt were torn, his limbs covered in deep scratches, or perhaps knife wounds. From the shelter of the trees, he checked Bea for a weapon, saw a knife, six, seven inches he guessed, hanging from a cord around her neck. The same kind of knife she had stuck into her mother's eye before she'd set her alight.

Len thought about the dead and dismembered animals he captured, animals caught for their beauty, killed to preserve them before they could be ruined by age and illness. Youth and beauty should always be preserved, including, in this case, the young Diz Osborne who, as far as Len knew, had never done anyone a disservice and whose only crime now, as far as Bea was concerned, was to be Rose Osborne's beloved son. Len knew without a shadow of a doubt, right at that moment, Bea's intention was that whatever Rose loved, whomever she treasured, was to be taken away from her. Unlike what she had attempted with Wally, this time it would be forever. Len had no doubt that Bea was going to kill.

He slid his knife from its sheath, tested its edge through his fingers. It brought a thread of blood to his skin.

An experienced stalker who had been known to catch even the highly tuned-in coyote unawares, Len skulked silently closer. He was out of the trees now. Bea stood fifty feet from where he was, at the very edge of the disused well, her arm resting on the boy's shoulder. Len saw Diz turn his head, lift his face as though to look at Bea, even though with his bound eyes he could not see her.

"My mother says you are a bitch," Len heard Diz say clearly. "And you know what, she's right."

Len's heart sank. He should never have said that. Now he was done for. As if in slow motion he saw Bea release her grip on Diz's shoulders, saw her face suffuse with anger, saw her give Diz a shove. Watched him disappear over the edge of the gaping black hole into the well.

Bea stood, with her head thrown back, listening; waiting, Len realized, to hear the boy's screams. Concentrating on achieving every last drop of pleasure from his terrible death, she trembled, mouth agape in a smile that sent a chill through Len's entire body. She did not even hear him coming at her.

He got her from behind, brought her down. She was on her hands and knees beneath him. His body pressed against hers, his hand searched for her knife, but she was too quick, it was already in her fist, already aiming at his throat as she rolled over. He moved out just in time.

She swung at him again. Again he rolled, realized she was on her feet, that she was coming at him. The knife was at his neck. He grabbed it by the blade, felt his blood gush.

Len summoned all his wiry, mountain-man strength. He leaped to his feet the way a young animal would. Bea took a step back, looking at him, surprised. Disarmed now, her knife gone, she turned and ran. Len caught her easily. He put both his arms round her from behind, felt her frail ribs crack as he increased his pressure, heard her shrill whine of pain that this time brought him pleasure. And then he cut her throat, the way he did the animals.

He stood, panting, staring down at her as she bled out. Rose-red velvet blood.

A couple of minutes passed. Finally, he knelt, lifted her wrist, tested for a pulse. Bea was no longer beautiful. To Len all that was left was bones, the entrails, the pelt.

He looked at her face, at the beauty that had been the façade all her murderous life. He leaned closer, inspecting her, wondering what had existed inside that blond head.

Suddenly her eyes opened.

For one last moment he was looking into the eyes of evil.

Then she was gone.

Len knew what he had to do. He moved Bea's body farther into the undergrowth, cleaned up his slashed palm with a pad of leaves, and went to the well to look for Diz Osborne's body.

Again, he found himself looking into a pair of eyes.

Diz was perched on a small outcropping about twenty

feet down, held from tumbling farther by a sturdy fern which probably had been growing there for decades.

Diz said in a trembly voice, "Are you going to kill me too?"

"No," Len said. Then, "Do not move. I will be right back."

He jogged swiftly down to his boat, took out the fishing line he always kept there, jogged back to the well, where he doubled up the line until he was satisfied it would take the boy's weight, then lowered it down the hole.

"I want you to tie this around your chest, right under the shoulders," he instructed. "I want you to tie a knot so tight it will take shears to cut it off. Do you understand?"

"Yes, sir, I understand."

Len thought it was good the boy obviously still had his wits about him. "Then here it comes." He began to lower the line. "Do not make any jerky moves, do not reach out for it, trust me I'll get it close to you."

"Yes, sir," Diz said again. He sounded frightened now.

The line touched Diz's chest. "I got it, sir, thank you," he called.

Len thought it a tribute to Rose that the kid remembered his manners even at a time like this. He thought of the dead bitch in the woods behind him, and of this poor innocent kid who she had meant to use to bring Rose Osborne down to her own evil level, to cut Rose to her heart, if not with a knife, then with despair and sorrow. And all under the guise of friendship.

"Now, tie it like I told you," he said. He wasn't sure but he had to trust his line would hold. "Test it, give it a tug, a real hard one. So, okay, now, swing your legs out first, then let the rest of your body follow, keep your hands on the wall, get any grip you can, push upward with your feet against the wall . . . that's right . . . that's it. You got it, son," he yelled triumphantly as Diz's head appeared over the edge of the well.

"Jesus H. Christ," Diz said, sprawling on the ground next to Len. "You're fuckin' amazing."

Diz heard Squeeze barking. He looked over his shoulder. Saw Harry heading up the hill toward him, and behind him came his brother, Roman.

"Oh look," he said, turning to Len, his savior. "They've found us."

But Len had gone.

56

Diz couldn't help crying, sitting on the ground next to the gaping hole of a well where he had so nearly died. Len had simply disappeared into the thick undergrowth. He hadn't even been able to say a proper thank-you to the man who saved him. And he was scared because he didn't know where Bea was either.

Squeeze loomed suddenly over him, giving his face an encouraging lick. Then Harry appeared, running, with Rossetti and Roman, like a pair of fullbacks coming in for a touchdown, Diz thought. It brought a smile back to his face.

Panting, Harry inspected him. "You're a friggin miracle, y'know that?" he said. "All you've gone through and now you're smiling?"

"I'm smiling because you and Rossetti looked so funny puffing up the hill," Diz said, almost becoming his old perky self again. "Only thing is I lost my binoculars."

Roman glanced around for them.

"In there." Diz pointed to the well.

The men went and looked down it. "Was it Len who got you out of there?" Harry asked.

Diz nodded. "Yes, sir. He did." He explained about the fishing line still tied around his chest. "He saved my life," he added. "That and the old fern, growing in there. It stopped my fall after Bea pushed me in."

Harry did not allow his feelings about what might have happened to Diz to show on his face. He knelt next to the boy and began hacking off the fishing cord with his Swiss Army knife, rubbing Diz's shoulders to ease the cramp, wishing he could also erase the pain that, despite Diz's bravery, he knew the boy must be suffering. The mental anguish of almost being murdered was the kind of trauma few people survived to remember.

"Diz, if you can, if you are able to even think about it right now, to remember, I would like you to give me some idea of what happened."

Roman was holding on to him, and Diz saw the tears in his eyes. He hid his face in Squeeze's thickly furred neck. "It was Bea," he said. "She knew I'd seen her, with my binoculars, y'know, and that I'd guessed what she had done to her mother, and to Jemima, and what she wanted to do to my mother. I don't know it all, only what I caught in my glasses. But I couldn't be sure. And then she said she wanted to talk to me, she had something special to tell me. And I listened and she did. She talked about my mom, said what an angel she was . . . and then . . ." Diz stopped. He buried his face deeper into Squeeze's fur. He began to sob. Harry glanced at Rossetti. "It's okay, Diz," Harry said quietly, "You can talk about it later."

"No. I must tell you now, because what Bea said was she hates my mother, she said she was going to kill me so she could watch my mom suffer, then she would kill her too. And now I don't know where she is and I'm afraid she's going to do that."

On the shore road, Harry saw the flash of lights on the sheriff's car. He picked Diz up and carried him carefully down the hill.

"Jeez," Diz said, awed. "You mean I get to ride in a cop car?"

You couldn't, Harry thought, keep a small boy down for long.

When he'd sent Diz off home, he called Rose.

"Where is he?" she demanded, frantic.

"On his way to you, and then you'll take him to get checked out. He seemed okay to me, Rose, no real need for worry. Except for the mental anguish of what he's been through."

"And where is she?" Rose asked, in a voice so quiet it was, Harry thought, almost a threat.

"That's what we intend to find out, right now. Take care of your son, Rose."

He turned to Rossetti, who had spotted a trail of blood. He'd pulled back the undergrowth and they both looked at the large red stain, almost beautiful in its scarlet depth.

"Somebody died here," Harry said, already on his phone to summon reinforcements, and forensics, and ambulances. "Either Bea, or Len Doutzer. Personally, knowing the clever Bea, I'm betting it was Len."

The two men waited until the reinforcements came wailing along the shore, bringing vacationers out of their cottages once again, wondering what was going on. Within the hour cops were combing the hillsides, going one more time through the wreckage of the Havnel house, searching the guest cottage where Bea was living, the woods, the fields, preparing to dredge the lake if necessary.

Standing on the hill, looking at the damage that young woman had wrought, Harry grieved not only for those she had killed, but for his beloved tranquil Evening Lake. The place where he had once come to rest his troubled soul.

A couple of hours later, he and Rossetti drove the dust-embraced BMW up the path that led to Len's cruddy A-frame, swirling to a stop with a honk of the horn right outside the always-padlocked front door. Squeeze was first out.

The dog stood for a minute, nose pointed in the air, sniffing, then without so much as a backward glance, he headed behind the house, to the shed.

This time the door was not closed. It swung open on its hinges. Ten feet away from it, Squeeze stopped dead. Ears flattened, he took a couple of paces back. Harry caught up to him, put his hand on the dog's neck.

"What's the matter, my friend. What's wrong?"

The door creaked, swinging gently back and forth.

Harry looked at Rossetti. He was right there, Sig Sauer already cocked.

"I fuckin' hate this place," Rossetti was muttering. "Gives me the fuckin' creeps."

Harry said, "What do you think we're gonna find in there?"

"I hate to think."

"Come on, Squeeze, let's go take a look," Harry said, but the dog backed away. He gave a long howl.

Harry looked at Rossetti again. "It's gonna be bad," he said. Rossetti nodded and the two walked together to the shed.

Harry opened the door, they looked inside, then

stepped back. Rossetti walked round the side of the shed and vomited into the bushes. The dog hunkered, way back, near the car. It was the first time Harry had seen his dog afraid.

He had to go in. Into that dreadful place. Check it all out. It was his duty. He was the cop.

He propped open the door with a couple of large stones and called to Rossetti. "You don't have to go inside," he said. "Just take a look from here."

Tethered to the crossbeams of the ceiling swung the eviscerated carcasses of several dead animals. Their pelts gleamed, their teeth shone yellow-white, their eyes were stitched shut.

Behind them dangled the naked body of Bea Havnel, strapped by her hands and feet, slit from belly to throat. She too had been eviscerated. Her entrails smoldered in a bucket in the corner. Her eyes had not been stitched shut though. They were wide open and seemed to Harry to be gazing straight into his. He was looking into the pale blue eyes of pure evil.

He went back outside, got his emotions together, his thoughts organized. He had never seen anything as macabre, as horrifying. Then he remembered Jemima with her throat cut, and Lacey Havnel with the knife sticking out of her right eye, and he thought whoever did this removed evil from this earth, by his own act of evil. He knew it was Len. What he didn't know was where Len was.

Within half an hour the place was surrounded by cops. Forensics were there again, "Having a field day," Rossetti muttered darkly. Photographers took their own pictures, detectives took their own pictures, videos were being taken, the ground searched inch by inch for evidence, for the knife, for blood. And the search was on for Len.

They soon found him, lying in his small boat, drifting across the lake. Dead from a shot wound to the chest. Right where his heart must once have been.

It was over.

57

Rose looked around, at the people sitting at her kitchen table, mugs of coffee, glasses of wine, bowls of her leftovers soup in front of them. Tonight it tasted strongly of basil because the plant outside the back door had suddenly gone into overdrive, sprouting all over the place so she'd had to put it to good use. Rossetti, the good-looking homicide detective who looked more like an Italian male model, told her it was as good as his mother's. "Better, even," he'd added with a grin that she knew he hoped would make her feel better about everything she had just gone through; she and her entire family, who were all also at the table.

Roman sat next to Diz, offering more soup, more bread, more Coke. The big brother was taking what had happened hard, having trouble keeping his emotions under control, while the girls, of course, did not even bother to try. They ate their soup silently, reluctantly, not seeming to notice when the odd tear rolled into their spoons. They ate only because Rose had told them they had to, adding with a smile the childish threat that otherwise there would be no ice cream.

Wally was another matter. Rose had thought Wally would die when she had told him what happened to Diz, the whole terrible story of Bea, and the well. They were in their bedroom, the French doors were open onto the porch with the view over the lake, so tranquil it seemed nothing could ever ruffle its timeless surface. Rose had read stories where people's faces "turned white with shock." This was the only time she ever experienced it. The blood seemed to drain from Wally's summer-tanned face and his eyes went blank, dark as though he were looking into that well, could see his boy there.

Wally sank onto the bed, put his head in his hands. "How could I have allowed this to happen?" he said. "Diz could have been killed and it was my fault."

Rose went and sat next to him. She put her arm around his shoulders. Her husband was crying. "It was no one's fault," she'd said quietly. "No one is responsible for a madwoman like that. That's what she was, who she was. If it had not been us she targeted it would have been some other family. It's over. Diz is safe, that's all that matters now."

Even as she said it, Rose knew Wally would always feel responsible for allowing Bea into his home, into his family. Rose was very glad Bea was dead.

Now her husband sat in his usual place at the head of the table, his notebook and pen at hand as always, in case he was struck by an idea for a location, a character, a twist in the plot. She thought, though, even Wally could never have figured out the twist in this plot. The next morning Wally was to leave for a place somewhere in Arizona that took care of people with his kind of problem. Not that Wally was "using" anymore, but he had been more than a "recreational user," as the euphemism went, of cocaine. It was his own choice to take this course, to be reindoctrinated into the world of normal living. "To become myself again," was what he said to Rose, and she agreed. She was no longer that young girl in the white bathing suit leaping into the lake, into his arms, thrilled with the very idea of "love," but she loved Wally. Always would. She was his and he was hers. The day they had made those vows still stuck in Rose's mind. She, and, she also believed, Wally, had made them till death did they part—and they would keep them. Rose was very glad of that.

Homicide Detective Harry Jordan was sitting next to her; well, almost next to her. In fact Squeeze had pushed his way between them and was leaning against her legs, his long head on her lap, eyes raised adoringly to hers whenever she looked down at him.

"I swear my dog's in love with you," Harry said, leaning back in his chair. Her eyes met his. "And I don't blame him," he added softly.

Rose gave him a smile, lowered her eyes, willed herself not even to go there. Not to think of Harry. Ever. Again. In that way. She turned to look at Diz, who had his brand-new binoculars slung around his neck, whose eyes were bright with the optimism and resilience of extreme youth, and whose black eye—a true purple shiner—and scabbed limbs were a lingering reminder of what he had gone through.

"He'll be okay."

It was Harry who said it to Rose, not her husband.

"How can you know that?"

"I've been through violence before, with kids. Some of them can work it out. Others can't. I'm guessing Diz is one of the 'cans.' All due to you," he added. "With a mom like you he'll be able to release the terrible memories, not all at once, of course, but we have people in place who'll help him."

"A therapist?"

Harry nodded. "One of the best. I told her about Diz and she's made her services available, immediately, if you wish. Personally, I think the sooner the better. Diz is a good kid, Rose, we don't want him harmed by this, long term."

"Of course not." She looked searchingly at him. "Are you sure, though, he'll be all right?"

Harry took her hand in his. "I'd bet the farm on it," he said.

Diz didn't need the binoculars to watch what was going on between his mom and Harry Jordan. They liked each other, even he could see that. And boy, was he glad. He'd never been so glad in his life to see anybody as he had been with Harry. "Detective Jordan," his mom said he should call him, but Harry said just call him Harry. So he did.

"Harry," he called across the table.

Harry turned his gaze from Rose. "Yeah, Diz?"

"My mom taught me always to say thank you and I've forgotten whether I did or not."

"You already did."

"Did I thank you too, Detective Rossetti?"

"You did, son." Rossetti felt Rose's gaze on him and he slicked back his hair, and gave her a warm, white smile.

"Detective Rossetti, is my mom's cooking as good as your mom's?" Diz liked to mix things up a bit and was happy when he saw that the detective appeared confused.

Then, "Listen, kid," Rossetti said sternly. "Everybody's own mom's cooking is the best. Keep that in mind and you'll never go wrong."

Everybody laughed and Diz sat back, satisfied. Even the dog came to sit next to him, like he really belonged. Everything was okay again, here at Evening Lake. Home.

EPILOGUE

It was dusk and Evening Lake was peaceful. Lights were coming on at the pretty homes and the water rustled like a sheet of gray moiré silk, dipped at the western edge with the last remnants of pale sunlight. There was not a cloud left in the sky. "Like an omen of good fortune," Mal said to Harry.

They were sitting together on the porch in the uncomfortable Adirondack chairs now padded by Mal, with memories of how painful it had been for her behind, with Harry's sofa cushions, which, looking at them critically, she decided he needed new ones anyway. Stars that somehow looked bigger and brighter at the lake were already beginning their glitter, and every bug seemed to have disappeared with the oncoming of night.

Mal stole a look at Harry, next to her in his Adirondack chair. His head was thrown back, his eyes were closed. An ice-cold mojito, made by her, was clutched in one hand. With his other, he slowly smoothed Squeeze's ears. The dog's big head rested on Harry's knee. They looked, Mal thought, the epitome of contentment. She did think, though, she should mention it was time Harry got some better outdoor furniture. Come to think of it, indoor as well. But perhaps now was not the time. This was a moment of quiet perfection, which, after all that had gone down the past few weeks, was to be relished and enjoyed with the long-awaited peace of mind.

She sat, swinging her legs, looking at the fading sky, thinking about how fleeting happiness might be, how rare these brief moments of pure contentment, how fortunate she was to have found this, to have found Harry. Or had Harry found her? She smiled as she looked at him again. He was half-asleep now, mouth slightly open. She reached over and took the glass from his hand before it fell, spilling a little onto the new slippers she had bought him. Black velvet loafers, with his monogram, HJ, embroidered in gold.

Without opening his eyes, Harry said, "Why did you get me these fuckin' rich old playboy slippers?"

Mal waved her own feet at him, also in the black velvet slippers. Monogrammed. In gold. MM. "I thought it was good for our image," she said, taking a sip of the mojito, which tasted deliciously of mint, handpicked by her from the jungle in back of the cottage that was Harry's "garden" and that she believed must have been planted by his grandfather because Harry was certainly not into gardening.

"Velvet slippers make me feel old," Harry said, sitting up and looking at her.

"Me too, I guess," she said with the smile that lit up her face. "But anyway, you are older than me. I'll bet when you first came to Evening Lake you hung at the soda fountain with your hair in a quiff and the girls in poodle skirts and ponytails, playing 'Blue Suede Shoes' on the jukebox."

"Jesus!" Harry laughed. "I'm not that old. Anyway, what's for supper?"

Mal heaved a dramatic sigh. She got up and walked, in her brand-new monogrammed black-velvet-loafer-slippers and her short white shorts and floaty flowered top, to lean on the wooden rail, looking out at the gently fading familiar view. "Now I feel like an old married couple. What's for supper, little wifey?"

"I know what's for supper." Harry got up and came to stand next to her. "Times like this, though, I miss Ruby's."

"You also miss your job." Mal glanced sideways at him. "So I guess you're not going to quit?" She asked a question to which she already had the answer.

"After what happened here, at my own special place, with all the people who came together to help, those who needed the police, their protectors, their keepers of the proper peace, I cannot think of any other profession that would hold my interest and my feeling for my fellow men as well as the job I do now."

Mal understood. It would make a difference to her sweet simple plan for their lives, their growing-old-together-by-the-fire dream, but there was always another dream. A new dream, that anyhow turned out to be pretty much like reality, the way she'd always known it would.

"So, how do you know what's for supper?" she asked, changing the subject back.

"I saw. It's takeout pizza from Tweedies."

"And a green salad," Mal added virtuously.

"By the way, Rossetti's coming for lunch tomorrow. Bringing his mother."

Mal's eyes widened. She knew the story of Rossetti's mother. "Wow, better hold off on the spaghetti Bolognese, then. I couldn't take the competition."

"It'll be steak on the brand-new Weber." Harry smiled proudly at his new grill that was pretty much the same model as his old one, but as yet without the layer of burned-on grease. "And baked potatoes."

"Diz's favorite," Mal suddenly remembered. "We could invite the Osbornes," she added, hopefully, daunted by the idea of entertaining Rossetti's mom alone.

"Let's do that." Harry leaned companionably on the rail next to her. The lake was its usual nightly ink by now, still rippling like silk though, under a sliver of a new moon. "Look, the lights just went on at their house."

Mal looked over at the Osbornes' house, so festive with its twinkling porch lights, filled as always with family and friends. Remembering, she thanked God. And Len Doutzer. And Harry and Rossetti. And even, in a small way, herself. She had played a tiny part in the unmasking of the evil that was Bea Havnel. Now gone, and please God, able to be forgotten by them all.

Squeeze brushed against her bare legs and she knelt over him, snuggling her face into his soft fur. His blue eyes looked steadily into hers. It was, Mal knew, a look that meant "love."

She got up and went and put her arms around Harry's neck. "I love Squeeze," she said. "He can have the front seat in the Jag anytime."

Harry turned from the lake, away from his memories of the horrors that happened, and looked at her.

"That's true love," he said, enfolding her in his arms. Next to his heart.

Read on for an excerpt from the next book by
Elizabeth Adler

ONE WAY OR ANOTHER

Coming soon from Minotaur Books

PROLOGUE

ANGIE
Fethiye, Turkey

The sea is aquamarine. Azure, now, as I sink deeper into it, the color and texture of bridesmaid's velvet. Translucent, though. Even with my water-pressed eyes I can see the two of them up on deck, champagne bottle aggressively in the woman's hand which a moment ago she'd swung at me, striking my temple where my hair grows in a soft coppery-red wave. Now bloody.

I'm surprised no one noticed my fall. I'm also surprised how little sound a body makes hitting the ocean. I slid in silently, with scarcely a bubble to mark my exit. I did not even leave a wake behind the boat as it sped on.

A watery grave was never my intention; somehow, I always felt I should pass gently in the night, safe in my own soft bed, to some other warm and welcoming place not too different from the one I already inhabited, where everything went on much as before, only more smoothly.

It seems I was wrong. I was going down again, for the last time, I knew it now. Swept along by a swift current, my lungs filled with water, the salt taste filled my mouth, stung my still open eyes that I seemed unable to shut.

I didn't see anyone, though I did hear the faint shrug of the small boat.

Heard an unknown male voice say, "She is dead." Then, "No, she may live."

I hoped he was right.

The woman who had wielded the deadly champagne bottle, and who stood in the stern of a fast departing black yacht watching as Angie disappeared into the ocean, was known only as Mehitabel. No need for a last name in her way of life where most people knew each other only by their first, some invented, as was her own, some real, as was Ahmet Ghulbian's, the billionaire owner of the fast gulet who saw no reason to falsify a name so world renowned, like Onassis, for its success story and his wealth.

Mehitabel was not Ahmet's mistress, not even a sometime lover; she was his long-term cohort, keeper of his secrets, of which there were many, and carry-outer of his commands, whatever they might be.

Mehitabel never refused to do anything Ahmet asked of her. Their deal was unspoken, noncontractual, but perfectly understood by both for the simple reason that they were essentially alike: both were immoral to the *nth* degree; both driven by needs unknown to most people; and both incapable of deep emotion.

Mehitabel cared for no one other than herself; she would never have *given* her life for Ahmet, but she would *take* other people's lives for him. That was what he liked about her and he compensated her well for her services. Personally, Ahmet was not a man that liked to get his hands "dirty;" there were people like Mehitabel for that.

Watching the red-haired girl struggle in the wake of the fast-moving boat, Mehitabel did not so much as crack a smile. A shrug was the most she could summon in response, as she walked away, barefoot, since Ahmet allowed no shoes on his immaculate teak deck, her black dress blending into the blackness of the boat, of her surroundings.

All she was thinking was, so, another one bites the dust, or this time, "swallows up the sea." She almost allowed herself to enjoy the thought.

1

Fethiye, Turkey

Marco Polo Mahoney sprawled happily in a listing sun lounger whose webbing straps would certainly not last much longer. Still, it was a comfortable spot to rest and sip every now and again from a bottle of ouzo, a bit acrid but it gave him a peaceful buzz. Pleasant for the time of the evening. Sixish? It had to be sixish, didn't it? A man certainly could not be found drinking earlier; people might think badly of him.

He reached out to stroke his dog's ears. What the hell, he was on holiday and he liked a drink or two. Maybe more. Sometimes. But drinking alone was not supposed to be good for you; he should stir himself, go out and find some company in the village. He got to his feet and stood surveying his own small part of the southern Turkish coast: a strip of white beach, a turquoise sea turning azure where it met the deeper blue of the sky now darkening with storm clouds, all set against a green, foresty background.

Marco was a well-known portrait artist. He was thirty-five, attractively craggy, currently bearded because he never shaved on holiday; brown hair brushed straight back and salty-stiff from swimming in the sea; dark blue eyes narrowed against the sun, eyes which seemed to see everything. At least that's what his sitters said, and it was true. He saw all their flaws, something they also said made them uncomfortable. But of course he was worth it.

Marco was in good shape though he never worked out. He'd played basketball in his youth; tennis too, but more often he was the one on the sidelines, charcoal in hand, sketching the action. The girls had been flattered, the boys called him a wuss. He'd laughed, but that passion was what made him who he was today, sought out by the rich, the famous; a man who knew how to play the social game but, when on his own, wore old shorts and went barefoot, like now. He was also a man who enjoyed solitude.

He was taking a short vacation, alone but for his dog, renting a cabin and sailing a small wooden boat known as a gulet out of the Turkish port of Fethiye. He was sun-brown and naked but for his bathing shorts, surfers' shorts, baggy-legged, hanging low on his lean hips, a scuffed pair of ancient flip-flops dangling from his toes.

He lifted his face to catch the last of the sun, welcoming its warm caress. He knew he should have remembered about the sunblock; had his girlfriend been with him it would not have been forgotten. The daughter of an English "Lord," the Honorable Martha Patron was consistent, persistent, and insistent. You knew exactly what you were getting with Martha; slightly severe beauty of the straight nose, high cheekbones, tightly-pulled-back blond hair variety. It would have been worn in a ponytail on vacation, but in what Martha would surely have termed "real life" she would have worn it in a neat bun sitting low on her long neck. In bed though, it hung, loose and soft over her shoulders.

On vacation too, Martha would have worn a designer bikini with a designer cover-up, which Marco knew from experience would probably be of some chiffonish material in a gentle green or blue, with rope-sole wedge heels, the real thing, made of canvas in Spain or somewhere like that. Martha was the kind of woman who always knew where they made things and where to get them, how to be first with them. With everything, actually.

Which was why Marco was still surprised she would go for a guy like him, a bit of a scruff really, his light streaky brown hair too long, always in shorts or jeans; didn't own a real shirt other than the ones she bought him and which were mostly still in their plastic wrappers. He did own a pair of shoes, though. They had belonged to his grandfather, handmade by Berluti in Paris many moons ago. Marco kept them polished to a rich gleam in respect for that grandfather who had raised him, and also in case he might one day have to wear them to a stylish event in some international city where shoes were the expected norm, though in any case he usually got away with sneakers.

In "real life," which this vacation most certainly was not, Marco was "an artist" as Martha kept on reminding him . . . "A *portrait artist*, in fact," she would add, pleased because Marco's clients included some of the top international CEOs, men whose likeness Marco painted to keep the wolf from his door, enabling him, financially, to slip away from that reality into the glorious reality of this vacation, where he could be alone. Apart, that is, from his dog, Em, who went everywhere with him.

Long story short, he'd reply when strangers were curious about the grizzled mutt always at his heels, always at his side in cafés, always tucked under his arm when he travelled. Small and unbeauteous, Em lived in a part of Marco's heart that understood the loneliness from which he had rescued her.

When he'd found her, a few years ago, he'd been alone on a terrace café in Marseilles. The place did not even have a view and he'd stopped there solely for the purpose of a quick caffeine fix, served in one of those short, dark-green cups with the gold rim all French cafés seem to use; plus, of course, a glass of wine made from local vines grown up on the hill near Saint Emilion *and* an almond croissant made with enough butter to die from. That's when he saw the animal catcher van with its wire cage drive slowly by. The dog sat, small, grayish/brownish, youngish, a street survivor. Until now. The van stopped. A man got out on the passenger side, strode across, reached for the dog. Marco got there first.

"Oh no you don't," he said, or words to that effect, quickly scooping the mutt from under the man's hands. "This dog is mine." And so of course, from then on it was.

He named the dog Em, for the Saint Emilion he'd been drinking when he saw her. It seemed to fit and she responded to the name from first go. Now, of course, that's who she was. Em. Marco's dog. She ate anything, which was useful since he took her everywhere. He would not visit a country that would not accept his dog, not fly an airline where she would be made to fly in the hold, would not stay at a hotel that did not welcome her as well as him. He was, Martha told him, more in love with that bloody dog than with her. Marco did not admit it, but it could be true. And that was why the dog was with him now, on this beautiful southern Turkish coast, sharing the small, whitewashed plain slab of a one-room house with the bright blue wooden doors and shutters he'd painted himself, and the even smaller boat, the old wooden gulet, as well as the orange inflatable from which he fished every day.

If he was lucky and caught something bigger than six inches, big enough not to throw back in, that evening Marco would grill it over hot coals on an improvised barbecue made with stones and a piece of wire mesh. He'd share it with the dog, sitting outside under the stars, moving on from the ouzo to that odd Turkish wine with the slight fizz that caught in his throat but which he enjoyed. Other evenings, they'd walk to the village café bar where they'd sit under the spreading shade of the ancient olive tree and devour roast goat and couscous flavored with lemon, or a sandwich on thick crusty bread with sweet tomatoes picked that very moment from the garden, with sliced onion and crumbly feta cheese.

The proprietor, Costas, a lean, haunted-looking man in his forties with a springy mustache, very white teeth, and deep blue eyes, knew them by now, and there was always something special for Em: a bone that might have come from a dinosaur it was so big and which made Marco pause to think twice about what he might be eating; or a bowl of fishy stew complete with heads and tails, of which Em seemed particularly fond.

Anyhow, of an evening and sometime deep into the warm night, Costa's café bar became their place, where they were known and there was always company and conversation, and where there was always somebody who spoke enough English to make sense of it all. It was a good, simple life, quite separate from Marco's life in Paris, and the cities where he painted rich mens' portraits and their wives in pearls and diamonds and small superior smiles. Still, he made a good living at that, and despite the drawbacks he enjoyed it. And it paid for all this. *This* kind of life, this village, this coast. *This*, he loved.

Sprawled in his sagging lounger, he swapped back to the ouzo, took another swig, pulling a face. He told himself he really should go a bit more upmarket, spring for the extra couple of bucks and drink something that did not make his eyes water. He turned to watch as a yacht chugged slowly out of the harbor, its black hull cutting smoothly through the waves. The sky had darkened, the air was tense with the threat of thunder and lightning flickered quick as a blink. A storm was approaching and pretty fast too, as Marco knew from experience they did in this area. The storms could be severe and in his opinion the boat would have been better off waiting it out in the harbor, or at least moored close to shore.

The boat was a hundred yards away by now, and picking up speed. Marco got to his feet, hitched up his baggy shorts and picked up his binoculars. It was a modern gulet, based on the old local wooden fishing boats out of Bodrum. This one though, was bigger, smarter, faster.

As he watched a woman emerged from the cabin and ran along the deck. Her long red hair caught in the wind that was coming with the storm, clouding around her in a coppery halo where the sun's final gleam lit it momentarily. She was wearing a blue dress that as she balanced at the very stern, whipped back from her slender body. She put a hand up to her head, her neck drooped in a gesture of what seemed to Marco to be pain. Shocked, he caught a glimpse of a gaping, bloody wound, her white skull. And that's when he saw her fall.

Marco stared at the place she had gone under, waiting for her to come back up. The gulet chugged on. There was no sign of her in its wake. No one had come running to help, no one on the gulet seemed to know she had gone. It had been maybe thirty seconds too long and Marco knew she was in trouble. He ran for the old orange inflatable, dropped it into the waves. The outboard started at first go. In a few minutes he was where he'd seen her go in. He circled, staring deep into the sea, but the water was less clear here, disturbed now by his boat. He stilled the engine and jumped over the side.

It was like falling off a cliff. He went so deep his lungs were bursting when he finally popped back up next to the dinghy. The sea was kicking up, the sky dark, the storm was getting closer. And then he saw her hair, long copper hair floating upward toward him. He was in there in a second.

But he could not find her. He dived, and dived again, but the storm had moved in and turbulence shifted the waves, shifted him. He had lost her.

And now the past came back at him, bringing memories he would never want to relive.